ACCORDING TO ARNOLD

ACCORDING TO ARNOLD

A Novel of Love and Mushrooms

GILES MILTON

ISIS

LARGE PRINT

Oxford

Copyright © Giles Milton, 2010

First published in Great Britain 2010
by
Pan Books
an imprint of Pan Macmillan

Published in Large Print 2010 by ISIS Publishing Ltd.,
7 Centremead, Osney Mead, Oxford OX2 0ES
by arrangement with
Pan Macmillan
a division of Macmillan Publishers Limited

The moral right of the author has been asserted

British Library Cataloguing in Publication Data
Milton, Giles.
    According to Arnold.
    1. Mycologists - - Fiction.
    2. Conspiracies - - Fiction.
    3. Married people - - Fiction.
    4. Large type books.
    I. Title
    823.9'2–dc22

ISBN 978–0–7531–8676–3 (hb)
ISBN 978–0–7531–8677–0 (pb)

Printed and bound in Great Britain by
T. J. International Ltd., Padstow, Cornwall

For Lindsay

"Curiouser and curiouser"

Alice's Adventures in Wonderland,
Lewis Carroll

PROLOGUE

I'm missing you, of course. And I'm missing Philippa. But then again, I'm standing by the window and there's this strip of brilliant powder and a shimmering slab of greeny-blue. Beach and lagoon. And the water's flashing and twinkling in the sunlight like thousands of dancing, jiggling specks of glinting silver and I can't look at it for long because the glare's so bright it's hurting my eyes.

And there are two white tufted tropicbirds hovering in the thermals and just waiting, waiting, waiting, to swoop down into the water and — ah, there they go *right* now — down-they-go-down-they-go — S-S-SPLASH! And bullseye. That's what I call fishing. They've each got one in their great pointed beaks.

And beyond, in the distance, I can see this foaming white water that's churning and roaring all day long. It's the reef at the outer edge of the lagoon, where they catch all the biggest pomfrets and triggerfish. And all you hear is this rolling, never-ending crash of waves on the reef — crash-sh-sh-sh, crash-sh-sh-sh, crash-sh-sh-sh. It's there when you go to sleep. It's there when you wake up. At times you don't even hear it. But then — when you least expect it — it suddenly looms back into your consciousness: crash-sh-sh-sh, crash-sh-sh-sh, crash-sh-sh-sh.

You must have both been wondering about me. You must have been wondering how I'm getting on. And I've been meaning to be in contact for the last three weeks, but it's all been so frantic I've hardly had a minute to myself. And, besides, I've been feeling so inside out it's as if my brain's working little more than a two-day week.

I'm sure you'd prefer me to scribble the whole thing down on paper, but it's so humid here and the air is so sodden with water that paper turns into a soggy face flannel before you reach the end of the page. And that's why, Peter, I've decided to record the whole saga onto my tape machine. I'll send it to you in instalments. On cassettes. I rather like the thought of you sitting there at home and listening to a story that's going to stretch your eyes.

It's strange to think that our nearest landmass is over a thousand miles away. *A thousand miles of ocean*. There's Tonga, of course, but even that's more than eight hours by boat from here. Eight hours to see your neighbours. By my reckoning, that must make Tuva one of the remotest spots on earth. And it must be the least accessible as well. For almost half the year the sea's too choppy for the monthly cargo boat to dock at the jetty. During the monsoon, they literally hurl the crates of supplies ashore. The locals are amazing at catching them — it's quite a sight. They're barefoot and they've got these great rippling muscles and they catch the boxes as they come flying through the spray. I watched them do it just a few weeks ago. Sacks of rice. Palm oil. Spare parts for the generator. You name it. They didn't drop a single crate, even though the jetty was as slippery as washing-up liquid.

Arnold Trevellyan was still living in France when I interviewed him for the *Daily Telegraph*. His was the sort of yarn that appealed to both broadsheets and tabloids — a happily married auctioneer (and by all accounts, a successful one) who had ditched his wife, got engaged to the queen of a tiny island in the South Pacific, and was about to head off into the sunset to rule his tropical realm. A year earlier we'd run a story about an English woman who had married a Ghanaian chieftain. That, too, had made a cracking read.

When I think back to that first meeting with him — well, it was on that very same day that my life began to be turned inside out. I found myself entangled in a series of extraordinary coincidences, and all because of him. I wasn't aware of it at the time, of course. It was only some months later that I came to recognize that Arnold was exerting a strange influence over my life. On that first evening in his company all I could say for certain was that I was in the presence of someone *unusual*.

And when I first saw the island from far out to sea, well, I couldn't help thinking it looked like a giant green bowler hat that had been all wrapped up in steam. It looked as if it had emerged dripping from the ocean, sweltering in the sunshine and cloaked in seaweed. And as we got nearer you could make out these spectacular waterfalls — they were hundreds of feet high — that came crashing and bouncing off the bluffs of rock. And when the spray catches the sunlight it refracts into a thousand different colours of rainbow and turns the whole place into fantasy.

It takes three or four hours to get to the peak of Mount Tuva and you need to hire one of the locals from the village as a guide. I went with Gilbertine — she's this great strapping woman, stronger than any man. She's got biceps like a bison's, I swear, and feet as big as cowpats. And you should see her wield a machete. Swish-whack. Swish-whack. She splinters the branches into matchsticks.

And the air is thick with the scent of blossom and there are these great clusters of creamy-yellow flowers that dangle from the mountain ribbonwood and look for all the world like Christmas decorations. And there are gigantic butterflies and humming birds no bigger than my thumb and geckos the colour of fresh mint sauce.

There's no path up the mountain and the creepers are so thick you literally have to hack your way to the top. And as you climb higher and higher, there's this steam that hangs in the air and there's moss underfoot and it's like a thick wet sponge. And even the trees are sweating in the heat.

And then, with a helpful yank on the arm from Gilbertine, you reach the top. And it's like opening the curtains on a bright spring morning. The view, Peter, the view! You can see the whole archipelago spread out like a string of jewels across the ocean. It's a cliché, I know, but you'll have to forgive me: imagine dots of brilliant green emeralds in a deep turquoise sea. There's Vanu stretching away to the west and Oloua to the north and diminutive little Kitu just across the channel from here.

Even Gilbertine gave a great cry to the heavens. "Ooiawaa! Ooiawaa!" she said. "O wonder! O wonder! Mr King, sir, look — there."

4

Far below us we could see whales basking in the deep waters just outside the lagoon. They were basking and blowing and having the time of their lives and Philippa would have loved to have seen it. She'd get spectacular pictures from the top of Mount Tuva.

And here's the strange thing. When you're standing up there, on the peak, it's amazing how distant it all seems. The lagoon is transformed into a miniature pool of water and the beaches are like coils of white string. And as for the coconut trees — they could have come straight out of Toy Town.

And off to our left — on the shore of the lagoon — I could just about make out Lipuko village, which is the little settlement where we all live. And as I looked at it all spread out below me, I said to myself, "Arnold Trevellyan, you're a king. You're a sodding real-life king." And although I was exhausted from the climb and aching all over and sweating like a sea cow, I had to struggle to stop myself from laughing at the absurdity of it all.

My coronation, Peter! *My bloody coronation!* If only you'd been here. To think that your old pal Arnold Trevellyan is the big boss in every conceivable sense. I can sign treaties with whoever I want. I can declare war if the mood takes me! It beats life back in London, that's for sure. Even the queen — our very own British queen — had to laugh when I told her some of the stranger things that had happened over the course of the year. "One really ought to write it down," she said, "although one must never *ever* make it public." Well I can't write to save my life and, besides, it's far too hot. And that's why I've turned to my tape recorder.

* * *

There was something else about Arnold — a certain *magnetism* — that I can't quite put my finger on. In one sense he was unremarkable. He was medium height and medium build — medium everything. Darkish hair (rather unkempt) and averagely good looks. No — more than average. He turned women's heads, even if he wasn't aware of it. It was his electric blue eyes that did it. They seduced and ensnared people, and at the same time they were quizzical. It was as if they were trying to fathom exactly who you were.

It didn't take me long to discover that his life revolved around mushrooms. For the better part of three hours he regaled me with tales of toxins, soil structure, beetles and the conditions that were necessary for the spores of mushrooms to burst into life. This was not at all why I had come to see him, but he spoke with such passion that I kept my dictaphone running for the entire evening.

"How," I asked him, "did you acquire so much knowledge about fungus?"

He took a long sip of wine and stared at a damp patch in the corner of the room (I do believe he was searching for signs of mould).

"Milkcaps and toughshanks," was his reply. "Deceivers and funnels and brittlestems. For the last four years, every Saturday morning, in weather fair or foul, I've scoured the woods and fields for them. I've examined them, dissected them, sniffed them, tasted them and photographed their spores. I've collected droplets of slime, I've measured their gills, their caps and their stems. I've got more than sixty test tubes containing the milk of the lactating mushrooms — the *volemus, subdulcis* and *blennius.*" His voice dropped to a whisper. "They actually lactate," he said, "like a pregnant, milk-filled breast."

And off he went, describing tastings with friends, cases of poisoning and outings in the woods. "Mushrooms," he said, "are our last living link with the empty vacuum of prehistory. They've been around for four hundred and fifty million years. When we hold a mushroom in our hand, we are holding a plant that the dinosaurs would recognize. Touch a mushroom, smell it, taste it: you are taking yourself very close to the beginnings of the world. You are holding in your own hands one of the earliest forms of life." He smiled. "What tenacity they've got!"

He told me why *Gyroporus cyanescens* turns blue when you slice it with an iron-bladed knife. And he described his excitement when he found a seven-pound cauliflower fungus — the largest he had ever seen. "It was like holding a large wet brain," he said, "dripping with dew and smelling of peat and old churches. A delicate brain, with subglobose lumps and fimbriated lobes."

He looked at me and saw I was lost. "Forgive me," he said with a smile. "I've gone back to my study and left you out there in the woods. You should never have got me started on mushrooms."

I had indeed started him off on the subject. I'd asked him a question about the grilled mushrooms that he was serving with the Chablis I'd brought. (I'd intended it as a gift, but we drank it during the interview.)

7

"Caesars," he said. "These are caesars. And they are among the rarest and most sublime mushrooms on the planet. They'll only grow in specific climatic conditions and even then they often fail to germinate. That's why they've been savoured as a delicacy for many centuries. They're amanitas, the dish of kings and princes. And you must approach them with care: they're a powerful aphrodisiac. You normally eat them raw, but I wanted to try them cooked."

He picked up a slice and held it between his thumb and forefinger. "They're always rare," he said, "but this year they're rarer than ever. What with the wet summer and the dry autumn — that spells death for a caesar. It took me three days to find this little plateful."

"Can't you propagate them?" I asked. "Grow them yourself."

He laughed. But he didn't answer my question, even when I asked him a second time. He just left it hanging in mid-air.

I thought that was strange.

The village is all terribly picturesque and just like you might imagine it. Twenty houses or thereabouts — they're knocked together out of palm trunks and corrugated iron — and a small mission chapel built by the Wesleyans. I'm looking at it right now. Eighteen seventy-nine — that's the date over the door. It was the year the Reverend Emanuel Bosworth first pitched up here and preached his "muscular" Christianity to the islanders.

My house is right on the beach. It's not exactly Buckingham Palace, but I'm not one to complain. And it's not all primitive on Tuva. No, I wouldn't want you to get the wrong end of the stick. We've got a few creature comforts — paraffin lighting, a primus stove and even a wireless. On a nice clear afternoon, when it's not thumping it down with rain, I can just about pick up the American Forces Radio from Samoa. *This is AFRrrr — and I'm your host, Jonny G.* And we've got a generator that flicks out electricity for a few hours of the day. I know some people would find life here too isolated, but, if I'm completely honest, I don't mind feeling cut off from the rest of the world, especially when I get to see furry bandicoots and humming birds and the shaggy green peak of Mount Tuva.

There are a handful of old colonial buildings alongside the mission chapel, all with tiled roofs and snow gutters (can you believe it — they actually designed them with snow gutters!) They turn into baking furnaces in the hottest hours of the day. Yesterday afternoon the chapel reached ninety-six degrees. And the pipe that feeds the cold water to my house was so hot you could've made a cup of tea with it.

It's as sticky as soap in the afternoons and I find my mind begins to wander. I get this dull ache in my temples — it's as if a weight's been clamped to the side of my head and finding the energy to do anything's a struggle and I keep losing my train of thought. So I strip off all my clothes (no problems with nudity in this corner of the world) and just drift and drift and I think of Lola. *Lola, Lola, Lola.* And before I know it, I'm fast asleep and dreaming sweet dreams and the two of us are lounging together under a shady palm tree and she's looking more gorgeously stunning than ever and there's a cool breeze blowing in off the sea and I'm sipping a chilled glass of mango juice and — and I don't wake up until six or seven o'clock in the evening. And every time she comes to me with a drink and she's invariably topless and looking like a queen peach. And I can't help pinching myself and wondering if I'm not the luckiest forty-two-year-old in the history of the world.

And that, Peter, is why you *have* to come. You *have* to see my little realm, to meet Lola, and to get away from it all for a few weeks. If you do come, you'll find yourself getting six holidays for the price of one. Each island has its own character. There's Oloua: it's lush and tropical, a great green blob. Then there's Tu'unoho island. That's very different. Flat and sandy and almost arid. Nothing whatsoever grows in the centre of the island because of the salty soil. There are these strange white lines of salt crystals streaking across the ground and when it's really hot, as it was on the day when I visited the island, hundreds of tortoises had assembled to lick the salt off the ground. And you stand in complete silence under a burning sun and all you hear is this rasping, rasping of their tongues on the ground.

It was the strangest interview I'd ever conducted. It was he who set the questions and he who chose the topics of conversation. At one point he launched into a discourse on the early Roman Empire, regaling me with tales of the Ninth Legion and anecdotes about Claudius's invasion of Britain. He told me how they'd beached their galleys and quinqueremes on the foreshore at Richborough; how they'd advanced through Kent in battle formation: "the human tortoise — *very effective*". He told me how Claudius's Batavian cohorts had annihilated the native British charioteers and how they'd celebrated their victory. It was typical of the whimsical manner in which he recounted his stories. I had no idea of the link between all of this and the mushrooms we were eating until — after a twenty-minute historical detour — he revealed that Claudius's favourite mushroom was the same as the one sitting on a plate in front of us. But even then we were only at the halfway point. The emperor, he told me, had died a horrible death because his beloved mushrooms had been contaminated with others from the same family — deathcaps — which happen to be the most poisonous mushroom in the world.

"So how," I asked, "did he die?"

"A good question," he said, "but with a very bad answer. Day one — nothing. He'd feel as right as rain. Oh, yes — nothing wrong with the emperor. Nothing at all. Day two — still OK, except for a niggling little stomach cramp that seems to restrict his guts somewhat."

I've still got the whole interview on tape.

"And then the diarrhoea begins. And his body starts to drain itself. His guts are soon in full meltdown and it's not a pleasant feeling. Not pleasant at all. And then, well, he suddenly feels better. It's over! He's fine! Bring wine for the emperor! And bring on the dancing girls. Whores and strumpets. And strike up some music. Faster, faster.

"Except that he's not fine. It's the toxins, you see. They're infiltrating every nook and cranny of his liver — the sneaky little buggers — rooting their way into every single cell that he possesses. Liver failure. Kidney failure. That's what follows. And a desperate struggle to

11

breathe. That's the worst of it. You gasp. And gasp. And you clutch at the little oxygen that comes into your lungs. Oh, help me. *Uuuaaagh*. Oh, God. *Uuuaaagh*. Air. *Uuuaaagh*. And then comes the coma — and, well, it's a blessed relief. For as your vision blurs and your mind wanders, the pain seems to slip peacefully into your unconscious and you're not even aware that the rhythm of your heart is beating a very slow pump-pump-pump.

"And pump.

"And pump.

"And. Stop.

"It was probably ten days before he actually succumbed. It's the cruellest of mushrooms. The cruellest of them all."

Arnold told me he had done a lot of research into these toxic mushrooms and had published two papers on them. One had even been printed in *Science*. He said that he hoped to find an antidote to the toxins. It was his reason for coming to France. He told me it was his life-long challenge. And then he laughed.

He was obsessed with mushrooms and fungal growths. I'd never met anyone quite so enthusiastic. One of the columnists here at the *Telegraph* once wrote an article about how you come to resemble your profession if you practise it for long enough. That's why butchers' hands look like slabs of meat, why bar owners take on the colour of old claret. Arnold didn't look like a mushroom, of course, but he did have the air of someone who was forever on a quest for rare fungi. His eyes flickered, his angular nose twitched, his left foot jiggled, his fingers tapped and he chewed his nails.

"You must treat them gently," he said. "Delicately. Touch them as your lover would like to be touched. They bruise easily."

And on he went — I swear he made me hungry when he talked about the wine and cream sauces, the freshly chopped parsley and the smell of it all simmering on the cooker. And he told me how he had once devised three hundred and sixty-five different mushroom recipes for Flora — one for every single night of the year.

"She loved mushrooms," he said (somewhat ruefully, when I think back on it). "I could make her melt with my mushrooms."

It was three whole hours before I managed to ask him about how he was soon to be crowned king of one of the smallest islands in the South Pacific. (It was — I was to discover — all tied up with the mushrooms.) But he was reticent about telling me the whole story, which was strange given that he was the one who had invited me out to France. He said he was toying with the idea of recording it all and that he'd keep me posted. But he didn't — at least, not in the way he intended.

It's a bathtub of a journey to get to Oloua and a stomach-churning extra half-hour if you want to make it to Tu'unoho. That's the most northerly in the group. Kitu and Ta'ula are much closer. Gilbertine and Doris (she's another of our larger ladies) often swim across to Kitu, even though there's a ferocious undercurrent and there are sharks and stingrays and jellyfish the size of bean bags. "Sharks, sir?" said Gilbertine when I asked her if she was scared of them. "I punch them. On the nose."

And there are also the two outer islands: Vanu and Niuapulapei. Nee-a-poo-la-pay. Try pronouncing *that* after you've just drained your tenth glass. They're much further afield: it takes more than four hours to reach them and you need to be certain the weather's going to hold. On a clear day I can stand at my study window and just about make out the cloud that permanently hovers over the peak of Mount Vanu. It's an old volcano — hasn't erupted in centuries. Local tradition — how they love their traditions — says it was formed from the tip of Gaou's thumb. He's the god of creation, or so they say, and he's supposed to have lost his thumb when he flung his daughter, Nauri, into the sea.

And then the sun melts into that very same sea and you go to bed and you find yourself wrapped in a great big eiderdown of silence. It's absolute. There's a complete absence of man-made noise. No cars. No sirens. No beeping of horns. No shouting. Never even a raised voice. I haven't heard a plane in all the time I've been here. And, come to think of it, I haven't heard the sound of a machine in the last two months — unless of course you count the little cargo boat that comes from Tonga. It's like being stone-tone-deaf. And that's probably been the hardest thing to get used to. Imagine, Peter, life without Monteverdi or Jonathan Richman. In fact, try to imagine life without any single noise at all. That's what they're used to here. That's what they're born with. And it's because of that, well, that I wanted to ask you a favour. Would you mind sending me a tape with *some sounds*? You could perch a tape recorder on your office window and catch

14

the buses going up and down the Strand. And, while you're at it, let's have some sounds of Taplow Bottom as well. Some traffic noise. The sound of an engine. A lawnmower or two. I'd like to play them to everyone on the island. They've never heard such things. Gilbertine actually asked me — as she was hacking her way up the mountain — what a bus sounds like. I tried to make the right noise but all I succeeded in doing was make her roar with laughter.

"That, Mr King, sir," she said with great solemnity, "is called breaking wind. And it's a noise we hear every day."

Here on Tuva there's nothing but the same old crashing of the surf on the reef and the two parrots squawking from the eaves of the mission chapel and the coconut trees, which you can probably hear rustling in the late afternoon breeze, and

— thud —

ah — did you hear that? If there's a hollow thudding sound on the tape, that's one of the coconuts falling onto the roof of my hut. I'll have that for my supper. They're at their ripest at this time of year and we eat them with tuna and guava and rice. They're meant to be very good for you. Doris even has a little jingle: "A coconut a day keeps them varicose veins at bay."

And if I leave my tape machine running, you'll soon hear the pitter-pitter-pitter of the rain. Wind first, then rain. It starts at six o'clock sharp every evening (you can time it to the second) and lasts for about half an hour — longer during the monsoon when the wind whips up a gale. That's when we really feel as if we're at the absolute end of the world.

It's that very isolation, of course, that brought Warlock here. You know, the explorer and naturalist, Ernest Arthur Warlock. He came just after the First World War — just after the assassination of the old king, Lola's grandfather. And he found that Tuvan beetles had evolved differently from the Tongan ones, even though there's only two hundred and fifty miles separating the two islands.

"You do realize, sir, that Warlock was up to his neck in it." That's what Gilbertine said to me.

"Up to his neck in *what*?" I asked.

"The Order. Everything. He'd been in it from the start, sir. That's why he came here in the first place. He'd been sent here by the committee. They wanted to know if it was viable, from a mushroom point of view."

Well, as a matter of fact, Peter, I didn't know that Warlock was up to his neck in it. Indeed, it came as a complete surprise. But when I thought about it further, well, it all added up. The whole bloody story began to fall into place. And it made me realize that they had — *have* — every chance of success. Yes, they have every chance of pulling the whole thing off. And it's going to change the world.

I'm told that there's a copy of Warlock's book in the University of London library, the one in Senate House. The big white building in Bloomsbury. You know the one. It's in the section on Oceania. If ever, Peter, you have half an hour or so to spare, would you mind photocopying the pages on Tuva? Just the introduction and the stuff about the island. I'd love to read what Warlock has to say about my new fiefdom.

Oh, yes — and I'd also like to know what he says about the mushrooms. He wrote something about Tuvan mushrooms. You see, mushrooms were his passion with a capital P. Indeed, I'd always supposed that it was because of mushrooms that he came here in the first place. And yet here's the strange thing, Peter. I've yet to find a single bloody mushroom on the island. It ought to be the perfect climate for *russula* and *hypholoma* and *tricholoma*, especially up on the mountain. And I was expecting to discover a whole regiment of sulphur knights. And yet —

Ha! Without so much as a by your leave . . . you see, I've been wanting to get myself onto the subject of mushrooms for the last ten minutes and now I find myself in danger of banging on about them without even realizing. So here we are — ladies and gentlemen, and Peter — a round of applause for the Mushroom. It's where I wanted to be all along.

Mushrooms, mushrooms, mushrooms. It all began fourteen months ago: you'll remember, Peter; it must have been — let me see — October 1988. Baddington's had a policy of granting a year's unpaid sabbatical to anyone who'd worked there for more than ten years. I'd been the head auctioneer for far more than ten years, of course. I joined in the May of 1967 (two days after your coming-of-age party, and still with a thumping hangover). And so my sabbatical was way, way overdue.

But I had no particular desire to take time off. *I know, I know* — everyone thought I was mad. Even you and Philippa (although you were too polite to say so). But I could see no obvious reason. You know how I lived for that job — I can admit that now. It was the perfect combination of everything I love most: history, camaraderie and a big fat dollop of showmanship. I loved being in the middle of it all. It was exciting. I guess that's why I didn't want to throw it all away, even if it was only for ten or twelve months.

But Flora — well, you of all people know how insistent she can be. And persistent. And she was desperate to get away from it all. She was fed up. She said she was bored. *Bored!*

She'd already given up her job at Foxtree and she wanted to "go somewhere green". That's what she said. But I couldn't see any reason to leave. I honestly couldn't have been happier. And there was plenty of "green", for Christ's sake, in our back garden. And on the common. There's about a thousand acres of greenery.

There was a volcanic eruption on the scale of Krakatoa when I told her I was happy to stay put. "*You're* happy," she said, "but I can tell you for a fact that I'm not exactly over the moon at this precise moment in time. And I can also tell you — although you won't listen — that there's something wrong with you, Arnold."

I put down my glass and as I did so, her voice suddenly dropped in volume. "My lovely Arnold," she said. "My gorgeous, fanciable Arnold — what *are* you doing with yourself? You say you're an auctioneer. You're forever telling people how you're an expert and a historian and a showman and bla-bla-bla all rolled into one. And you *are*. But can't you also see — I'll be blunt — that for all your claims and stories, in spite of everything you say, you're *nothing more than a salesman*. Yes, a salesman. And I only say all this not to criticize you or to be deliberately mean for the sake of it, but because it upsets me more than anything else. You're so talented and knowledgeable and unusual that you could be king of the world."

I'm paraphrasing what she said, of course, but it was pretty much like that. And she didn't stop there. "And then there's this house," she said. "You love it. I know you do. And I like it too. But I feel as if you're attached to it by strings. I feel as if it's got a hold over you. It *has* got a hold over you. I feel as if you're incapable of letting go. And it's not healthy. In fact, I find it rather odd."

That's what she said. But then that's what she'd been saying for the last ten years. And then she told me that I was "frightened to let go". *Frightened — I ask you!* And to "let go" of what? She couldn't give me an answer to *that*. And then we had the whole saga about children again. She said it was because I couldn't "let go" that I didn't want to have children.

"*Let go?*" I repeated. "You keep saying *let go*. What, exactly, do you want me to *let go* of?"

She slowly shook her head. "You can't see, can you? You just can't see."

And then she started telling me that she couldn't understand how someone with more vitality than the space shuttle — I quote — could take so much pleasure in the "little routines of work". The little *bloody* routines of work. She made my job sound so — *pedestrian*. It was incredibly unreasonable. It's actually highly skilled. And she said that someone with so much excess energy — that's me, apparently — should not be wasting my time selling "Pre-Raphaelite tit-tat" and "Georgian dinner services" to the highest bidder. And then she looked me straight in the eye and pleaded: "Arnold; my wonderful Arnold; my handsome and delicious Arnold; my confidant and friend; Arnold, the love of my life: for one time only be honest with yourself. What do you really *long* to do?"

"OK," I said, folding my arms in a very definite sort of way. "OK, if you really want to know. Mushrooms. That's what I long to do more than anything else in the world. Mushrooms."

"Then good," she said in a tone of voice that was suddenly so soft that it could have made peace with the entire planet. "At last, Arnold, at last. If you pursue your mushrooms, I'll follow you to the ends of the earth."

And that's how we came to be in Burgundy, you see. I applied for a sabbatical and old Mr Baddington reluctantly granted it. Flora found tenants for our house. We rented it. And off we went. It all happened in the space of a few short weeks.

We talked and chatted and then it was his turn to ask me questions. It was all so strange — he had four or five specific things he wanted to put to me. What, he wanted to know, was the longest river in Russia? And what was the capital of Botswana? These were two of them. I can't recall the others. All I remember is that I hadn't got a clue about the answers to any of the things he asked — and I told him so.

"Of course," he said sympathetically, shaking his head. "And why on earth should you?" He slapped his hands together and smiled. "Good, good." It was all very odd.

I wrote up the interview on the following morning and sent it over to the newspaper, But it was never published. It wasn't Arnold's fault and nor, in truth, was it mine — it was the fault of his new wife. She refused to be photographed, you see. Apparently she didn't want to be in the paper. And the editor gave me sharp words when I got back to the office. "You could have fucking well checked that out before you went, Tobias," he said.

Originally, there had been some talk of me accompanying them to the South Pacific in order to write a follow-up article about their coronation. But the costs of getting there were prohibitive and there was little point if his wife was not going to play ball. Besides, there was so much other news to cover. Events in Eastern Europe were starting to creep into the papers and the editor deemed it a waste of resources to send someone off to a remote South Pacific island. I was promptly despatched to Berlin and then to Czechoslovakia in order to report on the early signs of unrest: the riots in Berlin; the resignation of Honecker; the student rally in Prague.

And it was while I was in Eastern Europe — and in the strangest of circumstances — that I started to pick up rumours about Arnold Trevellyan. It really was peculiar. I felt as if his shadow was stalking me. It was as if he was waiting for me at every turn. I overheard his name being mentioned in the most unexpected places. I heard it being whispered in a bathhouse in Bucharest. I overheard a group of men talking about him in Albania. Yet whenever I tried to find out more, I was met with a wall of silence. The only thing I gathered was that there was some sort of conspiracy — a big one — and that Arnold was somehow implicated.

But I'm running ahead of myself, for this was all some months in the future. At the time it was his magnetic personality — and that alone — that struck me. For weeks after our meeting I kept wondering what had happened to him. I couldn't stop myself thinking about how he was coping on his new island home.

I'd hoped to contact him directly on Tuva — find out what was going on — but the island, as he'd told me, is impossibly remote. There are no international phone lines and I'd remembered him saying that even postal communication takes several weeks, as all the letters have to go via Paris and then Sydney and then Tonga. So I decided upon a different tack. When I'd met Arnold in France, he'd spoken at length about his friends in the Taplow Bottom Mycological Society. And it was to them that I decided to turn, hoping they might have had some news.

Their president was a certain Peter Rushton, a man who Arnold had mentioned when I'd interviewed him in France. I contacted Peter, explained that I'd met Arnold in France and was given an open invitation to Taplow Bottom. I met up with him one Sunday at the beginning of December. It was the eighth, I think, or perhaps the ninth.

Peter was diametrically opposite from Arnold in both looks and character. Chalk and cheese. And quite a smoothie. He must have been the same sort of age — early forties — yet he looked a good ten years older. In part, it was his clothing. Beige slacks, green Pringle and those diamond-patterned socks. His skin was a little too tanned; his hair was a little too groomed. His natural home would have been the clubhouse of a golf course, not the woods and forests that Arnold so loved sniffing around in. He was Home Counties through and through. It set me wondering why he and Arnold were such close friends. It seemed so *unlikely*. But they'd been chums since childhood and I now suspect — with the benefit of hindsight — that Arnold enjoyed his normality. With Peter you knew exactly what you were getting.

And then there were the mushrooms to bond them. Peter shared Arnold's interest in mushrooms, and certainly enjoyed eating them, but he lacked his friend's passion. I got the impression that for Peter it was little more than a hobby — it could just as easily have been stamps or coins — whereas for Arnold it was the very lifeblood that fuelled him.

We'd chosen Burgundy, or rather *I'd* chosen Burgundy. Flora was not so fussed *where* we lived, just so long as she got out of Clapham and into somewhere green. But I, Peter, had something specific I wanted to do. I was on a mission. I wanted to make a detailed study of the amanita genus — the fly agaric, the blusher, the deathcap. I wanted to collect as many species as possible and take a close look at their spores. I wanted to get to know them as intimately as you can ever get to know a mushroom. I wanted to study them, compare one against the other. I wanted to dissect them, photograph them, heat them, freeze them and do everything that you could ever do with a mushroom without being arrested and locked away. As you know, Peter, I'm already on first-name terms with all the amanitas. But I wanted more, much more. I wanted to determine why some in the genus are deadly poisonous — fatal — while others have extraordinarily beneficial properties. As you know, it's the great unsolved mystery of the amanita. In fact, it's the biggest, fattest mystery in the world. If you're into mushrooms, that is. And I felt sure that those microscopic little spores would hold the key to finding an antidote that would save lives. In the last ten years, sixty-seven people have died terrible deaths from amanita poisoning — sixty-seven deaths that could have been prevented.

I chose Burgundy for one reason: it's the best place in Europe to find amanita. Professor Blatthorn told me it was even better than the Black Forest. It's the dampness, you see. In late summer and autumn the combination of heat and dampness provides the perfect conditions. England's too soggy and never quite warm enough. That, Peter, is why we've always had such a struggle to find grisettes in Taplow Bottom woods.

Flora and I didn't have to look very far to find a place to live. We found one advertised in the *Journal of Mycology*. In the small ads at the back, sandwiched between a farmhouse in Calabria and a watermill in Normandy. This place was in the Morvan. More-Von. Rhymes with Moron, with an extra emphasis on the Ron.

The Morvan is a national park, a big one. North of Dijon, south of Vézelay. Look at a map and you'll see that scarcely any roads run through the centre. It's one of the wildest areas in France. A quarter of a million hectares of sparkling, pristine, untouched wilderness. A quarter of a million hectares of oaks and elms and beech and brambles and briars and old man's beard. And in the spring the ground is covered in bluebells and adder's tongue and hoary ragwort. A thick oriental rug.

Flora fell head over heels in love with the house as soon as she saw it. It was a half-derelict folly which had been built by Marshal Veuilly in the eighteenth century. Veuilly was the aide-de-camp of Louis the sixteenth — an old-style, stuck-in-the-mud Trojan warhorse. And this was his little hideaway. A place where he could indulge in romantic trysts with his mistress, Madame de Sévignac.

Flora liked the idea of a romantic hideaway and so, I confess, did I. Everything in life suddenly seemed exciting. I even forgot about Clapham and work and my friends and the auctions. "Will you be my Madame de Sévignac?" I asked Flora on our first day in the house. "Most willingly," she said, "if you'll be my dashing Marshal Veuilly."

It was quirky — I'll grant you it was quirky. But then Veuilly himself was quirky. According to Flora, he always had "his rumpelstiltskin" (her choice of words) with his mistresses while dressed in full military attire. I guess it helped him in his little fantasies.

He'd built his folly in the style of a military tent, complete with drapes and pitched roof — all of it carved from stone. It was in a poor state, that's for sure. No one had lived in it for years. Decades even. But it had water (yellowish-brown), electricity (with sparks) and a little kitchen that looked as if it hadn't been used since before the war.

The rent was cheap. The owner, a certain Monsieur de la Regnier, offered it to us for song. "You're in luck," he said. "No one's lived here for years."

I felt like telling him that *he* was the one in luck; after all, it was us paying him to live here. But I held my tongue and smiled politely. And so did Flora. And then, to fill the silence, I told him about my quest for mushrooms. And this provoked a most curious reaction.

"Yes, exactly," he said. "Yes, yes. Amanitas."

I gave a start. *Amanitas*. How the hell did he know? You see, I hadn't yet mentioned my interest in amanitas. I most definitely hadn't mentioned them.

"How did you know?" I said.

"Uh — eh —?" He was mumbling. I swear he was bloody mumbling. And he was visibly unsettled to have been caught out. (Flora didn't notice, but I was watching him intently.)

"Amanitas," he said, clearing his throat. "Yes, the woods are full of them." He nodded gravely and fumbled with his moustache. "Mushrooms," he said, "are the noble staff of life." And that brought our little conversation to an end.

The only drawback to renting the house — and at the time, neither of us realized just what a disastrous drawback it would prove to be — was its complete and absolute isolation. There were no houses for miles around. Nothing. The de la Regniers' chateau was the nearest place to ours, but that was six or seven miles away. We were on our own, stuck slap-bang in the middle of nowhere and surrounded by mile upon mile of thick-as-a-hedge woodland. I'd never realized such a wild place existed in France.

It was perfect for me, of course. The forest at the back of the house extended for twenty or thirty miles, perhaps more. The vastness of it all was almost frightening. The view from our upstairs window was of this gigantic green duvet — an endless, undulating eiderdown of greenery. On it went. And on. Over the hills and far away.

And if you were lucky, on the clearest days, you could just about make out Mont Beaumont. That's the highest point for miles around — it's more than six thousand feet — with spruces and conifers furnishing its slopes. We'd been told that in winter it was always covered in snow. Not like the old days, of course — but snow nonetheless. And it was true. The first snows arrived in November and the top of Beaumont still had patches of white at Easter time.

Our first evening in the house — I'll never forget our first evening there. We lit a fire, for the stone walls seemed to shudder with the chill (how funny to speak of the chill when I'm sitting here sweating and sweltering in ninety degrees) and we were huddled around the fire in all our clothes, trying to get warm.

When Flora spoke, she did so in a whisper. "Well, my dashing Marshal Veuilly," she said, "we're alone. We're miles from the nearest person."

"It's what you wanted," I said. "You were the one who wanted to get away from it all."

"Yes, but how strange it feels." She paused and then smiled at me. "I hope you'll protect me. I hope you'll save me from intruders."

"Perhaps I should change into my uniform."

"I think I prefer you without," she said. She nuzzled her nose into my neck. "Yes, I definitely prefer you without."

Flora was right about the isolation, Peter. It really did feel strange. It's funny — I hadn't thought about it until she mentioned it. But then — well: you see, in Clapham there are always lights. There are neighbours all around. Zara and Michael with their four children. The Austins. Old Mrs Hitchens. And there's always noise. Cars and lorries and even in the middle of the night you hear airplanes or sirens or something. But here — nothing. At night you heard nothing. Not a whisper. Not even the wind. I'd lie in bed, wide awake, and listen to the sound of my own ears. Pump-pump-pump. It's the blood racing round your brain. Pump-pump-pump. It's circulating all your thoughts and worries and fears. Pump-pump-pump. It's unsettling because you realize that it's the pump-pump-pump that's keeping you alive. If that was to stop — well, it would be curtains.

And even on the mountain itself there was no human life. We were told that the little observation station on the top was only manned in midsummer. For the rest of the year Mont Beaumont, with its wild slopes and its wild spruces and its wild conifers, was abandoned to the wild snow and the wild wind.

There was the chateau, of course. That was only seven miles away. But the owner spent much of his time in Paris and almost every time we passed it, the shutters were closed and the place seemed boarded up. And the nearest village — well, it was another eight miles beyond the chateau. And it wasn't exactly humming. So it was all a big, big change from what we were used to in Clapham.

I'd managed to convince myself that there was nothing frightening about solitude. I'd spent so much time in woods and forests that they no longer scared me as much as they once did. Besides, we were often together on our mushroom-picking expeditions. You. And me. And it's the fear of the unknown that unnerves people — I'm convinced that's what it is. Yes. The fear of getting lost. The fear that you are absolutely alone. But when you recognize the trees, know the plants, can put a name to the beetles and the ants and the slugs — well, you're no longer entirely alone. Even a large forest becomes a more friendly place.

It was our first night, remember. Our very first night. And as I stood at the window peering out into the darkness, I suddenly glimpsed the flash of a torch. It lasted for a second, perhaps less, but I swear it was there. There was a light. It

28

flashed. There was someone outside. There was someone outside our home.

I looked harder — strained my eyes — but I could see nothing but shadow. Night had fallen and it was by now so dark that even the tops of the trees had been swallowed into this big black hole. I waited by the window; stood there for more than a minute to see if the torchlight would reappear. But the forest had slunk back into its shadow — slipped away — and whoever was outside was somehow managing to move around without light.

My first thought was whether or not I should say anything to Flora. *No* — I thought not. To tell her that there was someone wandering about outside not wishing to be seen would have put the fear of God into her. So I said nothing. I closed the curtains, damped down the fire and suggested that we go to bed.

"You've bolted the back door as well as the front?" she asked.

I certainly had. I'd double-locked them both.

CHAPTER
ONE

Peter Rushton told me a lot about Arnold: about his job, his home life and his marriage to Flora. Flora was five years younger than her husband and was (in Peter's words) "like a stick of dynamite". They argued quite often, that's what Peter said, although he was sure they were very much in love. "Almost like childhood sweethearts. They shared their secrets. They shared everything." But when they fell out — "Crash, bang, wallop" — the sky fell in. It was World War Three with a full exchange of nuclear weapons. Peter didn't blame Flora for their squabbles. Arnold, he said, could be quite impossible. Inflexible. He pushed things to the wire.

I asked him more about the source of their arguments. "Well," said Peter, "*she* thought his job was the problem. She wanted to get out. Move on. Take Arnold away. And she wanted children. Yes, a family was what Flora really, desperately wanted. Biological time clock and all that. Happens to all the ladies. But Arnold . . ." He paused for a moment, as if reflecting on all that had happened. And then he leaned forwards, leaned towards me, as if he wished to say something in complete confidence. "It came as a great shock when people heard of their impending divorce," he said. "And when they learned the reason for them splitting up, well, there was outright incredulity."

And with good reason. Not only was Arnold marrying a queen — a genuine, real-life queen — but she was said to be extremely attractive and a great deal younger than him. Peter told me that although Arnold always kept one eye on the ladies — "It was as if he needed the attention" — he'd been one hundred and fifty per cent faithful to Flora since the day they were married.

"She was his wife and his lover and his friend," he said. "He adored her and she adored him. In fact, Arnold worshipped Flora in his own funny way."

Peter also told me that everyone in their mushroom-hunting club had been "gobsmacked" by the news. But he added that there was something in all of this that did not take him completely by surprise. Arnold had a side to him which was, well, a little odd. Those were his words. "A little odd." He'd known him for more than thirty-six years, yet there was a part of Arnold he didn't know at all. Certain things that didn't make sense.

Peter wondered if it was "an attention thing". Arnold, he said, relished the limelight. That was why he so enjoyed giving talks and lectures. "He could talk away on any subject you might happen to throw at him. Regency chairs. King Charles the second's mistresses. And, of course, mushrooms.

"His last talk on mushrooms was at the Royal Geographical Society. A packed house. Full. And virtually all of them female. Hundreds of women on the edge of their seats. Hundreds of women with their tongues lolling out. He held them entranced. And when he spoke of the aphrodisiac qualities of the husky puffball, well — you could almost hear the hormones."

"But wasn't Flora annoyed?" I asked. "I can't imagine many wives taking kindly to hundreds of women eyeing up their husband."

"Well, she was used to it," said Peter. "And she knew that Arnold would never be unfaithful. She had absolute, implicit and total trust in him. Even though he was unpredictable."

I asked what he meant.

"Arnold doesn't do things the way other people do things," said Peter as he tapped his fingers on the table. "Not at all. How can I explain . . .? Perhaps — yes — let me tell you about the Soup Kitchen. D'you know about the Soup Kitchen in Bayswater?"

This rang a vague bell.

"It was for homeless people. A place where they could get hot food. Once a day — in the evening."

"And what's it got to do with Arnold?"

"He set it up. It was his idea. And —" Peter laughed — "they always served mushroom soup. Day in, day out. Mushroom bloody soup."

"Why?"

"Ah, that's where Arnold steps in. He said that mushrooms were free for all. A democratic food. They sprang up everywhere, even in central London. Hyde Park. St James's Park. Wimbledon Common. You could find them anywhere, if only you looked."

"Is that true?"

"Yes, yes," said Peter. "I suppose it is. And then, one day, he turns up in Taplow Bottom with a coachload of homeless people. Forty-two of them. He'd hired a coach and brought them here. And he leads them into the woods. And he teaches them all about mushrooms and how to find them and identify them.

"Philippa, of course, was not best pleased. She didn't take kindly to finding forty-two stinking homeless people hanging around in our house that afternoon. In fact, she was furious. She spent the next two days disinfecting the chairs and carpets in case they'd brought in any infectious diseases. By that time, of course, Arnold had taken his tramps back to London and told them to look for their own mushrooms. 'Go and find you're own bloody food, you lazy homeless sods.' That's what he said to them."

"And did they?"

"That's the amazing thing," said Peter. "Most of them did. Eighty per cent. They really liked Arnold. They looked up to him. Somehow — and I've never understood how — he was able to work on their wavelength. And he rang me the next afternoon, pleased as punch, and told me they'd found more than thirty pounds of shrooms."

"And what about the twenty per cent that didn't go searching?"

"He told them to sod off," said Peter with a laugh. "To sod right off. He wasn't interested in slackers. And he refused to give them any soup."

The above conversation had taken place at the Red Lion, a little pub on the village green at Taplow

Bottom. I was intrigued by what Peter had told me: it only increased my curiosity about Arnold.

When we'd finished our beers, Peter proposed that we go back to his house because he had something that he thought would interest me. Arnold, it transpired, had recently sent him the first in what he intended as a series of cassettes about his new life in Tuva. Peter wanted me to listen to it because he had this vague sort of feeling — one he couldn't quite pinpoint — that his old friend might be in some sort of trouble.

There was the clunk of the play button; a moment of fuzz. And then Arnold's voice burst into life: *I'm missing you, of course. And I'm missing Philippa. But then again, I'm standing by the window . . .* He sounded so close — and his voice so familiar — that it was as if he was there in the room. His kingly duties on Tuva hadn't changed him in the slightest. It was him all right. The same Arnold I'd met in Burgundy.

We listened to the section of the tape about France, the part where Arnold spoke of his arrival in the Morvan.

"He never mentioned anything about the person outside when I went to interview him," I said to Peter.

"No," said Peter. "Nor did he ever mention it to me. It's typical Arnold: you only ever get half a story."

It *was* typical Arnold. I'd only spent a few hours in his company but it was long enough to have become familiar with his discursive manner of speaking. Yet *this*: this was strange. Was it for real? Had someone really been poking around outside his house?

"Dunno," said Peter. "He doesn't say anything else."

"And what's all that stuff about Warlock?"

Peter shrugged his shoulders. "News to me," he said.

We listened to the cassette for a second time and concentrated on the bits about Tuva.

"I'd never heard of the place," I said to Peter.

"No, nor, I have to confess, had I. It's not in this atlas —" he pointed to *The Times Atlas of the World* — "but then again, nor are half the other islands in the Pacific. Even Tonga seems to have been put there as an afterthought."

Peter said he was intending to go to the University of London Library, the one in Senate House, in order to photocopy the pages that Arnold had asked for.

He told me that I was welcome to join him, if I wished. I did indeed, for I was intrigued, and so we agreed to meet at lunchtime on the following Wednesday.

"Until Wednesday, then," I said as I turned to leave.

"Until Wednesday," replied Peter.

Wednesday was grey, wet and miserable: it had rained all night. I thought of Arnold, thousands of miles away on Tuva. He'd complained about the heat and humidity on his island, but I'd have been more than happy to have exchanged the London sky for some tropical sunshine.

Peter was waiting for me at the entrance to the Senate House. "Another tape," he said. "Arrived this morning. Philippa called me at the office to tell me. I haven't had a chance to hear it yet. I'll listen to it tonight. If you'd care to be there . . .?"

I'd have liked nothing better, but it was impossible. I had arranged to meet with Kate, my half-serious girlfriend, for what was likely to be the last in a series of increasingly lukewarm evenings in each other's company. Both of us had come to realize that we were going precisely nowhere.

Peter and I registered at the library (a formality), paid the day fee and then headed up to the sixth floor, where we'd been told we'd find the section on Oceania. And there it was: *Fungal Spores in the Tuvan Archipelago* by Ernest Arthur Warlock. It was a short book, little more than a pamphlet, with less than two dozen pages. Inside, on the title page, was a subtitle: *With a Brief Account of the Recent Assassination of the Late King of Tuva.*

I pointed it out to Peter. "I wonder when *that* was. The assassination, I mean."

"Well, nineteen nineteen or thereabouts," he said. "Look — that's when the thing was published."

The opening section recounted how Warlock's vessel, the *Challenger*, had arrived at Tuva in October 1918, dropping anchor in the deep water between Tuva and Wei-Kitu. Warlock had clearly been captivated by the natural beauty of the Tuvan archipelago for he had written a colourful description of his arrival.

As we sailed into the bay of Tuva, a wall of green vegetation appeared to rise from the water like the plush velvet stage curtain of the Royal Court Theatre. The flying fish were dancing their courtship in the mercury waters of the lagoon and, in the sky overhead, a couple of white tufted tropicbirds were hovering in the thermals. It was a very vision of paradise.

"That's what I call flowery prose," said Peter.

Warlock's original reason for coming to Tuva was to study the tiger beetle, but he was also an expert in mycology (according to the title page, he was vice-president of the Royal Society of Mycologists) and he was hoping to study the fungi of Tuva. But in this quest he was to be disappointed. There were no mushrooms of any kind to be found on the island, despite the rich soil and near-perfect climatic conditions.

One of the great surprises of my professional life was to discover that fruiting fungi were wholly absent from the Tuvan archipelago. After extensive research in these islands, and many others, I came to conclude that although the humus is filled with spores, these rarely if ever attain maturity. This may have something to do with the twice-yearly monsoon, which creates an unstable humidity in these maritime realms.

I enquired amongst the native islanders as to whether they had ever seen mushrooms — and indeed showed them photographs and lithographs of some of the commoner genera — but they looked puzzled. To my astonishment, none of them had ever seen a mushroom fruit.

"And to think," said Peter, "that Arnold's ended up on an island without mushrooms. That's ironic with a capital I."

The book contained a crudely drawn map of the Tuvan archipelago. All of the islands that Arnold had spoken about were there: Tuva, Oloua, Ta'ula, Wei-Kitu and the others. The reefs and atolls were also shown and it was immediately obvious why no large vessels could come anywhere near the place. Although there were deep channels of water separating the islands, each one was ringed with reefs and shallows.

"Well that certainly explains their isolation," I said. "If you can't get ships there, then you can't get tourists."

"Hole in one," said Peter. "And I guess that's how they've managed to preserve their traditions. Most islands around the world have done away with the old customs, but it sounds as if Tuva's held on to its colour."

We flicked through to the end of the pamphlet where there was the account of the assassination of the king of Tuva. Warlock, who'd arrived on the island a few weeks before the killing, recounted how the king had been shot in the head. There was no mention of the Order, or whatever it was that Arnold had spoken about. Nor had Warlock himself actually witnessed the killing.

The assassination of King Tuva brought regicide to the South Pacific for the first time in many decades *[he wrote]*. The manner of the killing was curious and has yet to be satisfactorily explained: two professional assassins who were believed to be of Russian extraction. I, alas, was on Ta'ula island at the time and was unable to examine the cadaver of the assassin who was killed. But I was fortunate enough to cast my eye over the bullet that was extracted from the deceased king's brain. It was of Russian manufacture and I was later told of rumours that the killers had been sent on the orders of Yakov Mikhailovich Yurovsky.

"Yurovsky?" I said, thinking aloud. "Who's he, then?"

Peter shrugged. "Never heard of him."

There was little more information about the killing, apart from the fact that the king's children all fled the island in the wake of the bloodshed. They didn't go back, or so Warlock said, which was presumably why Arnold and Lola were the first reigning monarchs since 1918.

"Is Lola a descendant of the old King Tuva?" I asked Peter.

"I guess so," he said. "I'm pretty sure he said that. And I suppose that's why she was allowed to go back."

I glanced once again at the map of the Tuvan archipelago and was suddenly struck by the ludicrousness of Arnold's situation. Why would anyone in their right mind want to uproot from England (or France, in Arnold's case) and settle on a tiny atoll on the furthest side of the world? These islands were beyond remote. I tried to work out the nearest landmass. It was probably

Australia, but that lay some two thousand miles to the west, perhaps more.

I couldn't see how the Arnold I'd met in Burgundy could keep himself sane in such surroundings. He said there were only twenty or so houses on the island, and it sounded as if most people spoke only broken English. Little wonder he sounded homesick: the stinking heat; the lack of companionship; the isolation; the boredom. He had the "delectable" Lola to keep him company, that was true, but how long would he retain his interest in her?

"Well, that," said Peter, "depends on what she has to offer." He let out a lurid laugh and then mumbled something about Flora.

Flora. I was suddenly struck by a desire to meet Arnold's ex-wife. She, perhaps, was the only person who could describe the strange circumstances in which her husband had left her. She alone might be able to explain what made Arnold tick.

"Not possible," said Peter. "She's in Singapore. At her sister's. Hasn't been back to England since the crisis blew up, I think I'm right in saying. But I'd like to see her again: she's as bright as a spark. And very attractive. Always had a soft spot for Flora, although I wouldn't want to live with her in a million years."

We photocopied the pamphlet and then put it back on the shelf. "I think," said Peter, "that we need to listen to his new tape. How are you placed next week?"

"Monday?" I said.

"Done."

CHAPTER
TWO

And then there was my wedding. If only you'd been here, Peter. Lola wore a dress decked with great garlands of taramora blossom. They hung from her neck like tangerines. And I wore my long white shorts and old mirror sunglasses.

Everyone was invited, of course. The entire population. And they sang their socks off during the ceremony, especially when we got to the Tuvan national anthem. It was a strange old service, a Tuvan take on traditional Church of England. The vicar was from Vanu (we haven't got one on Tuva). He's called the Reverend Kenneth Taupu — strange fellow — and he was so nervous he had to nip out for a pee twice during the ceremony. And when it came to the vows —

"Do you, Arnold Trevellyan, take this woman —"

"I do."

"To have and to hold —"

"To have and to hold —"

"To love and to cherish —"

"To love and to cherish —"

"And do you solemnly promise —"

"I solemnly promise —"

"That you will never in this life —"

"That I will never in this life —"

"Take more than nine other wives —"

"Take more than nine other wives —"

"Before the age of fifty —"

"Before the age of —"

Holy Moses! That's what I was thinking. *Nine other wives! Before the age of fifty!* Now I'd already been forewarned about the whole marriage thing: how they've practised polygamy, etcetera, etcetera, for centuries. It's the same on all the islands — Oloua, Tu'unoho and even Tonga, although I'm told they're trying to suppress it there. But even so — . When you actually hear it spoken by the vicar — . And you think to yourself that over the course of the next eight years, well, you're legally entitled — under Tuvan law — to marry nine more wives. That makes one a year. Or, to be precise, one every ten-and-a-half months. And on an island that only has thirty-one women.

"You don't *have* to take more," explained Lola later that evening. "It's not obligatory. And there are some women that count for two, the really big ones, like Gilbertine and Doris. If you married both of them, you'd probably be considered as having five wives, if you included me."

I blinked and laughed as I tried to take it all in.

"But wouldn't you mind?" I asked.

"*Mind?*" She looked puzzled. "Why on earth should I mind? A man like you needs several wives. You're a king, don't forget. Didn't your Henry the eighth have lots of wives?"

"Six," I said. "And he killed two of them."

"Well you're not allowed to do that on Tuva," she said. "You have to look after us. To have and to hold — remember? We take the wedding vows very seriously on Tuva."

"Well, I guess I could *have* Doris," I said, "but I'm not sure I could *hold* her. I wouldn't be able to get my arms round her."

Lola frowned at me for the first time. "I'm not sure you're taking this very seriously," she said.

So there you have it, Peter. If you ever want another wife — or another eight — you'd better get yourself over here.

Now, what else did I want to tell you? Ah, yes — you made everyone's day by sending that tape. I've been playing it to the islanders over and over — last night *and* this morning — and they can't get enough. But you forgot to write down what the noises were, so I've had to take a punt. Now then: here we go, here we go.

The first one's a lawnmower, one of those petrol ones. I guess it must be yours. Number two sounds like a strimmer or hedge-cutter. The third one's a Routemaster. Recognized that one immediately. That's Lola's favourite — reminds her of the couple of weeks she once spent in London. Then there's an ambulance — or is it a fire engine? The children like that one best. You've started a whole new craze for sirens: waaa-waaa-waaa-waaa-waaa. You can probably hear them all running around in the background.

What next? Ah yes, a train then a tube then a plane then a boat. Then come the bells of Big Ben — ding dong ding dong. Everyone likes that. But after that, Peter, you lost me. Sounds like you spent the next twenty minutes drilling holes into a bowl of jelly.

You've amazed everyone. If only you could see their faces. You see, most people here hardly ever leave the island, except to fish, and those who do never go beyond Tonga. They simply can't believe England is so noisy. "You could eat that sort of noise, sir," said Gilbertine. "You could eat it off a spoon." And she *would* eat it, Peter. And she'd eat her mother as well, if served with sweet potatoes and pawpaw sauce.

But I'm digressing. I'm straying off the beaten track. I was in the middle of telling you all about Burgundy. About the house. About the torchlight outside. Yes, that's where we were, seated in front of a roaring fire (how long ago it all seems!) with the front door locked and bolted and someone wandering around in our garden.

Flora, of course, didn't know anything. I hadn't told her I'd seen a light. I didn't want to scare her unnecessarily. And it would have been unnecessary, as it transpired, for the night passed off peacefully enough. The torchlight didn't reappear and there was not a sound to be heard outside, except the moaning of the wind in the trees. Moaning and whining as if it was exhausted from the effort of bustling its way through the forest.

We were woken by this brilliant sunlight streaming in through the windows: it was one of those glorious autumn days that make you happy to be alive. I remember opening the window and poking my nose into the chill. The air smelled as fresh as it comes: sharp, crisp, resinous, as if it had been polished with one of those beeswax-style lotions that we used to use at Baddington's. As I smiled into the sunshine, I half-convinced myself that I'd imagined the whole episode from the night before.

I went downstairs to heat up some water, leaving Flora in bed. We hadn't yet done a big shop so there were only the things we'd brought with us — coffee, tea, butter, that sort of stuff. As the water was heating on the stove, I struggled into my boots and stepped out into the garden. It was sharper than I'd expected; I didn't want to stay out long. But there was something I wanted to check — I wanted to put my mind at rest. I walked across to the edge of the garden, to the point at which the grass stopped and the forest began. And I took a careful look at the ground. It didn't take me long to find them. There, clearly imprinted in the squelchy mud, were footprints.

I bent down to examine them more closely. I was in no doubt, Peter, that those footprints were not more than a few hours old. They were not mine. And they were not Flora's. Someone had indeed been wandering around on the previous evening. Someone had been observing us, keeping an eye on us. And at that very moment — as I stood in my pyjamas staring at the footprints — I knew, I just knew, that someone was studying our every movement.

And then, quite without warning, there was a piercing shriek from inside the house. My heart froze for a second. Froze stock still. And then I realized that it was the kettle boiling.

"Arnold . . . Arnold." Flora was calling me from upstairs. "The kettle —"

I went inside, made tea and clambered back into bed.

We found ourselves slipping into a routine without really thinking about it. Yes, we found that our lives began to take on a new rhythm. And that's what I was used to, I suppose. Wake up. Breakfast. Bus to work. Routine — I think it's no bad thing. Tick, tick. That's how you keep yourself on the tracks. And while life wasn't quite the same in the Morvan as it had been in Clapham, it was all pleasant enough. I'd make tea and we'd drink it in bed and it was often nine-thirty by the time we'd sit down to breakfast.

But after a few weeks — well, it was then that peculiar things started to happen. Everything started to go odd. And it's no exaggeration to say that the things that happened were the original cause of all the problems between Flora and myself.

It was a Tuesday — I remember it as if it were yesterday — and the morning began like this. We got dressed, had a coffee and talked over our plans to explore the area to the east of our house. We'd not yet walked in that direction — or not very far — and I wanted to check out the vegetation and ground cover.

"Boots, waterproof and a knife," I read off our checklist as Flora picked up her basket.

"And keys," she said. "We ought to keep locking up, even though there's no one around."

"I've got the keys," I replied. "Come on, let's go."

Flora hung back for a moment. "Hey, Marshal Veuilly," she said. "You're looking particularly handsome this morning. How about a kiss for Madame de Sévignac?"

I kissed her — a big fat kiss on the lips — and then double-locked the door. And then I stood back to admire the house, as I did every morning. The place really was an oddity, Peter. It was small — little more than a cottage — and it had these sweeping stone roofs. They'd been designed to look like drapes of canvas — or so we were told — and in a funny sort of way it worked. They seemed to sag in the middle. And they even leaked, just like canvas. The house felt incredibly damp; there was a great rash of mould in the corner of the living room. Most of the gutters and drainpipes were blocked when we first arrived and when it rained — as it did all the time — water poured in under the back door. The owners of the chateau had already told us that no one had lived there for decades and I could well believe it. The wiring was so dangerous that we gave up on electricity and used a couple of old paraffin lights instead. They made it feel like an adventure.

There was a track that led away from the house in two directions. One branch led to Creux, the nearest little hamlet (I say nearest — it was still fourteen or so miles away.) The other seemed to continue eastwards, deeper into the forest. It was little more than a bridle path — it certainly hadn't seen vehicles for many years — but must once have served as a road because we found several moss-covered milestones set into the earthy banks. We walked and walked and, after we'd been going for twenty minutes or so, we unexpectedly stumbled across another house.

"What've we got here then?" I said to Flora.

"Certainly not neighbours," said Flora, "that's for sure."

The place was in a poor state. Part of the roof had slumped in on itself and all the windows had been smashed long ago. I gave the front door a kick and it promptly gave way. It fell into the hallway and broke in two.

"Hey, Muscle Man," said Flora with a laugh. "Don't waste all your strength on kicking down doors."

I picked my way over the front door, tiptoed down the hallway. A door on the right led into a front room which still bore the traces of carpet. The second door led into a kitchen with a tiled floor and rusting cooking range.

"*Arnold?*" It was Flora outside.

"Yes, yes — don't worry, I'm still alive. I'm coming out."

I retraced my steps down the corridor, sticking my head back into the first room before stepping inside to have a closer look. It had a thick smell of damp and I had to pick my way across the floorboards with care as many of them had the telltale black stains of rot. It was only when I glanced back towards the door that I noticed an old photograph hanging lopsidedly on the wall. It was faded and the glass was fuzzy with mildew, but there was no mistaking who was in the picture.

"That's the Romanovs," I said to myself. "The Russian tsar, tsarina and the rest of the family." They were posing together in the formal garden of a palace and looking directly at the camera. I tried to wipe the glass with my sleeve, but as I did so the corner of the frame snapped apart and the whole thing dropped to the floor.

"Arnold."

"Coming, coming."

I stepped back into the corridor, musing on who might once have lived here and why they'd had a picture of the Romanovs in their house.

"They were very popular in France," said Flora by way of explanation. "Think of all the Russians who came here after the revolution. Thousands of them."

She was right, of course, and I thought very little more of the matter at the time. Indeed it was some days before I was to discover the full significance of this picture being there.

We pushed on down the track, which was by now little more than a tangle of briars, until it opened out into a little clearing. And here we found two more abandoned houses.

"Why's everything boarded up?" asked Flora. "It's all rather sad. Every single house in the entire area is abandoned and in ruins. It's as if everyone upped and left about thirty or forty years ago."

"It is a little odd," I said, "but I suppose that's rural France for you. No one wants old houses. They don't like old things. They don't see the romance of it."

"But these are *so* romantic. They'd make fabulous homes."

"They would," I agreed. "But then again: how would you earn a living, stuck out here in the middle of nowhere?"

That, I assumed, was why they'd been abandoned. (When I think back on it now, with the benefit of hindsight, I can only smile at my naivety.) But it all made sense at the time. We'd already been told that the Morvan was one of the poorest areas in France. Jobs were few and far between. President Mitterrand had tried to create employment — he'd cut his political teeth in the Morvan — but it had proved an utter waste of money.

"Well, I don't know why some rich Parisian hasn't bought them," said Flora. "If these were in England, they'd have been snapped up long ago."

We looked around both houses: they were in much the same condition as the first. Flora wanted to buy all three of them, immediately, until I pointed out the costs of restoring them.

"Well, couldn't we buy the one we're in?" she asked. "We should sweet-talk Monsieur de la Regnier at the chateau. I'm sure he'd sell it to us."

"I'm sure he wouldn't," I said. (Buying a house here, Peter, was the very last thing on my mind.) "Let's see what happens. We might get bored. We might want to get out."

We pushed deep into the forest, started looking for mushrooms. We'd agreed that Flora would pick the edible ones — the penny buns and trumpets — while I'd restrict myself to poisonous amanitas.

Flora had the first success. A long line of hedgehogs and a fine collection of velvet brittlegills. I feared it might be too cold for amanitas: the temperature had fallen to about forty degrees during the night, and that — as you know — is very much the lower limit for mushrooms. And what with the wet summer and dry autumn — well, it was a disaster for deathcaps and caesars. In the wood itself, the trees and undergrowth seemed to have provided a blanket of insulation for there was a surprising amount of fungal growth, although nothing of great interest. The dead trunks were covered in smoky brackets, porecrusts and hairy curtains and I found more than two dozen turkeytails.

And then — bingo — I found what I was looking for. Clustered under a small group of pines was a solitary deathcap, a gorgeous bugger which had yet to be nibbled by slugs. And I noticed that it was surrounded by a little ring of thistles — blessed milk thistles, to be precise. Spiky leaves, fat purple heads — you know the one? And it set me thinking, it got my mind a-whirring. That humble plant on that chill morning was the genesis of my great idea . . .

It was easy to lose your bearings in that forest, Peter. It was quite unlike any other forest I'd explored. I don't know what it was — I still can't explain it — but my natural bearings seemed to go askew. You know how I'm normally very good on directions. I know my north from my south; I can work out where I am by the position of the sun. But here — well, it was strange. It was as if the forest was playing a trick on us. As if the briars and brambles were chuckling to themselves, having a good laugh, as we tripped and stumbled and lost our way. I kept having to take mental notes of specific trees or rocks or fallen trunks in order to find my way back to the track. And yet my mental compass still went wrong. At one point the sun seemed to be in the north-east. A few minutes later I could swear it had swung round to the south. The fir tree that was on my left just a few moments earlier now reappeared on my right. And even the track seemed to lead off in a different direction from before.

"Don't expect me to lead us out of here," said Flora. "I'm relying on your sixth sense." And she laughed.

We continued our search, creeping through the undergrowth and staring intently at the ground. You know how it is when you're looking for mushrooms. Your horizon is below you — four feet from your eyes — and you hardly ever look up. There's an invisible cord that keeps your eyes down, anchors them to the ivy carpet and somehow changes your vision.

We must have been searching like that for the better part of half an hour, picking our way through ferns and bracken. When I finally looked up — straightened my back — Flora was nowhere to be seen. I looked all around me, peering through the trees in search of her bright yellow cape. I stopped. I listened. There was not a sound. The forest was eerily silent. Silent like an empty cube.

"Flora!" I called her name. "Flora!"

"Flora, Flora, Flora, Flora, Flora." It bounced back off the trees and returned to mock me.

I tried again, only this time much louder. Floooooooooooora. There was a crashing overhead, a violent beating of wings, as a panicking bird fought its way out through the canopy of leaves.

I suddenly realized that I was lost. I'd been staring at the ground, not noting where I was going, and now I'd completely lost my bearings. And for the first time in my life

I felt a little wave of panic. I was well and truly lost. And so, I guessed, was Flora.

Calm yourself, calm yourself. It's not the time to panic.

I glanced over to my left, about two hundred yards through the trees, to where there was a patch of sunlight. It was a clearing in the forest, a large one, and I was surprised I hadn't noticed it before. I pushed my way through the bracken calling Flora's name several more times. "Flora! — Flora!" This time I shouted really loudly, but there was no reply. Just a horribly still silence, a warmish sun and the long wild grasses swaying like drunken metronomes in the breeze.

I can't remember if something caught my eye or if I heard a sound. But, whatever it was, it drew my gaze over to the far side of the clearing where there was a stumpy outcrop of rock. It seemed to rise from a hollow in the ground and it also seemed to have an opening like the entrance to a cave. I walked towards it and saw that this was indeed the case. The clearing dipped down into a natural bowl and inside this bowl there was a crag of limestone that reared up in a series of tooth-like towers and pinnacles. I half-closed my eyes, deliberately fuzzing the image before me. And my imagination did the rest. The blur of shapes metamorphosed themselves into a fantasy palace, with bastions and ramparts and crenellated battlements. All that was missing was a carved stone escutcheon, some pennants and a medieval jouster or two.

Water was dripping off the limestone portal, even though it hadn't rained for several days, and had collected into a deep puddle at the entrance. It was immediately obvious to me that this had once been a quarry. There was a big red sign: *Proprieté privée: défense d'entrer*. Well I ignored that; I've always been the questioning type. And this was certainly a curious place. Even before I stepped inside I could see that the rocky walls of the interior bore the imprints of vast geometric shapes. Rectangular chunks of rock had been gouged out, leaving a hollow space that looked like the empty negative of some sort of cubist sculpture.

I eased my way down the path — it was as mud-sticky as grease — and into the mouth of the quarry. The entrance was large, perhaps ten foot wide and thirty foot in height, and the ground sloped steeply away once I was inside. That first room, if I can call it that, was like the narthex of a Romanesque abbey — a giant box of a space that had been scooped out of solid rock.

It was not entirely enclosed, nor was it entirely dark. In places chunks of the ceiling had tumbled in on themselves, allowing shafts of light to shine down from above, like so many spotlights on the stage of a theatre. And wherever the light fell clusters of blessed milk thistles had burst into life, just like the ones in the forest.

"Well this is a discovery and a half," I said to myself. "This'll be something to tell Flora." I'd completely forgotten the fact that I was lost. I'd even forgotten the fact that Flora was on her own in the forest. I could only focus on what I'd found.

That first room opened into several other chambers — and each one seemed to be on a grander scale than the last. The rough stone ceiling, fifty feet above my head, was held up by these thumping great columns which the stoneworkers had left in situ in order to keep the whole place propped up. But in numerous places the ceiling above had caved in — gravity or tree roots had done their worst — allowing me to pick my way through the gloom quite easily.

I wondered when it had last seen human activity, when the Morvan's quarriers had last hacked out rock from here. It must have been at least a hundred years earlier, if not more, for the sawn stone edges, the fretted planes and jagged angles, were as smooth as skin.

I pushed deeper into the quarry, taking great care to remember my way. I was very worried about getting lost. I left an arrow of stones on the floor of each chamber, just like Hansel and Gretel. I was now about three or four hundred feet into the gloom and still there was no sign of the quarry coming to an end.

The next chamber was considerably lighter because an entire corner of the ceiling had fallen in on itself. And there, resting among a great heap of coal-black soil, was another cluster of blessed milk thistles. I remember thinking to myself, "Arnold Trevellyan, you're one lucky bastard." Because it had ticked through my mind that if these grew here, why, there would be no reason why amanitas wouldn't grow. Perhaps — yes — perhaps I could even cultivate death-caps and agarics. Perhaps I could grow caesars, Peter. That's what I was thinking. You see, this place — with its near-constant humidity — was like a semi-underground laboratory. All that was missing was my magic potion.

I stooped down to examine the soil. And as I did so, well, I swear to God — I heard the sound of voices. They were a long way off, little more than a distant echo. But — yes — there it was again. A babble-babble-babble of voices.

Holy cow — . That's what I said to myself. *Holy cow* — . My first thought was that I'd been followed, that someone had trailed me down into the quarry. I felt my heart going bump-tr-thump-bump-tr-thump. But then again: no. These were not the voices of people who were worried about being overheard. The noise that I could hear, and hear quite distinctly, sounded more like idle chatter. It was as if whoever was down here — down inside the quarry — was having an after-dinner conversation.

Bump-tr-thump-bump-tr-thump.

My next thought was that it must be a guided tour, a group of people brought down here to trawl through the old quarries. But it didn't sound like a guided tour. There was no voice of a tour leader. No shuffle of feet. I could hear raised voices and quiet voices, men's voices and women's voices. I couldn't work out what they were saying for they were too indistinct. I couldn't even determine what language they were speaking.

Follow the voices, Arnold. That's what was going round in my head.

I passed through one, two, perhaps three more chambers. And still I could hear the voices, sometimes louder, sometimes softer. And they seemed never to get any closer. Were my ears deceiving me? Or was the quarry playing tricks?

As I passed into yet another chamber, the ninth or tenth. And here — *stop* — I noticed something peculiar. The floor was no longer scattered with fallen rock and broken shards. This floor had been swept — swept recently — and was entirely free of debris. The stones and rocks that had fallen from above were piled up neatly in a corner.

And then everything seemed to happen very quickly. You see, I immediately noticed something, Peter, that wasn't quite right. Even in the half-light, I could tell that the wall in front of me was fake. It was not rock. It was made of wood and had been painted to look like rock. A trompe l'oeuil. And there was a door in the wall and when I leaned against it — pushed it — it burst open. And there was a short narrow corridor behind it with just a whisker of light coming from the room that lay beyond.

I made my way along the corridor — I had to grope — and eventually found myself in a rock-hewn hall. And it was now that I got my biggest surprise of all. For there, in the far corner, was a tall double door, all varnished and mahogany. It had polished brass handles and a key in the lock. It looked like something out of a bloody country chateau.

And, well, you don't exactly stumble across a door in an underground quarry and not open it, do you? So I place my hand firmly on the handle and I squeeze it gently downwards. And before I know it — CLICK — the door opens a fraction.

And this, Peter, is what was so strange. You see, it was almost as if I was expecting it. It was almost as if I knew what I'd find behind that door. That's not to say, of course, that I didn't gulp. Of course I did. I gulped like a bloody goldfish. Imagine: no sooner have I opened the door than — stone the sodding crows — I find myself peering into a ballroom. Yes, you did hear correctly. A sodding great ballroom. Seventy feet long. Thirty feet wide. And on the upper levels there are these kind-of moulded splodges of stucco that look like white blancmange. Big blobs of white blancmange.

And that's only the half of it. Three chandeliers *dripping* with baubles and droplets. And above them — but wait. Let me pause for a moment. I can picture you shaking your head. You're pulling a face. You're looking at Philippa. You are, aren't you? Well, Peter, I swear to God on all that's holy that

I was staring at a room that would have looked quite at home in Versailles or the Brighton Pavilion or any other palace or chateau you care to mention. And yet here I was, standing in a damp and dripping underground quarry in Burgundy.

Tapestries hung on the end wall. Peasants with leery eyes and fawns and satyrs, all getting their end away. A magnificent piece of rip-roaring debauchery, Flemish. Sixteenth century. And in the centre of the room, stretching from one end to the other, was this long dining table. You could have seated two hundred people around that table. And there were porcelain beakers and faience platters and delftware bowls and majolica vases. I could have flogged it off for a fortune at Baddington's. Silver forks, knives and spoons. Six goblets and six platters for each setting. And in the centre, the focal point, was this quite magnificent silver epergne — Louis the fourteenth — that was spilling with tulips, roses and pergaloniums. And I remember thinking to myself, "That's strange. Not one of those flowers are in bloom at this time of year."

It's odd how you react at moments like this. If I'd had time to process it all through my brain — think about it in a logical fashion — then I guess I'd have entered the room, snooped around, investigated further. But I can tell you this, Peter: you react in strange ways when you're put into strange situations. And I'm no different from the next man. I suddenly panicked. Yes, I was struck with a terrible, chilling fear. I'd stumbled across something I was not meant to see. This was clearly meant to be secret. And so I shut the door to the room and made my way back through the corridor, quickly, quickly, quickly, retracing my steps through the outer chambers of the quarry. And after stumbling and tripping and going the wrong way on several occasions, I suddenly found myself back at the entrance, where, to my immense relief, there was the same muddy puddle and the same late-autumn sunshine and everything was more or less back to normal. And I thought to myself, "I need to find Flora."

CHAPTER
THREE

I drove out to Taplow Bottom on the Monday evening, arriving twenty minutes earlier than I'd agreed with Peter. His wife, Philippa, answered the door when I reached their house; it was the first time I'd met her.

"Aha," was her opening word. "You must be the *investigative* reporter." She said it in a tone that simultaneously expressed disapproval and mild admiration.

I explained to her that I actually worked on the foreign desk.

"How terribly glamorous," she said, softening somewhat. "*And* it's my favourite newspaper. That and the *Mail*. I do like the *Mail*, but only for the showbiz gossip, mind. Peter's embarrassed, of course. But, believe you me, I've caught him reading the celebrity interviews on many occasions. Oh, yes. Only yesterday I noticed he was paying rather too much attention to an article about Madonna."

"Don't listen to a word Pippy says," interrupted a dishevelled-looking Peter as he appeared at the top of the stairs. "Now — come in, old boy. Settle yourself down in the living room."

Philippa offered me a cup of tea, but Peter once again interrupted her.

"Tea?" he exclaimed with an air of feigned astonishment. "He's come all the way to Taplow Bottom, Pippy darling, and you're offering him tea! I think we need a couple of pintingtons and a few chunkingtons of Cheddar."

I'd noticed that this was one of Peter's favourite expressions. He liked adding "ingtons" on to the ends of words. Pints became pintingtons. Crisps became crispingtons. There were even occasions when he called his wife Pipingtons.

He disappeared into the kitchen, leaving me momentarily in the company of Philippa. She was the very epitome of the Home Counties housewife: tweed skirt, sensible shoes and half a can of hairspray. She wore a pair of dark-rimmed glasses, giving her a severe look. My first impression was that she was exactly like the women who answered the readers' letters at the *Telegraph*. Only later did I realize that I'd got Philippa all wrong. Her common-sense approach to life was overlaid with a mischievous sense of humour. She was actually quite funny, although I was never sure if she intended to be.

I took the opportunity to ask a few questions about Flora while Peter was out of the room. "Flora," she said, "is a vision of loveliness. She is the most wonderful, divine, darling woman on earth. Vivacious. A little hot-headed at times. Sometimes fragile. But —" she smiled to herself — "you would be if you were married to *him*."

I asked her what she meant.

"Arnold's got a stubborn side, you see. Oooh yes. Stubborn, stubborn. *She* wanted to up sticks long ago. I don't know why, but she never really seemed at home in London. She wanted a change of scene. Some country air. But Arnold was addicted to his job."

She let out a little snort. "And that stubbornness," she continued, "was a real sticking point for Flora."

"But surely," I said, "it wasn't the reason for everything that's happened?"

"No, no, no. There was also the children thing. She was desperate for little kidlets. And . . ." She stopped in mid-sentence, folded her arms and let out a sigh. "But still, it just doesn't add up. You see, they were in love with each other. I'm *sure* they were deeply in love. Those two were made for each other — that's what I'd often said to Peter. And Arnold needed Flora. He needed her more than anything else in the world. Oh, yes. Behind every man and all that. And now he's met this Lola girl, who seems to be about half his age, and he's run off to the furthest corner of the planet. I know that men are men and most of them are ruled by their toggles. But still — I can't quite make sense of it. There's something that doesn't add up. I don't understand it."

"And what about Flora?" I asked. "How's she taken it all?"

"Well, that's a question and a half," said Philippa, "I've only spoken to her once in the last six months. Not through want of trying. But after her experience in France and everything she went through, well, she went off to stay with her sister in Singapore. And then the two of them went trekking in Thailand and Burma. And the only time I managed to have half a chat with her was when she first arrived in Singapore. But she didn't want to talk about what had happened. Said she was trying to put it behind her. So that was that. We chatted, of course, but not about Arnold."

"But isn't she trying to get him back?" I asked. "From everything Peter's said, they sounded like the perfect married couple. Surely she'd want to try —"

"I think this must have been the straw that broke the proverbial camel's back. I think she realized that Arnold was having an affair."

"But he wasn't," I said abruptly. "He told me he hadn't even met Lola when Flora walked out."

Philippa looked at me with an air of disbelief. "You men are all the same," she said. "Do you *really* believe that? You — a journalist of all people. But since you seem so keen to know more about Flora, I can tell you one thing —"

"Now then," said Peter as he burst back into the room, "two beers. One for you. And one for —"

"What in heaven's —" said Philippa, swallowing her words. Peter was wearing a green rubber bath cap, flippers and swimming goggles. "So," he said, "how do I look?"

"Er — fetching," I said. "Very fetching." I wasn't quite sure what else I could say: Peter and Philippa got stranger by the minute.

"We've been asked to a fancy-dress ball next weekend," explained Peter. " 'Come as pond life.' That's what it said on the invitation. So I'm going as a frog."

"Well it's certainly effective. And frog-like."

I turned to Philippa. "And you —?"

"The frog's princess," she said with a smile. "Isn't that obvious?"

Peter peeled off the bath cap, put down the beers and then handed one to me.

"Mr Edwardes was asking —"

"Tobias — please."

"Mr — Tobias — was asking about Flora. I haven't even had a chance to tell you, Pottle dearest, but she's coming back. Yes, she's returning to London in a week or so. I'm not sure how long she'll be staying: I only heard this from Annabelle — she's a mutual friend — this morning. But she'll have to be in London for at least a day or two because the tenants are quitting."

She turned to me as she was saying all this and added, "And if you'd like to meet her, then I could arrange a dinner party. No promises, but I'll see what I can do."

"He only wants to meet her because she's single," said Peter with a laugh that was bordering on the lewd. His comment irritated me, perhaps because there was a part of it that was true.

"Enough chitter-chatter," he said. "Let's listen to the tape. Come on, beers are open; make yourself comfortable. I'll put it on. Feel free to push the pause button whenever you want."

And then there was my wedding. If only you'd been here, Peter. Arnold told the story of the peeing vicar and his wedding vows and then proceeded to list the noises that Peter had recorded for him.

I pushed the pause button. "So, *did* he get them right?" I asked.

"Almost," said Peter. "Number two was a hedge-cutter not a strimmer. The fourth was a fire engine. But he was spot on about the bus and the train and the others. And the holes being drilled in jelly was a bunch of bananas in my electric blender."

I pressed the play button and Arnold was off again, discovering houses and mushroom picking and wandering into an underground banqueting hall. We listened to the tape in its entirety and then sat in silence for a moment, digesting everything he'd told us.

"*So?*" said Peter. "An underground banqueting chamber. And underground voices. And abandoned houses. What d'you make of it?"

"He spins a good yarn," I said.

Peter shrugged his shoulders. "I thought you said you saw the abandoned houses when you were there."

"I did. Well, I saw one. But the quarry — he never mentioned that to me. In fact, he didn't tell me much at all about his time in France. I remember playing back my tape of the interview on the following morning and realizing just how little he'd revealed about himself."

Peter swigged his beer and Philippa tutted. "Oh, it'll all be some great excuse as to why he's run off with this Lola girl," she said. "Men, men, men." She sighed. "And men in their forties — tuh. Toggles, pure and simple."

"I'm not so sure," I said. "From what Peter's told me, Arnold could have run off with any number of women over the years. But he never did. So why would he now? There's got to be some other reason. Surely?"

"Precisely," said Peter, looking at his wife with an air of triumph. It was two against one and he was happy to take safety in numbers. "Well said."

"And this underground dining room," she said dismissively, as if this was supposed to prove something.

"I've no idea what he's going on about," I replied. "But I can tell you one thing I discovered the other day."

"Yes?"

I explained to them how a colleague of mine on the newspaper, Tim Burton, was writing a book on the Russian revolution. I'd asked Tim about the assassination of the tsar and whether or not he'd heard of Yakov Mikhailovich Yurovsky, the man who'd apparently ordered the killing of Tuva's king.

"*Yakov Yurovsky*. That name does indeed ring bells," was his response. "It rings loud and clear bells. Yurovsky was the man who shot the tsar. He personally killed Tsar Nicholas the second. Put a bullet in his head. He brought the Russian royal dynasty to a bloody end."

"So why," I asked him, "would he also have killed the king of a tiny island lost somewhere in the south Pacific?"

"Beats me. But Yurovsky was a senior member of the Cheka, the Russian secret police. Important man. Answered directly to Lenin. I've got a whole file of stuff about him at home. I'll bring it in if you want. But there's nothing about any Pacific islands. I've no idea where all that's come from."

I told Peter and Philippa all that Tim had told me. They both nodded slowly as they digested the information.

"I see," said Peter in the sort of tone of voice that suggested he was as confused as me. "But why the king of Tuva? And why the connection with Russia?"

"I've no idea," I answered, "but now we have Arnold going inside an abandoned house in the middle of Burgundy. And what does he find?"

"A portrait of the Romanov family," said Peter excitedly. "A photo of the bloody Russian royals."

"Yes," I said. "A photo of the Russian royals."

"Well, bugger me backwards," said Peter.

"Just listen to you both," interjected Philippa, ignoring her husband. "You sound like you're looking for clues where none exist. It's all just coincidence. I've got a picture of the queen in our upstairs toilet. And I've got that new biography of her in the downstairs toilet. But that doesn't mean that I'm about to assassinate her."

"Talking of the queen," I said, interrupting her, "he said something about having met her. I wonder what he means by that."

Peter put up his hand, as if to signal that he had something to say. "While you were investigating your Russian assassin," he said, "I was also hard at work. I took myself off to Westminster Library and checked through all the Court Circulars — looked at the lists of all the queen's engagements. Took me bloody hours. I wanted to see if she'd visited Burgundy at the time when Arnold was living there. And I also wanted to see if she and Prince Philip had been anywhere near Tuva."

"And?"

"Not a sausage," said Peter. "Well, not a Tuvan sausage, at any rate. The last time they went to the south Pacific was in nineteen seventy-eight. And they haven't even been to Australia recently, either. Not in the last few years."

"What about France?"

"It's just about conceivable," said Peter. "The queen went to France on at least two occasions last year. But there's no record of her going to the Morvan — and Arnold makes no mention of having gone to Paris. So we're none the wiser."

"Then I suggest, gentlemen," interrupted Philippa, "that we call it a day. It's getting late and I'm sure we all want to be fresh for the morning. Pottle needs his beauty sleep, don't you my little Pottle-head? We'll get Flora over here in just over a week. Let's hope she can come. But in the meantime . . ."

I took the hint and got up to go. I had a long day ahead in the morning and it was already nearly eleven o'clock.

"You'll call if you get another cassette?" I asked.

"You'll be the first to know," said Peter.

CHAPTER
FOUR

My coronation. My bloody coronation. If only you could have been here, Peter. King Arnold the bloody first and his delectable Queen Lola. A crown and sceptre. An orb the size of a football. "Zadok the Priest" blasting out from the organ. OK, OK, it wasn't like that at all, but it was still quite an occasion.

All of Lola's brothers were there, along with the other six monarchs in the archipelago. We had it in the Wesleyan chapel on Tuva, same one as for the wedding. The building's tiny — it can only hold about fifty people. We had about three hundred guests from the other islands, as well as Lola's extended family. Most of them had to stand on the little lawn outside. *And* we had visiting dignitaries. The queen and prime minister of Tonga. *And* the king of the Solomon Islands. *And* the junior bloody foreign minister of New Zealand. He was as green as a parrot when he arrived and had apparently been seasick all the way from Tonga.

We got cards from kings, queens and princes from across the globe. Prince Charles sent one of his watercolours of Windsor Castle. Princess Anne sent us a picture of a stallion. And as for Prince Andrew — you'll never believe this: a Beryl Cook card that played "God Save the Queen" when you opened it. And inside there was a note saying that he and

Fergie intended to come on holiday to Tuva, "so long as we can get free flights". Cheeky bastard!

You're probably wondering why so many people showed up for the coronation. Well, this was Tuva's first bit of pageantry for decades. What you said in your letter was spot on: the island has indeed been without a monarch since the assassination. Almost seventy years. (Many thanks, by the way, for the photocopied pages. I've been chuckling to myself at the thought of Warlock traipsing through the village showing people photographs of mushrooms.)

You can just imagine how enthusiastic they all were about a restoration to monarchy. I honestly think it was one of the greatest days in Tuva's history. And it was extraordinarily satisfying to be at the epicentre of it all. I felt as if I was back on centre stage for the first time since I left London.

No champagne, alas, but we did all feast together after the coronation. Grilled porcupine fish, guavas, rice. All washed down with a ton of euchooe. We were all very merry by the end. The foreign minister of New Zealand had bounced back from his boat trip and was well enough to drink about a pint of the stuff. I'll leave you to guess what happened next.

And then, later that night, they did pig wrestling. It's the local sport. They whip up one of these wild pigs into a frenzy and try to jump onto its back. Kau was the first to try — he's a big strapping fellow. But the pig threw him off by dashing itself at a tree. Then Djenna had a go. He's quite small, which can be an advantage, and he's also quick on his feet. But he, too, got chucked off. And then came the moment everyone had been waiting for. Sound the trumpets, roll the drums. Gilbertine strode into the ring and glared at the pig. You could almost smell the fear. The pig was bloody petrified. (And so would you be, Peter, if you were about to be jumped on by Gilbertine.) She walks over to the pig — stomp, stomp — and then throws herself onto the animal. And the next thing we can see is two sets of buttocks — hers and pig's — whirring around the ring. And the crowd's roaring and the drums are beating and buttocks, buttocks, buttocks.

And then, all of a sudden, the commotion's stopped and Gilbertine is standing on her own two feet and she's holding the pig above her head: one hundred and eighty bloody pounds of pig. And then, with this great big surge of energy, she launches the thing skywards and the next thing the poor unfortunate creature knows, it's flailing around in the sea.

I tell you, Peter, it beats bull fighting. And no one gets hurt, not even the pig. It emerged from the water — dripping, sullen and looking a little disappointed with itself. And then it ran off into the coconut grove.

Ishmael and Solomon — they're two of our villagers — lit a huge fire and we sat up till the early hours eating and drinking and dancing under the stars. The only downside was the heat. It was a hundred and ten degrees and the humidity clutched you by the throat. We all stripped off and went for a swim in the lagoon, but it wasn't very refreshing. The sea's about the same temperature as bath water in England and there were weeds floating in the water, like thick wet pullovers. They brush against your arms and thighs, which is a particularly disgusting sensation. Each time you have this feeling that you're about to be ensnared by the tentacles of some giant jellyfish. You often find that type of weed at this time of year, or so I was told. They're washed in on the warm currents.

And the next thing I know it's long past midnight and someone shouts, "Giant whelks! It's time for the giant whelks." They're these crispy things that the locals pull out of the lagoon. You squeeze on some lime juice, sprinkle a few speckles of raw onion, and then — sluuuuurp — you suck the thing from its shell. Ping. It flies into your mouth (I nearly choked the first time I ate one) and you have to chew it before you swallow. Crunch, crunch, crunch — three bites usually does it. It's a peculiarly horrible sensation, like chewing through gristle, and made even worse by the fact that the sodding thing is very much alive. You can actually feel it wriggle on your tongue. It's as if it's trying to get away. That's why you have to swallow — swallow as soon as you've bitten the unfortunate creature into three not-quite-dead parts.

It's supposed to be an aphrodisiac, that's what everyone says. And I'd better not go into the details of what happened later that night. All I can tell you is that they slipped down — one — two — three — eight — nine — ten. And, the next thing you know, you're stark naked and hopping into bed with one of the most delicious women in the world. And three hours later, yes, three hours — you're lying there covered in sweat and thinking to yourself, "Blimey, perhaps I overdid the giant whelks."

And so here I am, sore of head and aching of body, and I'm sitting on my veranda relaxing in my deckchair and gazing out over my island realm. The sky's blue. The sand's white. The water's flickering. And the only slight irritation is the children, who are running around pretending to be English ambulances.

But I can't really grumble because as I speak to you right now, a spectacular red-tufted trumpet bird has just landed on the railings of my veranda. Cheepity-cheepity — there! Did you hear it sing? Listen — it's got the most exquisite melody in the whole wide world, especially in the mating season. It's this cheepity-cheepity-oola-oola-cheepity-cheepity. If you're lucky it will — there it goes again — can you hear? It's just started. Ah, now it's flown off. They're very shy: they're not used to humans.

But where was I? Where was I? Ah, yes, I'd left the quarries and I was back in the forest and I was desperate to find Flora. There was a little path that led out of the clearing — it was probably an animal track — but it eventually led to a bigger path. And then, after wandering for ten or fifteen minutes, I found myself back at the abandoned house.

"Flora — Flora." I shouted at the top of my voice. I kept shouting: all the time, as I fought my way through the bracken, I was calling her name. And eventually, thank God, I was met with an answer. *"Arnold!"* She was only about twenty yards away and yet the trees were so thick that I still couldn't see her.

"Oh, Arnold," she said, emerging from the brambles. "Thank God. I can tell you, I've never been happier to see you." She wrapped her arms around my shoulders. "What happened? Where have you been?"

I had to think on my feet. I couldn't tell her about my discovery. I just couldn't. Not yet. You know what Flora's like, Peter. She'd panic. She'd get paranoid. And before we'd know it, we'd have a whole bloody saga on our hands. And, besides, I had another reason for not saying anything. I wasn't even sure if I could trust my own eyes. Here I was, standing in the dappled sunshine of a forest in Burgundy and it suddenly seemed too preposterous for words. Had I *really* seen what I'd seen? Well, in one sense, of course I knew that I had. And I knew it was for real. And yet I also knew that there was something sinister going on in those quarries — something untoward — and I wanted to know more before I said anything to Flora.

"I got totally and utterly lost," I said. (I didn't want to lie to her. I'd never lied to her.)

"And so did I," she said. "It was so strange. One minute you were there. And the next you'd vanished."

"And I called and called your name," I said (which was also true), "but I guess you didn't hear."

"Well, I did the same," said Flora. "Over and over."

It made me think, Peter, what with all our shouting and that; it made me think that somewhere in the forest, those airwaves created by our voices must have met. The vibrations must have collided with each other, like ghostly spirits whispering secrets into one another's ears. "Arnold-Flora, Arnold-Flora" until those two sets of airwaves would have slumped in on each other. Arn-ra. Arn-ra. It's a rather charming thought, don't you think? The conjunction, I mean. That's real love. Body and spirit, whisked away on the breeze.

"I can officially declare," said Flora with a happy sigh, "that we're no longer lost."

We made our way back to the house and I put the key in the door, turned the lock and stepped inside. I remember kicking off my boots and putting my basket of mushrooms in the living room and then going straight into the kitchen. Flora followed me in, and we both washed our hands under the kitchen tap.

You may wonder why I'm including all these mundane details. Well, Peter, they're an important element in the story. You see, it's essential for you to realize that I was acutely aware of everything I was doing: that when I reflected later on all that had happened, I could recall with absolute clarity every event and every detail that occurred when we entered the house.

It was as I was drying my hands on a dishcloth that I heard her cry of alarm. Flora had gone into the living room and the next thing I heard was her calling my name.

"Arnold —" she said in a tone of voice that betrayed real panic. "*Arnold.*"

I hurried next door.

"Arnold, look," she said. "Look . . ."

I froze. Yes, I froze when I saw what she was pointing at. You see, I realized in an instant what was wrong. We had a little candle-holder on the table; a brass candelabrum that held three small candles. We'd been burning them on the previous evening when we were eating our supper. The candles had been *white* — it was the only colour we could find when we'd bought them in Avallon. And they'd burned down to the halfway mark when we'd snuffed them out and gone to bed. They were white, Peter: mark my words. They were as white as a sheet of paper. As white like snow. White like your Volvo.

And yet *these* candles now — the ones that Flora was pointing to — well, they were red. Bright red. They were burned down to exactly the same point. They were in exactly the same position. And yet they were red.

It was — well, the only word to describe it is chilling. It was one of the most genuinely chilling moments of my life.

74

Like *Psycho*. I didn't know what to say. I didn't know how to react. I had that feeling you get when you're told something terrible. For a split second you're frozen in time. Your mind numbs — stiffens — as if it's drawing a deep breath before preparing itself to take on board reality.

I remember telling myself to stay calm. I remember walking over to the candelabrum and inspecting it more closely. At first I hardly dared to touch it. And a thousand questions shot through my brain — stupid ones, when I think back on it. Could we both be deluded? Had we actually bought red candles? But no — even *I* realized that was ridiculous. I'd held the white ones in my hand. I'd stuck them onto the candelabrum. And besides, the molten wax that had collected around the bottom — the wax from the previous evening — was one hundred per cent white.

Had we been poisoned by the mushrooms? Were we hallucinating? You may laugh, Peter, but I actually thought about that. But I also knew that it was not possible. Both of us had been scrupulously careful when picking our haul.

It occurred to me that the house might be haunted. Perhaps there was a poltergeist living here. Flora later told me that this thought had run through her head as well. And whyever not? We've all heard stories of malevolent spirits playing tricks on people, hurling things across rooms and appearing as shadows on walls. Do you remember the story of that house in Marlow, Peter, the big one down by the river? The owners were sitting in their living room one evening when a vase came flying through the air.

But there was no bad feeling in our house, nor were there any other signs of change. Nothing was broken. Nothing had been moved or touched. And everything else seemed just as it should be. There we were, standing in the warmth, and the sunlight was streaming through the windows and the house seemed the most friendly place on earth.

"Someone must have broken in," said Flora.

"But *why*? Why would anyone want to break in and exchange three half-burned white candles for three half-burned red ones?"

"I don't know," said Flora. "I don't know."

I went to check the doors and windows, just to be sure. The front door had definitely been locked when we'd got back from the forest — I remembered turning the key. And the kitchen door at the back was still locked and bolted. Three of the windows were glued shut with paint — they can't have been opened for years — and the fourth was jammed from the inside.

"I can't see how anyone could have got inside," I said in all honesty. I couldn't see how and I couldn't see why. And why the candles?

"What are we going to do?" asked Flora. I noticed a tone of panic in her voice. It was as if she'd suddenly been struck by the strangeness of it all. "Arnold . . ." she said, "we can't stay. We can't stay in the house. *We can't stay*."

That was so typically Flora. Just because one, admittedly very strange, thing had happened she wanted to get out.

"What do you mean — we can't stay?" That was my immediate response. "Don't be ridiculous. You're seriously proposing to leave the house because of three miserable red candles? It's a mystery — in fact, it's really rather bizarre. But *leaving?*"

I stopped for a minute, but then I realized I had more to say. I suddenly felt angry with her. "We're staying put," I told her. "At least, *I'm* staying put. And I'm rather hoping that you're going to stay put with me. You promised me, remember? Yes, it was your absolute cast-iron promise. 'If you pursue your mushrooms,' you said, 'then I'll follow you to the end of the world.'"

"Yes," said Flora quietly, "but I hadn't counted on this."

And then — I still can't quite explain why, Peter — I lobbed a hand grenade into an already tense situation. "Besides," I said, "this whole sodding thing was your idea in the first place. You were the one who wanted to get away. You were the one who wanted to drag me into a sabbatical. I'd have been very happy to stay at home if it hadn't been for you —"

Now it was her turn to flare up. "Oh, I see!" she said with a flash in her eyes. "Oh — that's *typical*. It's all my fault, is it? Just like it's always my fault. You should be thankful, Arnold. You should be grateful. I've got you out. I've helped you to escape from that stupid place. I've got you away from it all. And you're still too thick-skinned to see that it's going to change your life."

And we were off. Ding, dong. Round one. Arnold in the blue corner. Flora in the red corner. And yet — this was the surprising thing — I could only half-concentrate on the verbal fireworks that were shooting across the room. I was thinking about Clapham, you see — and about our house — and about the fact that there were tenants sleeping in *our* beds. And I was thinking about all the changes that had taken place in the last month or so (although they were nothing in comparison to what was to come). And then suddenly —

"*Arnold* — you're not even listening."

And then, not for the first time, I was suddenly overcome with remorse. Yes, a great fat tidal wave of remorse. And I apologized to Flora and told her that I was sorry, sorry, sorry, which I genuinely was. "We're both a bit on edge," I said. (That, too, was true.) And she turned to me and she smiled. She had a lovely smile, especially when she was really happy. In that smile, all the human misery in the whole wide world suddenly came to an end. We made up. The storm was over. And when calm had once again returned and the last ripples of anger had subsided, Flora ever so calmly picked up the candelabrum and went over to the kitchen door. And then, after fiddling with the bolt and locks, she opened the door and flung the thing out into the trees at the end of the garden.

I watched it curve through the air in a great arc — one of the candles fell off in mid-flight — before it crashed into a pile of brambles. Flora brushed her hands, as if to remove any contamination left behind by the candelabrum and then lit the stove.

"I'll start preparing the omelette," she said. And she flung her arms around my shoulders.

It's six o'clock in the evening and I'm looking out of my window and I'm going to wax all lyrical because I think it's the only way I'll ever get you and Philippa to come out here and visit me.

There's this flat, flat sea which looks like a sheet of huge green plastic and this open emptiness of sky. And it's the palest possible blue at the top, far above, but as your eyes travel downwards from above they collide with a burning disc of sun. It's magnificent, Peter. A great lump of molten cheese.

A polished cymbal. Or is it egg yolk? Yes, think of a big runny egg yolk just after it's been pricked with a knife. You know, when it begins to bleed into the white of the egg and then oozes across the plate and goes all smudgy at the edges. Except for the fact that what I'm looking at right now is more orange than an egg; it's orangey-red and it's getting redder by the second. And I've never seen the sun so huge: it's taking up half the sky. And it's mirrored on the surface of the sea, except that there — on the sea — it's no longer round. It's been stretched into this long, elongated blob of orange that's rippling and twinkling with the play of the wind on the water.

In less than a minute — I know this for a fact — it will start to melt into the horizon. I timed it the other night. It took five minutes and thirty-three seconds to sink completely. And then you have about twenty minutes of gloaming, when the sky is washed with pink. If you tried to paint it, you'd end up with a gaudy smudge. But when you see it in real life, well, it's simply spectacular. And then the heat begins to subside and there's a slight breeze in the air and you realize why it's good to be alive.

CHAPTER
FIVE

It was more than two weeks before I next saw Pottle and Pipingtons. On 20 December the foreign desk sent me to Bucharest to cover the rapidly unfolding events in Romania. Ceauşescu was said to be in deep trouble and people were beginning to think the unthinkable.

"He'll be shafted," said my foreign editor. "Mark my words. And you, Toby, will be there to see it."

I was indeed there; I witnessed everything. But I was also privy to the strangest and most unexpected of conversations, which had a direct bearing on the fate of Arnold Trevellyan, some five or six thousand miles away on Tuva.

I arrived in Bucharest on a bitter Wednesday evening, stepping off the plane into an icy wind. A taxi had been arranged to take me to the Intercontinental Hotel, which was being used by all the foreign journalists in town and quite a number of the Romanian ones as well. I went straight to the hotel bar and saw some familiar faces: Michael Brown from *The Times* and Jonathan Howard from Reuters.

"We meet again," I said, offering them both a drink.

"Berlin, Prague, Bucharest," said Michael. "Wherever next?"

"Moscow," I joked.

"*Now* you're talking," said Jonathan. "I'd like to be *there* when the whole thing explodes."

The bar in which we spent the next three hours was gloomy and depressing. It seemed to be caught in perpetual twilight.

"You've heard the rumours?" asked Michael.

"And counter-rumours?" added Jonathan.

I sat in silence, listening to the gossip that they'd picked up from "sources" — in this case the hotel doormen.

"There's going to be a public rally tomorrow. In Palace Square. Ceauşescu's going to address the crowds. If he makes it back from Iran, that is."

It's strange to arrive in a foreign city when something big is about to happen. In Bucharest you could feel the excitement. There was unease and uncertainty and everyone was busily inventing theories about what was going to happen.

There was good reason to expect that something might indeed be under way. Just a couple of days earlier the army had fired on a crowd of demonstrators in the western city of Timisoara. But they hadn't kept up their firing for long. When they discovered why the crowds were out on the streets — they were trying to protect a popular priest — the soldiers started to fraternize with the people. As Michael said that very evening, "When the army switches sides, the regime's in deep bloody shit."

There were dozens of journalists at breakfast the next morning. Every publication and television station had its own table. Everyone was discussing tactics and trying to work out who they should interview.

Print journalists operate differently from those in television. No support teams, no television cameras, no technicians in tow. We either work alone or with a local stringer who knows the ground. And it was the stringer that had been hired to help me — Andrei Georgescu — who I was now waiting to meet.

And this is where Arnold Trevellyan re-enters the story. It was Arnold who had first put me in touch with Georgescu. I'd been telling him that I specialized in Eastern Europe, that I'd covered stories in Bulgaria and Hungary and Poland, when he suddenly interrupted. "If you ever find yourself in Romania," he said, "you must look up Andrei Georgescu. He's an old friend. Runs the Bucharest Mycological Society. A mushroom man. Speaks English. And he's a journalist. You might want to team up with him." And he gave me his card.

And now, some six months later, there I was, sitting in Bucharest's best hotel and waiting for Arnold's friend to arrive.

"Mr Edwardes?" A slight, dark-haired man approached my table and tentatively extended his hand. I stood up and held out mine.

Andrei was an occasional reporter for *Scînteia*, one of Romania's dailies. He spoke excellent English — just as Arnold had said — and had contacts in several government ministries. He also had the use of a fax machine, an important plus, which he was willing to put at my disposal.

I offered him a coffee and then quizzed him about Arnold. I asked how well he knew him and how often they'd met.

"Only once," he said. "Some years ago. At a mycology conference in Leipzig. It's not so easy for us to travel, you see. But, well, we share a common interest. The amanita genus. I also study the deathcap. And so we keep up a regular correspondence. I like him. He reminds me of a cousin of mine: he's a university lecturer *and* runs an open-air museum *and* plays the violin in quite a well-known quartet. And when you called, well, I owe Arnold a favour or two and so I was happy to help out."

I asked if he knew the whole story about Arnold. About how he'd left his wife, was living on Tuva and had been crowned king of the island.

"King!" He spluttered into his coffee. "And of an island in the Pacific. How did that come about? He told me in his last letter that he'd soon have some news for me but that really is —"

I told him everything I knew and he laughed. "D'you know," he said, "there's one part of me that's not even surprised."

We talked a little more about Arnold, about my visit to France and my interview with him in his house in the forest. But then, as everyone began to drift away from their breakfast tables, I felt that we should also get going.

"You've heard about the gathering tonight?" Andrei asked.

"Yes," I said. "What time's it kicking off?"

He passed on the details he'd picked up from colleagues and added that thousands of people were expected. "If they got that many in Timisoara," he said, "you can expect ten times the number in Bucharest."

Andrei told me it was pointless trying to secure interviews with anyone in the government. "No one's answering their phones and no one's in their offices," he said. "And even if they were answering their phones, they wouldn't tell you anything."

He suggested we try a rather different approach. He proposed going to Fundeni Provincial baths in the northeastern suburbs of Bucharest, a place where he had gathered much useful information in the past. "It's frequented by the Securitate," he said. "Many of their senior officers go, especially on Thursdays. We're more likely to pick up stories there than at any of the ministries."

When my look revealed that I was unconvinced, he laughed. "We don't *have* to go," he said. "You're in charge. But I don't think it'll be a waste of time."

I nodded my agreement. "OK — when?"

"When you're ready," he replied. "I'll just finish my coffee and then we can go."

While we waited to pay, I asked the question that was on everyone's lips. "If Ceauşescu falls," I said, "who d'you think will replace him?"

Andrei laughed. "*If*," he said. "A little word but also a very big one. You've seen the security forces on the streets. The police. The army. They're in control, believe me. But *if* he should happen to fall — or flee the country — then, well, that's anyone's guess. Perhaps the army will step in to take control. Or someone from the Securitate. It's even conceivable that the king might try to return."

"The king?"

"Yes, King Michael. He's been living in exile for years. In Switzerland. And there are all sorts of rumours flying around about him. He's said to be itching to come back and he has a lot of Western money behind him. He's still very popular here, he could prove a figure of unity. He's one of the few people who could bring people together."

"I can't imagine the Securitate taking very kindly to the return of the king. They'd probably try to kill him."

"Yes," said Andrei. "They would. Knowing that lot of thugs, they'd almost certainly try to assassinate him. But who knows what will happen? As I said, things might become clearer tonight. In fact, I predict that things *will* become clearer tonight."

We finished our coffees and made our way out into the street. It was a twenty-minute ride to the bathhouse, by which time we were deep in the city suburbs.

"They're careful who they let in," said Andrei. "It's the closest you'll come in Romania to a private club."

"Can you get *us* in?" I asked.

"Don't worry about that," he said. "Contacts."

He explained that he had an uncle working at a senior level in the Ministry of Water and Sewage. "This is his favourite bathhouse. He's quite a well-known figure, Grigore. That's his name. Uncle Grigore. Perhaps he'll be here."

We pushed open the door and stepped down into a dimly lit vestibule. Andrei said something in Romanian to the concierge and handed over a few coins. In return we were given keys and towels.

It was almost completely dark inside the steam room. The atmosphere was a thick fog and the only light came from the glass panels in the domed ceiling.

"See those men over there?" said Andrei, pointing discreetly to a row of pot bellies. "Securitate. Senior ones. That's who you need to get to know."

"And how do we manage that?"

"Not sure." Andrei laughed.

He peered into the steam, trying to work out if any of the bellies belonged to his uncle.

"He's not here. A pity. He's acquainted with several of them. A couple are neighbours of his. But — come — let's sit a little closer to them. I'll listen in, see what they're saying."

After a few minutes I nudged Andrei and asked what they were talking about.

"They're discussing where they're going to go drinking tonight," he said. "See the fat one with the dark red birthmark?" He pointed to the largest in the group. "It's his fiftieth birthday today. They're planning to take him out."

"So *they* won't be at the rally tonight," I said.

"No," said Andrei. "Clearly not."

He carried on with his eavesdropping while I grew increasingly annoyed at having wasted my time by agreeing to come here. After a few more minutes I tapped Andrei once again and suggested that we should leave.

"No," said Andrei. "Wait — it's strange."

Their conversation had become increasingly animated, yet at the same time they were speaking much more quietly.

"What are they talking about?" I asked. "Have they mentioned tonight's meeting?"

"Wait, wait," said Andrei, straining to hear. "I thought . . ."

He paused and then whispered in my ear, "What's the name of the island where Arnold's now living?"

"*Arnold* —?" I told him it was Tuva.

"T-u-v-a." He repeated the word slowly. "Well, that's — *Tuva?* Are you sure? That's —"

"*What?*" I said. "It's what?"

"They're talking about Tuva. Yes, they're actually talking about Tuva. 'Dimitri will go to Tuva — . He must be despatched.' That's what they said. Despatched. In Securitate talk, that means killed. Murdered."

"What, *Arnold?*" I said.

"No . . . I don't know. They didn't say his name. And now they've changed the subject. They're talking about birthdays again."

There was a chorus of laughter from the group of men and then they all got to their feet. One plunged into the hot bath. The others returned to the changing room.

"What the hell's it all about?" I asked Andrei.

"I've no idea," he said.

The first shots rang out later that evening. We were in Palace Square, watching it all, and the effect on the crowd was instantaneous. Suddenly everyone was scattering in every direction. One old man stumbled and fell at my feet. Andrei and I picked him up off the ground.

From the moment Ceauşescu had appeared on the balcony, it was inevitable there was going to be trouble.

The crowd began chanting, "Timisoara, Timisoara", a reference to the demonstration that had taken place on the Wednesday.

"I've never seen anything like this in my life," said Andrei. Nor had I. I'd been to Eastern Europe on three or four occasions over the past twelve months, but I'd never seen a crowd behave in such a fashion.

Within less than a minute, everyone in the square was shouting the same words. Ceauşescu continued with his speech as if nothing had happened until the people were bawling so loudly that you could no longer hear his words.

For decades he'd been used to adulation and polite applause. Now he found himself facing a crowd that was enjoying itself for the first time in years. He paused for a second, turned and then headed rapidly into the building. The balcony doors swung shut behind him.

More shots were fired. It was impossible to pinpoint where they were coming from. There was a flash from one of the palace windows. There must also have been gunfire on the far side of the square, for there were constant flashes. There was a burst from a machine gun and then an armoured personnel carrier entered the square.

"We must go," said Andrei, "before things *really* get out of control. The Securitate won't stop at anything."

I took him at his word. We returned to the hotel, where many of the other journalists had already gathered.

"He's done for," said Michael when I met him in the lobby.

He was right. Four days later Ceauşescu was tried and shot.

CHAPTER
SIX

"Let's hope we won't have any more bad surprises." That's what Flora said as we got back from another mushroom outing in the forest. I couldn't have agreed more. I'd had quite enough surprises.

We stepped inside the house and took a cursory look into the kitchen. Everything was in perfect order. Flora placed the panniers on the table and I stepped back into the hall and struggled out of my boots.

It wasn't until I walked into the living room — bang — that my jaw dropped to the floor. You'll never believe, Peter, the sight that confronted me. There, on the table where we'd eaten our supper and breakfast; there, on that very table, was the candelabrum — the very same candelabrum that Flora had thrown out of the back door just days earlier.

I'd *seen* her throw it out. I'd *seen* it fly across the garden. I'd *seen* it land in the briars. And now here it was — back on our table. And this time the candles were white. Three sparkling white candles which had never been lit.

Flora gave a start when she entered the room. And then she screamed: yes, she actually let out a scream. "Oh no," she said. "That's too much. Arnold, I don't think I can handle this any more."

I didn't say anything. For once I was lost for words.

"Someone is coming into our house," said Flora slowly and deliberately. "They're breaking in and they're trying to scare us. Either that, Arnold, or this place is haunted. And whichever it is, I don't like it one little bit."

"We must go to the chateau," I ventured. "Ask *them* what's going on."

"They're away for weeks," said Flora. "The de la Regnier family have gone to Paris. And besides, what could they tell us? For all we know, they're up to their necks in this."

"Not if they're in Paris."

"*Arnold*. Don't be ridiculous." That's what she said. She told me I was ridiculous. "This is serious. And I will NOT spend another day in this strange house. Why do you think all the other houses we've seen are abandoned? Well, I can tell you. It's because something strange is going on, that's why. We must leave. We must get out immediately. And if you refuse to leave — if you refuse to get out while we're still all in one piece — then I shall quite simply have to go on my own."

Well, Peter, you can only imagine what followed. We had one of those explosive rows that most couples only manage once or twice in their lives. *She* swore. *I* swore. She walked out; she came back in. We'd had rows before, of course. When Flora and I didn't agree, it was always the end of the world. And Flora always stuck to her guns. She *had* to, I guess, because I'm a stubborn bugger. But in the end we'd always find a compromise. I tell you, Peter, after more than ten years of marriage we were so good at diplomacy that we could have freed bloody Terry Waite if we'd been asked. But not on this occasion.

"I'm not staying," she said. "I am NOT staying in this house." She kept repeating the same thing, over and over. "I'm not staying, I'm not staying." She must have said it six or seven times, or that's how it seemed. She'd lost all sense of proportion. And I kept telling her that if it wasn't for her we wouldn't be living in a stupid remote house in the middle of nowhere.

She tugged at her hair. "Well, I don't like mental games, thank you very much," she said. "I find them disturbing and I find your complacency disturbing and I'm alarmed that you're not taking this at all seriously. The next thing that'll happen is that one of us will get hurt. They'll come and get us, whoever they are. This *thing* — it will escalate. I know it will. No, Arnold, I'm not into mind games," she actually called it a mind game, "and I'm not staying. I am NOT staying. You can come with me if you want — yes — I'd very, very much like you to come with me. But *I'm* not staying a minute longer."

"You have to stay," I said in an unnaturally calm voice. "I *insist* that you stay. It was for *your* sake that I came to France. It's for *my* sake that you must stay."

"This has got nothing to do with 'your sake' or 'my sake'," was Flora's response. "It's to do with something very odd that's taking place here."

"Nothing will happen," I said, "if only you stay."

Now that, Peter, was probably the midway point. We'd gone about as far as we could. And what I *should* have done, of course, is back down. I should have said, "Yes, darling; of course, darling," and agreed to pack up our stuff and leave that very night. That would have been the right thing to do. But there was a niggling little voice inside of me — a big fat demon with horns, in fact — saying I should stick to my guns. You're right, Arnold. That's what it was telling me. You're right.

"Besides," I said, "where will you go?"

She thought for a moment; I could see her thinking. Whirring it over in her mind. "Well, I don't know. Perhaps, well, to . . ." She smiled to herself. "To Paris. Yes, Paris. I'll stay at Simon's."

And it was those four words that did it. They took our argument to a whole new level. D'you remember Simon? That old flame of hers. A "friend" from university. He was living in Paris at the time. And Flora knew all too well that in proposing to stay at his place she was twisting and turning the knife. She knew I couldn't stand him. And she also knew that he couldn't stand me. It was jealousy on his part, of course. I'm sure he still loved Flora.

"Well, just bugger off," I said, pushing the candelabrum so hard that it fell to the floor, "if that's what you want."

"No, that's not what I want, you stupid, stubborn, annoying, infuriating idiot." Those were the last words she ever said to me. And then she fled from the house in tears.

And that, Peter, was how it ended. *You stupid, stubborn, annoying, infuriating idiot*. Just like that. In one instant, we'd gone from married couple to estranged couple. It seems so incredible when I think back on it. She ran outside, climbed in the car and drove off down the woodland track. And then there was silence. The house fell deathly silent. And I felt very much alone — alone in an empty forest and no one for miles and miles and miles.

I spent a miserable evening wondering what to do. I thought about going to Paris. I still had my scooter, you see.

The little scooter I'd bought when we first arrived. And I thought about begging her to come back. I thought about many things that night, Peter, and revisited all the good times we'd had together and managed to convince myself that that was exactly what I had to do. Yes, I had to go after her. Follow her. Yes, it was the right thing to do, even though it was a personal defeat for me.

But in the event I never got the chance. For on the very next morning, my world was flipped head over heels upside down. I made the discovery that was to transform my life.

CHAPTER
SEVEN

I returned to London on 2 January and found three messages awaiting me from Peter. Flora, it transpired, was going to be in Taplow Bottom on the Friday night. Peter and Philippa wanted to invite her — and me — to dinner.

I rang Peter and accepted.

"Glad you're alive," was his reply. "We looked out for you on the old box."

I asked if he'd heard from Arnold.

"Another tape," he said. "All about France. You need to hear it."

I contemplated saying something to Peter about my own discovery, alerting him to the strange conversation that Andrei and I had overheard in the Bucharest bathhouse, but I decided it could wait. My first priority was to meet Flora; I wanted to hear her version of the stories that Arnold had been telling us.

I arrived early in Taplow Bottom — so early that I took Peter and Philippa by surprise.

"Come in, old boy, come in," said Peter. "Not a problem. Gives us a chance to sneak in a quick beer and listen to the tape before we serve the main drinkingtons. Pipington's still in the bath. We've got ten minutes to misbehave."

He led me into the living room and left me alone while he went off to get the beers. I looked at the photos on the writing table. Peter and Philippa on their wedding day. Peter and Philippa in Greece. Peter and Philippa with Arnold and — . So *that* was Flora. Tall, blonde and slightly ferocious. I picked it up and looked at it more closely. She looked older than Arnold, a good five or ten years older. And she looked very different from what I was expecting.

I sat down in an armchair, still holding the photo, and wondered about the best way to ask Flora about Arnold. She was undoubtedly the only person who knew every aspect of his personality, but I thought it unlikely she'd be willing to talk about him to a complete stranger. My best hope was that she'd confide in Philippa and that Philippa might pass on any information to Peter and me.

I also wondered if Philippa would have told Flora I was a journalist. I wasn't even sure if she knew I'd met Arnold in France. The only thing I could guarantee was that Philippa would have told her I was single. Indeed, I half-suspected that she'd decided to invite me over because she loved nothing better in life than match-making.

"Philippingtons is a one-woman dating agency," said Peter, reading my thoughts as he reappeared with two beers. "Take care not to disappoint, Tobias," he said. "Philippa doesn't like disappointments."

I pointed to the photo. "I didn't imagine Arnold's wife to look like that," I said. Peter laughed. "That's not her," he said. "That's Philippa's sister, Madge. She's ferocious. A jackal with fangs. We wouldn't set you up with her."

So there I had it — straight from the horse's mouth. They were setting me up.

Peter went over to the table and looked through the photos, strumming his fingers on the worktop all the while. "*Flora, Flora, Flora* — no, sorry, old chap. You'll just have to wait."

We listened to Arnold's latest tape from beginning to end without saying a word. Peter was about to play it for a second time when the doorbell rang. It was Flora — and we could hear her being given a rapturous welcome by Philippa.

"Oooh, my dearest, darling Flora. At last — the return of the prodigal daughter. How are you? How *are* you? You look as lovely as ever. In fact, you look better than ever. You look a million dollars."

I could hear Philippa's voice booming out down the entrance hall, but what I wanted to hear was Flora's.

"Well, it's lovely to see you," she said. "It's been so long and it's been so very difficult. It feels so terribly — *empty* — to be back on my own."

She sounded very different from the Flora that Arnold had described on the tapes. He'd made her sound strident and argumentative. "But —" she was still out of sight — "all these things can come later. How are *you?*"

"Tip-top and shipshape," said Philippa in her customarily forthright fashion. "Come — let's go into the living room.

Come and meet our new friend, Tobias. He's driven down from the big smoke especially to meet you."

"*Me?*"

I noticed that Philippa hadn't said *why* I'd travelled all the way to Taplow Bottom, nor had she revealed where I worked. It was as I suspected. She'd decided to be selective in the information she fed to Flora.

In my mind's eye, I'd already formed a picture of Arnold's ex-wife: dark-haired, petite and well groomed. And now, as she entered the room, I found that I was not far wrong.

"Hello," she said, extending her hand. "I'm Flora."

"Hello," I replied, taking the offered hand. "Ouch, you're an iceberg."

"Well, let's hope I don't melt," was her reply.

It was meant as a perfectly innocent comment, of course, but we both immediately realized — and so did Philippa — that it was possible to find an unintended ambiguity in her turn of phrase.

Peter came to the rescue. "Well, we don't want any puddles on the carpet," he said.

We all sat down, all except Peter, who was about to perform his favourite role in life. "Beer, wine, vodka, gin, ouzo." He reeled off his customary list of drinks with all the professionalism of a fully employed bartender. "Or perhaps a spritzer for the ladies?"

"Do you know what I'd *really* like?" said Flora.

"Try me," said Peter.

"I'm sure we'll have it," chimed Philippa. "Pottle's well equipped in the drinks department."

"A spicy bloody Mary," said Flora. "I'm still shivering. I spent too long in Singapore and now I'm continually freezing. I think it's the only thing that will inject a bit of warmth."

"One spicy bloody Mary on its way," said Peter, who was clearly delighted with her choice. He liked nothing better than to concoct mixes and cocktails.

Fragile. That's how Philippa had described Flora. But I found it hard to believe that she was fragile. And if she was, then surely she'd have liked the stability that Arnold gave her. But everything that Peter and Philippa had told me suggested that this was precisely the side of him she found so impossible.

Flora was also meant to be impetuous and fiery: wasn't that what Peter had said? "Quite a stick of dynamite." Arnold, too, had made her sound both fiery and neurotic. And yet my first impression of her was that she was remarkably composed.

"You asked for spicy and you've got spicy," said Peter, returning with a large bloody Mary. Flora stirred it slowly with the celery and tentatively took a sip. We all sat there expectantly awaiting her judgement.

"Oh, yes, a big step up from Raffles," she said with a smile. "Theirs were far too spicy. And not nearly enough vodka. But this is, well, perfection."

Peter brushed his lapels as a conscious acknowledgement of his new-found role as barman and then took a long glug of Adnams.

"I bet they've got nothing like *this* in Singapore," he said, tapping his tankard with a certain smugness. "I suppose they only drink lager out there."

Singapore had come up quite naturally in the conversation and it led Flora to talk about her time there. She explained how she'd headed straight to her sister's after leaving France and spent the better part of eleven months with her.

"You were always close to Anna," commented Philippa. "I guess this whole thing must have brought you even closer."

I admired Philippa for the wonderfully English way she had of talking about sensitive issues. The "thing" itself was never mentioned. She alluded to their rift; she passed comment; she even pronounced judgement. Yet she never actually mentioned the word itself.

Flora's tone suddenly changed. "I came so close to falling apart," she said. "It all happened so quickly. That's what was so — *odd*. That's what still puzzles me. I lie awake at night — every night — wondering why I didn't spot that something was . . ." She sighed. "Oh, Philippa, I didn't have an inkling: I had no idea that anything was wrong. Arnold's such a talker when he's got an audience. He can keep a room spellbound with his tales and anecdotes and charm. But sometimes, when you're on your own with him, well, it's as if the gates come crashing down. I often wondered what was really going on inside the depths of his head. If only he'd told me that something was not quite right. Given me a clue."

She turned to me and smiled. "I'm sorry," she said. "This must be so boring and tedious."

She couldn't have been more wrong. It was exactly what I wanted to hear. I was so intrigued by Arnold and his new life on Tuva that I wanted to know every detail of what had taken place between the two of them. I also wanted answers to all the questions I'd singularly failed to ask when interviewing him in France, but there was a voice inside me urging caution.

Philippa did, at length, ask Flora if she'd heard from *him*.

"Not a thing," she said. "Nothing in more than six months. Not a word. It's as if he never was. As if he never existed. It's not even as if he's dead — it's worse than that. It's as if he's never even been a part of my life."

"And have *you* tried to contact him?" asked Philippa.

"Well, of course," said Flora in a tone of voice that was almost indignant. "I wrote half a dozen times from Singapore. And again from Malaysia. I tried to explain why I'd left. And what I wanted. But I also said that I'd never go back to Creux. Not in a million years. There was something about that place that scared the hell out of me."

"And?" asked Philippa.

"And nothing. He never replied. There was complete radio silence. And that was something that really did surprise me. It made me realize that perhaps we really *had* reached the end."

"And . . .?" said Philippa for a second time. I had to hand it to her. Her method of gathering information was unsubtle but effective.

"So that's where I find myself," said Flora. "What do I do? Short of going to Tuva, I can't see any way of finding out more. Unless you, of course — . Have *you* heard from him? Have *you* had any news?"

"Yes," said Peter, a little sheepishly. He mumbled something about the tapes. "Yes. And he seems well enough. Except for the heat. He doesn't seem to like the heat."

I could scarcely believe the matter-of-fact way in which Peter was speaking. He made no mention of the quarries or of Arnold's coronation or his strange new life on the far side of the globe.

"He *seems* well." That was not *my* interpretation of the facts to hand. True, I knew more than Peter, but even if I hadn't been to Romania I would have drawn the conclusion that all was not well. There was something in all of this — many things — that didn't quite add up.

Philippa announced that the food was almost ready and we stood up at the same time. "Boy, girl, boy, girl," she said, pointing to where we should sit. "And, Flora, perhaps you can be mother and pour the water."

Peter had shuffled off to get wine and we found ourselves alone for the first time. "And what," she asked as she filled my glass, "do *you* do? Philippa said you live in London."

"Yes," I said and proceeded to tell her how I'd just got back from Romania.

"That must have been quite a trip," she said. "Were you there for all the rioting and shooting? It must be terrible to see such things for real. Rather than on television, I mean."

I played with my glass, turning it round and round. It *was* terrible to see such things — it was almost unreal — and yet —

"Well, I'm there to report on them," I said. "I try to let them wash over me. I think you have to, otherwise they come back to haunt you."

I found myself mumbling. I wasn't even sure what I was saying. And I certainly wasn't prepared for Flora's response.

"But that's amazing," she said. "How does it go? 'Oh, dreadful is the check — intense the agony — when the ear begins to hear and the eye begins to see.' It's Emily Brontë. I'm sure you know it. I think I'm too like her. I'd be hopeless at your job. I'd examine things endlessly; I'd think about them and turn them over and over in my head. And then I'd worry and panic. And before I'd know it, I'd be just like Emily."

I smiled. "You've managed to make me sound rather boring."

"Oh, no," she said brightly. "I'm so sorry. That's not what I meant at all. I'm impressed. It's a good thing. You control what happens to you. And that's a great advantage."

"And you?" I ventured. "What about you? Can I ask — would you mind me asking what *really* happened? You see, I have to come clean. I met Arnold. I interviewed him. For the newspaper. I thought Philippa would have told you. I went to France and spent an evening with him. And there are so many things that don't quite add up."

"You met him!" she exclaimed. "You've met Arnold! Well then you know exactly what he's like. Arnold's Arnold. And that's what I found so exciting. You never knew what was coming next."

"And so," I said, "tell me —"

"No," she said. "Not now. Not tonight. Perhaps another time."

Her eyes flickered. For a second I thought she might even cry.

"Ahem," interrupted Philippa as she entered the dining room with a large dish of moussaka. "I think, young Tobias, it's time to change the subject."

It was nearly eleven o'clock when I left Peter and Philippa and long after midnight before I was back in London. I lay awake for more than an hour, turning the evening over and over in my head. I was none the wiser about anything. Eventually I fell into a deep sleep and would probably have slept until mid-morning had the telephone not rung at just after nine. It was Peter.

"The post's arrived," he said. "And there's another cassette from Arnold."

CHAPTER
EIGHT

We have a little schoolroom here — we've only got six pupils — and they're all taught by Miss Rose. She's from Wei-Kitu island: she just arrived a few days ago. Young, pretty as an orchid and with these dark ringlets of hair that float down over her shoulders.

I sat in on her first English lesson earlier today. If only you could have been here, Peter; I promise you, we'd both have been sniggering away in the back row.

"*My* name is Miss Rose," she says to one of the children, "and *your* name is Kawa."

"*My* name is Miss Rose," repeats Kawa, "and *your* name is Kawa."

"No," she says patiently. "*Your* name is Kawa. You're a boy."

"No," repeats Kawa. "*Your* name is Kawa. You're a boy."

"No," says Miss Rose. (She's beginning to get exasperated.) "*My* name is Miss Rose."

"No," repeats Kawa. "*My* name is Miss Rose."

"Oh dear," says Miss Rose "Why am I so —"

"— *AiooeiA* —" I stand up at the back of the class and declaim it in my finest Tuvan. And the whole class collapses into giggles. And Miss Rose looks somewhat abashed. And I realize I've made a terrible mistake. You see, Peter, what I

105

meant to say was "patient"; I wanted to be nice to Miss Rose. But it didn't quite come out right. "AiooeiA" actually means "hairy": hairy like a sloth. And Miss Rose blushes and the children snigger and a few of them let out whistles. (On all the islands around here, hair is considered very seductive.) And they all found the whole thing a scream.

And now everyone's saying I've got my eyes on Miss Rose and that there'll soon be another wedding. And they've started making ding-dong wedding noises and throwing rice over Miss Rose when she walks through the coconut grove. And even Lola said to me, "I hear you've been making advances on Miss Rose." And when I tried to explain that no — no — oh, please, God, I meant to say "patient" and it was all a terrible mistake, she said calmly, "Well I think it's lovely. Miss Rose is very beautiful and she's also very clever and for all I know she's very AiooeiA as well. But —" she paused — "I still think it would be diplomatic to choose a Tuvan girl for your second wife. Someone like Gilbertine. She's AiooeiA. She's got beautiful black locks. Or Doris. She's also AiooeiA. And don't forget you'll get a lot of woman if you choose either of them."

I told her I'd think about it.

"And by the way," she said. "If you really did mean to say 'patient', it's aiOOeia not AiooeiA. The stress in on the OO."

She sat down and suddenly looked sad. "You've never told me I'm hairy," she said quietly.

"You are," I said. "You're very hairy. And it's lovely."

She smiled. "Thank you," she said. "You're hairy too."

And now it's almost noon and I'm sitting comfortably in my deckchair with the tape recorder on the table in front of me and the sun's shining and the sand is glinting and the sky is a bright, bright blue and — wooooah — there's a — wooooah — a shoal of flying fish that are leaping, leaping, leaping out of the water. And — splosh — back they go. And wait-for-it-wait-for-it — wooooah — there they go again — they're out of the water and they're looping in this huge great arc and — splosh for a second time. There must be forty or fifty of them, Peter, and it's like a great silver semicircle that's bursting from the water. It's a flashing rainbow that keeps dipping back into the lagoon.

And I'm trying to think of all the things you wanted to know. *What*, you asked, *do you actually do?* Well, let me fill you in with a bit of background. I've been in such a rush to tell you everything that's happened that I now realize I've given you hardly any background. The Tuvan archipelago is unusual in the sense that each island is completely independent, even though we're a federation — one of the three federations of Micronesia. We're recognized individually by the United Nations, just like Tonga and Vanuatu. And we've got our own constitutions and flags. And although everyone uses the Tuvan dollar — it's worth about seventy-five pence — we issue our own stamps. They're not real ones: I mean you can't post a letter with them. You need Tongan stamps for that. But I'm told they're quite sought after as collectors' items. I could sell them a thousand times over at Baddington's.

We don't export a great deal. In fact, the only thing that's shipped out in any quantity is the shell of the Tuvan clam. It's this bright pinky colour inside and it's ground down into some sort of pigment that's used in nail varnish. When I first arrived here I was taken aback to discover that almost everyone on the island, men and women, was sporting nail varnish. Some of the men even paint their toes. Pink, for God's sake!

They did mine, of course — fingers *and* toes. ("You must have it done, sir. You're the king.') I tried to conceal them at the coronation, but the foreign minister of New Zealand spotted them when we were on the beach. "Stone the blinkin' crows," he said. "Next thing you'll be slipping into a woman's bra."

Well, I haven't got around to that yet, you'll be pleased to hear, but there are quite a few men on the island who could do with a bit of support in the upper-chest department.

So that's us in a nutshell. Stamps, pink toes and daylong sunshine. And, as I said before, I really am king of the castle — an absolute monarch by name and nature. (With a spot of help from Lola, of course.) You won't find a second chamber on Tuva. No members of parliament. No one to challenge my decisions. Of course, we're officially called constitutional monarchies, but King Bulawei of Oloua likes to joke that his island is not a constitutional monarchy but a monarchy that happens to have a constitution.

It's funny to think that I have far more power than the queen of England. When I met her a few months ago, she asked if treason was still a capital crime on Tuva. I had to confess that I didn't know and it made her laugh. "One really ought to know if one can chop off heads." That's what she said. "Philip and I talk about it all the time. He wants to cut off Kelvin Mackenzie's. And I shall chop off Margaret's."

So there you have it. It's official. She *hates* Maggie T. And you heard it from me first.

What else did you ask in your letter? Ah, yes. The population. *How many people do you rule?* Well, we're not terribly numerous, I'll be the first to admit *that*. Sometimes our little world out here can feel terribly — *empty*. And it makes me think back to London and to the really big auctions, when the room is packed with people and there's a buzz of noise and bustle and I'm up on the rostrum waving my arms and controlling every single action in the room. And there are eager faces, all looking at me, staring, excited, and the price is clambering higher and higher and higher — but then again — none of the islands in the archipelago has that many people living on them. Niuapulapei has just fifty-two. Ta'ula only has thirty-five. Even Oloua, which really *is* a big island, has less than two hundred.

We've got a respectable sixty-three people on Tuva, no more, no less. It struck me the other day that if I married ten wives, I'd be husband to one-sixth of the population. Two of our women have recently fallen pregnant, which caused such a flurry of excitement that there were festivities involving everyone on the island. They caught this sodding great tuna in the waters between here and Kitu — it was bigger than a cow — and lugged it back to the beach. Then they gutted and roasted it over an open fire. Oh, how I'd have loved you to have been here. Singing. Some fabulous topless dancing. And we all drank far too much of the local euchooe, which — perhaps I've already told you — is this disgusting sort of fiery spirit made out of coconut milk. Next morning I woke up with a head like a combine harvester.

Ah, here's Lola. And she's carrying a plate and a glass. My lunch.

"Lola, Lola, come and say something to Peter. Here. Come a bit closer, *chérie*, or this machine won't pick up your voice. You *must* say hello to Peter. He's my oldest friend."

"No, Arnold, no. Please. I don't know what to —"

"Well, it's recording so say something — anything — just so they can hear your delightfully sexy voice. Go on. I want them to hear you speak."

"*Oui, mais qu'est-ce que je peux dire?* Well — er — hello. Hello, Peter. This is — Lola and — well — Arnold wants me to say, um, hello to you. So — hello. Or, rather, *aleimako*. That's what we say here in Tuva. And — well — Arnold told me much things about you. And — I think you must come out here to visit us. With your wife. Yes. I really don't know what Arnold has been telling you about Tuva but — it is, well, *un paradis*. What's that in English?"

"Paradise."

"Paradise — of course it is. I forget all my English. It's very beautiful here. White beaches and coral reefs and *les palmiers* —"

"Palm trees —"

"Yes, and sun. And whales. Arnold tells me that you're interested in whales —"

"Yes, it's Philippa. She loves whales."

"Well, Philippa, if you wanted to see whales, you *must* come — . And, well, I don't know what else I can tell you. What else is there —?"

"Recite them a poem. In Tuvan. Say the 'Haaiehwo'. They'd like that."

"The 'Haaiehwo'? Well, OK — if I can remember it. It's an old Tuvan song, you see, a *chanson de pêcheur*. That's what they're calling it — a fishing song. And it's what they sang a long time ago when the fishing expeditions went out on the ocean. They'd go out for three or four days, hunting the big fish, and this is what they sang:

"Eoiee Houewieo Moeno aaekone eio kloeoem
    taeo
Eoiee houeweomeoneke oiechi eio Iham
Eoiee houelleoine ekemonei sloeimek obeoi
Aoi ghereoimee gher ee gher ait uleuo.

"There — it's very beautiful."
"And can you say it to them in English? So they can understand the words."
"In English? Er — if I remember. It was years ago when Papa got me to learn it in English. Now, um, let me see —"

"When Lady Sun lifts her drowsy head
When the dawn is pulled from her sleepy bed
When the sun — no, the light — is floating in the
    palest sky
The fishermen fish for the fish that fly.

"Well, it's something like that. Except that it doesn't quite work in English. Because in Tuvan there's a rhythm on the vowels. But, well, it gives you an idea. And the fish they would catch: well, according to my father, it was the best in the world. And once — I've been telling Arnold about this — on my seventeenth birthday, he took me to Maison Lipuko on the Ile St-Louis: it's one of the best restaurants in Paris. And the food, according to Papa, was the closest you'd ever come to Tuvan cuisine.

"It's still there, I believe. On rue le Regrattier, I think. Opposite a florist called Bonsai. I remember because my father gives me a little bonsai tree for my birthday. And, well, for me the outing was a great treat. I so rarely got to see the

111

world, you see. The threats had grown ever more alarming and my father insisted that it was, well, too dangerous for us to remain 'in society'. That was his expression — very nineteen thirties. But on my birthday, just once, we risk rejoining society.

"And we eat grilled trumpet fish and pawpaw. It's very Tuvan, mixing fish and fruit. Poor Papa was almost in tears by the end of the meal. He left Tuva in nineteen eighteen, you see, when he was eleven, and each time he goes to Maison Lipuko it brings back memories of his childhood. And poor, poor Papa — he died before he had a chance to come home. He was buried in Paris. In Père Lachaise. And then — well, I've said enough. Arnold is — how do you say? — *itching* to tell you more. So I hand you back to him. And, please, do come. It will make his day."

So that was Lola. I hope you liked the sound of her voice. She means it when she says you're all welcome. We'd love to see you here . . .

But I wanted to tell you — now she's out of earshot — I wanted to tell you more about Flora. Yes, you see, I was telling you how she'd left after our argument and I was alone in the house and I'd made up my mind to go and find her as soon as it was morning. But when I woke I felt in desperate need of a walk. Clear the brain. I wanted to go back to the quarry, you see. And I wanted to think things through with a fresh head. Work out my next move. That, at any rate, was the plan. But as you know, Peter, things don't always go according to plan. And they most certainly didn't on that particular morning.

I awoke to find it was a dishcloth of a day: a drip-drip-drip sort of day when the sky looks so sullen and bruised that you can't help wondering if the sun hasn't put out its lights for good. Inside the house it felt as damp as a towel and the only noise I could hear was this pittong-pittong-pittong-pittong of the rain spilling out of the gutter and onto the corrugated roof of the lean-to. Pittong. One. Pittong. Two. Pittong. Three. It dropped with absolute regularity every second — a metronomic beat that seemed to offer some sort of comfort.

I like walking in the rain and I was looking forward to getting out. I struggled into my leather coat and boots, stepped into the fresh air and double-locked the door. The pittongs were even louder once outside and each one sprinkled me with five or six splashlets of bouncing water. It was only when I glanced back towards the house that I realized something was missing. *My scooter.* My scooter, Peter, had gone. It was not there. I had left it at the side of the house (unlocked and unchained, for it hadn't occurred to me that someone might steal it). And now it was gone. I could even see the tracks in the mud where it had been wheeled away. And it dawned on me that — well, now I was well and truly stuffed. Stranded. Cast adrift. My only way out was on foot.

I returned to the quarries. They were like a magnet pulling me forwards. I climbed down through the opening and picked my way through the outer chambers, retracing my steps through room after room. And then I found myself back in the neatly swept chamber and I opened that strange wooden door in the fake wall for a second time and I squeezed through the narrow corridor. And there I was again, in front of the door to the banqueting chamber. I hadn't dreamed it: it really *had* existed. I opened the door: peered in once again. It was just as it had been on the previous day. Nothing had been moved. And I was about to enter the room when — without hearing a single noise — kerchunk — I was seized from behind by two men.

"You've got some explaining to do." That's what they said to me.

There have been several occasions in my life when I've been really terrified. Once I was on a plane which was struck by lightning. *Peeehow.* The whole thing lit up in a frazzle of electricity. And then there was the time on my honeymoon when we were on an elephant safari and the elephant was attacked by a tiger.

But here's the truly strange thing, Peter. On this occasion, I wasn't scared at all. It was almost as if I was expecting it to happen. You see, everything had been so *topsy-turvy* over the previous twenty-four hours that I think just about anything could've happened and I'd have been ready for it. I'd already worked out that something deeply weird was going on down in the quarries. And I knew full well that I was placing myself in danger. Yet I let myself be carried along by it all. I think it was because I had precious little to lose. You mustn't forget that Flora had walked out on me the previous evening and wasn't going to come back unless I actively sought her out. And I remember thinking that the only way I could make her listen to me — reason with her — would be if I could tell her exactly what was going on down here.

My two captors led me back through the chamber in which they'd seized me. We turned into a stone-hewn corridor that had rows of doors on either side. It was like those long, low tunnels you get in the London Underground — you have the impression that they go on for mile after mile.

It was only later, of course, that I realized that these were the service tunnels. They were only ever used by the staff. And the reason they twisted and turned all over the place was because they connected all the principal rooms, the banqueting halls and libraries and drawing rooms and — . But once again I'm racing ahead of myself. There I was, being frogmarched along the corridors, when suddenly we stopped.

"Here," said one of them. There was a door embossed with a small shield that had a maxim in Latin: *Orbis mea urbs"* — "The earth is my kingdom".

"Inside," said one of the men. "Nice and gently."

Both spoke perfect English, although they had strong French accents.

"Now, Mr Trevellyan, we have a few questions for you."

It was only now, as I sat down on a chair in the centre of the room, that I saw their faces. And that was important to me. I could get their measure.

I could see nothing particularly threatening. They were dark: well-groomed, middle-aged. And both smelled of eau de cologne. These were no gangsters and I knew in that instant that they intended me no harm.

My eyes flicked from their faces to the room. Faces. Room. Faces. Room. And I was suddenly struck by the splendour of it all. Three gilded chairs with elegant legs (French, seventeen seventies) and a rather spectacular walnut bureau from the Dutch East Indies. On the walls there were paintings by Caillebotte and Jean Béraud.

"You are Arnold Trevellyan?" asked one of the men as we all sat down.

"Yes."

"You are forty-two years of age?"

"Yes."

"You moved to Creux in November 1988?"

"Yes."

"You formerly lived in Clapham, south London?"

"Yes."

"You are married?"

"Yes."

"To Flora Trevellyan, née Watson?"

"Yes."

"You like vanilla custard, particularly when served on a nest of meringues?"

"Y-y-yes." I was thinking to myself, "How the hell do you know that? Next you'll be telling me the colour of my underwear."

"And —"

"I'm wearing blue and green underwear," I said.

They gave each other a surprised look and then turned back to me. "No," they retorted. "I think you'll find, Mr Trevellyan, that your underwear is orange."

I looked down and — here's the strange thing — I saw they were right. I'd put it on that very morning.

"And then," said one of the men, "if you'll allow me to continue, you argued about some candles and Mrs Trevellyan left and — where is she?"

"In Paris, I think."

"When will she return?"

"I don't know."

The answer to this last question clearly raised their suspicions as well as their eyebrows. They asked for more details. I told them that she was quite possibly staying with Simon Leach at his flat in rue Mouffetard and suggested — for the life of me I don't know why — that he was potentially dangerous.

"Yes," said one of the men, "but only to you."

They asked if Flora knew about the existence of the quarries, to which I answered a truthful no. And then they asked a series of other questions. Why had I chosen to live in the Morvan? Why did I spend my time snooping around the forest? And why and why and why?

"Mushrooms," I said to them in all honesty. "Mushrooms, mushrooms, mushrooms."

"Mushrooms?" said both men simultaneously. "*Champignons?*"

They looked at each other and I noticed the merest flicker of a smile.

"*Voilà.* Just as Claude said." They turned back to me with another question. "And what can you tell us about mushrooms?"

It was a red rag to a bull. Oh, Peter, you should have heard me. For the next three hours — perhaps more — I bombarded them with a complete lorryload of information about mushrooms. I told them about girdled knights and leaf parachutes and wrinkled shields. I told them why lactaria produce milk and why pezizas expel spores when you breathe on them. I lectured them on habitat, I gave them recipes, I told them how mushrooms could be propagated.

And this, finally, was when they stopped me.

"Aha," said one. "This is what we wanted to know all along. You mean to say that you can propagate *any* type of mushroom? Even wild ones?"

"Yes," I said. "I do believe I can."

"Any?"

"Most."

"Amanitas?"

I looked the men hard in the eye, giving them a dose of their own medicine, and said with all the confidence I could muster, "Yes, I do believe I could cultivate amanitas."

And I did, Peter. I did. The humidity in those quarries and the temperature and the level of lighting: everything was perfect for the cultivation of a family of mushrooms that — to my knowledge — no one had ever cultivated before in the history of the world.

But it wasn't just that. I'd become increasingly convinced that the key to germinating amanitas was the alkalinity of the soil. They could only grow if the soil was absolutely perfect. And — well, I won't bore you — but I'd made a liquid, my magic potion, which could do just that. Twenty-three different ingredients, seven chemical compounds, and a dollop of genius. It was a bespoke liquid specifically created for amanitas. I'd already mentioned it in my article, the one in *Science*. But now I'd perfected it even further.

"Then Claude was right," said one of the men. "You shall be our guest. And you shall stay with us a while. You are most welcome." And then they both started laughing. And soon they were laughing so much that one of them had tears in his eyes. And when they finally stopped they asked how long I needed.

I said it would take seven weeks, perhaps more. Again they burst out laughing. Indeed, they laughed so hard that they set me off. I remember thinking how strange it was. I was under arrest in an underground quarry and I didn't know what was going on and I didn't know if I was in danger and yet here I was roaring with laughter.

You must remember that, up to this point in the interrogation, I still had no idea as to the identity of these men. Nor did I have any idea what they were doing down there. In fact, I knew nothing at all. Yet I felt suddenly as if the tables were beginning to turn. I was the one who had launched the conversation about mushrooms and now they were hanging off my every word. It began to cross my mind that perhaps it was for mushrooms — and mushrooms alone — that I'd been seized in the first place.

When my two interrogators eventually stopped laughing and we all came to our senses, I asked them what they wanted me to grow. Deathcaps? Panthercaps? Fly agarics?

They tutted and exchanged glances.

"No. We want you to grow caesars."

"*Caesars!*"

"Yes. Amanita caesarea. Twenty-five kilograms. That's fifty-five pounds in your English measurement."

I let out a low whistle.

"A tall order," I said. "That's a very tall order. Do you realize what you're asking? It's never been done before. Not to my knowledge, at any rate. They're the fussiest mushroom in the world. And they're almost impossible to cultivate. I could try, of course, but I need to know why. And I want to know what's going on. And I'd like to know . . ." I sighed in exasperation. "Could you please tell me," I said, "*everything?*"

And all this time, Peter, I was thinking, "Caesars — that's strange." Because this was the one year when there were no wild caesars in the woods.

"All in good time," was their response.

"And if I refuse?" I ventured.

"Just do it," said one of the men, "and it'll be hugely to your advantage. You'll be treated like royalty. You'll be free to come and go. You'll be free to explore. But don't think about trying to leave the area. You'll be caught — you have our word."

"I can't leave," I said. "My scooter has —"

"You're with us now," said the smaller of the men. "And there's no escape. You are under surveillance at all times. You're being watched. Everywhere you go."

They both stood up and moved to the door.

"I'm *free*? To go?" I looked at them in astonishment.

"Yes. Go back to your house. Get your spores — get whatever it is you need. And then get planting. We need those mushrooms in less than eight weeks. But do not leave. And do not contact Flora."

"But —" I said. "But — ."

"I'll show you out," said one of the men. And he led me back to the room with the fake door and shook my hand.

"We'll bring you everything you need," he said. "Nothing will be lacking." And then he turned and left, and I found myself alone.

I don't know if you've ever been in that situation, Peter, where you dream that you're somewhere truly odd yet deeply real. And then you suddenly wake up and for the first few seconds you're unsure if you're in the real world or the world of dreams. And it takes a few moments for your eyes to trundle a message to your brain with the news that you are indeed in your very own bedroom and this is your very own snug bed and — yes — you've just woken up and all is well with the world.

Well, that's exactly how it was for me, except for the fact that I'd not been asleep and I'd not been dreaming and I was most certainly not in my bedroom. I blinked once, twice, and — yes — I found that I was still inside the quarries and each time I pinched myself it hurt. *Yes, Arnold, you're awake.* Pinch. *Yes, Arnold, this is for real.* Pinch. *Ouch!* I pinched so bloody hard that the pain shot deep into the muscle. And, yes, I was standing in the neatly swept chamber with a fake wooden wall.

I remember glancing at my watch. *Four hours!* It felt like a few minutes. And yet it also felt like a world away. Had my watch stopped? Or had it speeded up? Was it another day completely? But then I noticed natural light filtering in through the glass ceiling panel — confirmation that it was still daytime and still pissing with rain and that nothing had changed and yet at the same time everything had changed.

I kept asking myself how all of this could have been concealed for so long. That had been my first thought when I originally saw the banqueting hall. And the more I saw of the place, the more it made me wonder. But then I thought of the caves at Lascaux, the ones with the Stone Age wall paintings. They'd lain undiscovered for millennia, hadn't they? And so had the Dead Sea scrolls. And then, one day, along comes some French farmer or bedouin shepherd or whoever it was and stumbles across them. So perhaps it was indeed possible.

And yet this was on an altogether grander scale than the caves at Lascaux. And there were people living down here. And furniture and lighting. And the place was heated. This was some sort of James Bond fantasy. And whoever was running it had the pockets of a multi-millionaire and the support of — well, of who, I wondered? The state? The local mayor? The family upon whose land these quarries were situated?

And that's how it was. I returned to my house. Had something to eat. And later that day, when I went for another walk, I noticed them for the first time. There were cameras. In the trees. Hidden amongst the rocks. I swear that the entire bloody forest was under surveillance. And the house as well. There were closed-circuit television cameras everywhere. That's how they knew about the custard and meringues. I couldn't believe I hadn't spotted them before.

And, well, it was some days later that I first met Lola and she told me about Soufflot and the buildings and everything else. And it all began to make some sort of sense. And apparently all the documents — everything — are in the Bibliothèque Nationale in Paris. That's the national library, You should take yourself to the manuscript room, Peter, and place an order for the following: have you got a pen to hand? It's this — hang on — ah, yes, here we are, I've got it written on a piece of paper: Cartes des France: Ms C3512.OE (Bourgogne-Creux). It has a subheading: *Les carrières de Soufflot*.

And in that document — or the three documents rolled together — you'll find everything you need to know.

CHAPTER
NINE

It was Saturday, 6 January, and I was sitting at my desk at the *Telegraph*. I'd asked Peter on the previous evening for Flora's number. I wanted to know what she could tell me about the quarries in France. And I also wanted to discover, more out of curiosity than anything else, what had gone wrong with their marriage.

"Excellent, excellent, excellent," was Peter's response. "Good lad. It's all going like clockwork. Pippingtons will be pleased."

"*Peter!* I only want to ask her a few questions."

"Yes, yes, understood and all that. Now — have you got a pen? Of course you have. You're a journalist."

I dialled the number he'd given me, but it was engaged. I tried again a few minutes later, but it was still engaged. On the third attempt, it rang — rang twice before her voice said a simple, "Hello?"

"Hello. It's Tobias. Tobias Edwardes. I just wanted to say that — well — I'm sorry if I upset you last night. I really didn't mean to —"

"You didn't, I promise. I'm over-sensitive. It's one of my weaknesses. I shouldn't be so — I should be more like you. Your words stuck in my head, you know. And I think you're right. I think too much. And I read too much Emily Brontë. I should let it all wash over me and —"

We spoke for fifteen minutes and the conversation came easily. We spoke of Peter and Philippa. Of Singapore. Of work and food and —

"I was wondering if I could persuade you to meet up. For dinner. On me, of course. One evening this week."

"I'd love to," she said. "I haven't been taken out since I got back. What a treat."

And before I knew it, it was a done deal. At 7.30p.m. on 9 January — just three days away — I was to meet Flora at Grenouille, the little French place on Frith Street.

"Should I bring a chaperone?" she asked with a hint of mischief.

"No need," I said. "That's my role."

We arrived at the restaurant at the same time and she kissed me on my left cheek. I took half a step back — she'd taken me by surprise — leaving her second kiss in mid-air.

"Don't you want the other one?" she said with a nervous laugh.

We chatted, drank and ate. Flora started with a warm salad with goat's cheese. I had carpaccio of beef.

"Here," she said, proffering a crust of toast. I was struck by the fact she handed it to me on her own fork — a minor detail, but one that stuck in my mind.

I returned the compliment with the beef.

"Yum," she said. "Nothing beats red meat. Red meat and cheese. I'm a dedicated carnivore. I've never understood vegetarians."

124

We finished our starters and drank some wine. "I'm sorry about the other night," she said. "I felt such a — I don't know — I felt I wasn't really making sense. And I felt so stupid afterwards. It's just that it was so odd to be back in England after such a long time away. Back to Clapham. Back to the old house. Back to everything, except for the fact that everything had changed.

"And to step back inside the house. It was — well, the last time I'd been there, it had been with Arnold. We'd still been together. We'd left that place as what is usually referred to as 'a happily married couple'. And now, coming back to this lonely-feeling place which was still furnished with our furniture, and there was our big double bed but it had been slept in by tenants and, well, it was all so odd. I thought I'd feel anger. I thought I'd feel bitter. But I didn't — not either of those two things. I just felt sad."

"But what happened to the house during the divorce?" I asked. "Why wasn't it sold? Did he let you keep it?"

"The divorce?" She said the words slowly and with a tone of slight surprise. "The divorce. Ah, you don't know. Of course you don't. And why should you? The thing is, Tobias, nothing's been settled. There's not been a divorce. Nothing's sorted. Nothing has even been discussed. I've never received a call from a solicitor. I've not spoken to Arnold about it. I am completely in the dark. I've been left without even a sliver of light. And I'm absolutely at a loss to know what to do. If I could see Arnold — if I could only see him. My God, I think I'd attack him. I'd scream at him and I'd shout at him and —"

"And then what?"

"I don't know," she said quietly. "I don't know."

There was a pause while she composed herself. She was flushed and visibly upset. "But he's married Lola," I said. "They're living as a married couple."

"I only know what Philippa has told me. She said they married in a Tuvan ceremony. It's not the same thing at all. It's not legally recognized in this country. Nor anywhere else. Except on Tuva. And all the other stupid islands. So it's valueless; it means nothing. Not worth the scrap of stupid paper it's written on."

"Except, presumably, to Arnold."

"Yes — and his wife." She said the word "wife" in a tone of heavy irony. "You see, by going through with the ceremony — which is, Philippa tells me, recognized in Tuva — he was able to become king. And that, it seems, is what Arnold so wanted. It's bizarre. I know, I know. It's so totally bizarre that I still can't quite get my head around it. Arnold has always been obsessed by absolute monarchs. The whole idea fascinates him. Catherine the Great, Louis the fourteenth. It's like a fantasy to him. 'Imagine,' he said to me one evening, 'imagine being able to control the lives of all your citizens. Imagine having the power of life and death at your fingertips. You cease to be a mere mortal at that moment. You become a god.'

"And then he smiled. 'Little wonder the Romans deified their emperors.'

"And now his unhealthy little fantasy seems to have taken on its own reality. But instead of robbing other people of their heads, he seems to be in the process of losing his own."

I listened to what she said. I could almost hear Arnold's voice as she recounted such things. I had many more questions to ask, but the main courses arrived and interrupted us.

"Mmm. Duck and cherries," said Flora as it was set down in front of her. "What a treat."

"And I have a thing about venison," I said. "Want to try?"

She nodded and we went through the food-swapping experience once again. "There's much I simply don't know," she said, returning to the subject of France. "But all I can tell you is this: there was something deeply strange going on in the whole area that surrounded where we were living. Not a single house was inhabited for miles around. The owners of the chateau were decidedly odd, although they were rarely there. And I had this feeling — often — that we were being watched. It was as if someone didn't like us being there. That they wanted to get us out."

She paused for a second and I wondered if I should tell her what I knew about the quarries. It occurred to me that she knew nothing of what Arnold had told us. She hadn't communicated with him since he left for Tuva and she hadn't heard any of the tapes.

"And then I read in some magazine or other that when the Soviet Union was ruled by Khrushchev — in the late fifties — the KGB used to specialize in psychological instability. That's what they called it. Foreign diplomats living in Moscow would experience exactly the same sorts of thing that were happening to us. Odd things. Things that make you question your sanity. Things that make you think you're going crazy. And, yes, I really had an impression that I was starting to go crazy. And Arnold — well, I got no support whatsoever."

"Who lived in the chateau?" I asked. "Do you know their name?"

"An old French family," said Flora. "Nobility. A family called de la Regnier. But we only met them once or twice."

I noted it down in my pad. "I'll check them out," I said. "Find out who they are. Maybe they've got something to do with it."

"And then," continued Flora, "well — as I've told you, we had this blockbuster of a row. And I walked out."

"Well, you were right," I said. "You had every right to walk out. You'd put up with a nightmare."

"I don't know if I was right or wrong. And you can imagine how many times I've asked myself that question. But — oh, I don't know. Arnold's wonderful, he's passionate, he's sensitive. But there's a side of him that's never truly grown up. He's handicapped by his inability —"

"His inability —?"

Flora folded her arms. "Oh, why am I telling you all this? It's not interesting for you. And it's the last thing I want to talk about right now."

There was a pause, giving us both a chance to eat our food. Grenouille did us proud that night. It had long been my favourite restaurant — cosy, intimate, French. And now, well, the evening was proving to be as enjoyable as it was unexpected. Flora was interesting company.

"So?" I asked at length, "Let me get this straight. You walked out. You got in your car. You drove away. And what next? Where did you go?"

She wiped her mouth and laughed. "Well, that was the problem," she said. "I had nowhere to go. Nowhere obvious. Except for an old friend, Simon — an ex-boyfriend — in Paris. So I went there; just to spend a night there. I wanted to annoy Arnold. Make him jealous. And — yes — force him to come to Paris. But —"

"He didn't."

"No, he didn't."

"Chocolate mousse, madam? *Tarte tartin?* Coffee?"

She nodded enthusiastically when the waiter proposed a *tarte tartin*.

"And your friend Simon. Can I be indiscreet? Did anything —?"

"No, no. Of course not. And nor did I ever intend it to. Not with Simon. He tried to jump on me, of course. That's Simon. But I most certainly didn't allow myself to be jumped on. So after a few days there I decided to go to my sister's place in Singapore. I wanted to get away. I couldn't have gone back to Arnold. Not there and then. I needed some breathing space. And it was while I was there — in June, I think it was — that I heard from Philippa about everything that had happened."

The coffee arrived and we drank it slowly, as if neither of us wanted the evening to come to an end. Flora spoke less, now that the meal was nearly over. She looked at the candles and I looked at her. And then it was time to order the bill and then we asked for our coats. A few seconds later we found ourselves back outside in Frith Street.

"So —" I said, clumsily filling the pause.

"So," she replied.

"Would you like to meet again —?"

"Yes," she said. "Very much."

CHAPTER
TEN

It was my second night alone and I was knocked sideways by it all. I was suddenly struck by the realization that everything had gone strange and would remain strange for weeks, months, perhaps forever. I went to bed and buried my head in the crumpled pillows. They smelled of Flora. Of when she's asleep. And I breathed in long and hard.

What would *you* have done, Peter? Put yourself in my position. I had no means of contacting her. No phone. No car. And I'd been told that on no account should I try to leave the area. Yet I suddenly had an overwhelming desire to tell her that there *had* been something going on: to tell her that all along there was something spectacularly odd happening in the forest. She'd been right to be suspicious. And all the weirdness — the candelabrum and all that sort of thing — had been for real. There'd been a reason for everything and that reason was to be found in an underground quarry that she didn't even know existed.

I lay on the bed and thought a lot about Flora. I could actually see her — I felt I could reach out and touch her — and I was thinking to myself what it would take to get her back. And as I thought these thoughts, I don't know why, I suddenly flung the pillows onto the floor, right there and then. They smelled too much of her. And that's where they remained. At that moment our marriage was a crumpled snowdrift of pillows piled up in the corner of the room.

I woke at first light, went downstairs to focus on the matter in hand. Mushrooms. I had seven or eight weeks to produce fifty-five pounds of caesars. That's what I'd been told and there was no time to lose. It must have been soon after nine in the morning when I made my way back to the quarries. I'd already selected the best place to experiment with the mushrooms. There was one hollowed-out chamber, half-open to the sky, which had a perfect level of light and humidity. At one point I measured it over a twenty-four-hour period. It was constant — absolutely bloody constant.

"Your lucky day," I said to myself. "You've hit the jackpot." And then came the hard work. I shifted some of the rich black soil of the forest into the chamber and began creating a series of beds. Back and forth, back and forth. In all this time I saw no one. No one came. No one went. But I knew that they were watching what I was doing because on my second day a wheelbarrow appeared from nowhere, along with half a dozen tools: a watering can, spade, that sort of thing.

By the fourth day the beds were pretty much ready and I prepared myself for the big moment — sowing my precious spores in the soil. I brought them all into the chamber, put on my sterilized gloves and was just about to dampen the soil with my magic potion when I heard this voice from behind me.

"Can I help? Can I be of any assistance —"

I spun around and found myself face to face with quite the most enchanting vision of loveliness I'd seen for many years. There's beauty, Peter, and there's beauty with a capital B the size of Bali. And I'm not just saying that because of everything that's happened. It was all in the eyes: a creamy-milky-turquoise-blue.

"Mushrooms." That was my first word to her. Couldn't think of anything else to say.

"Mmmm," she said. "My favourite. And it'll make you very popular here." She spoke English with just the whisker of a French accent. It was her "h"s that gave it away.

I showed her my envelope containing several ounces of caesar spores.

"You're Arnold Trevellyan," she said with a note of excitement in her voice. "We've been expecting you for ages. And now you're here! You're the mushroom man. They all call you Mr Caesar."

"But how do you know —"

"Oh, it was Claude — Claude de la Regnier. He said you'd be coming. You're coming to help with the banquet, that's right, isn't it?"

"*The banquet?*" No one had mentioned a banquet, Peter.

"Well, it's great you're here," she said.

"Well, I didn't exactly choose to come. I was — How shall I put it? I didn't have much choice."

"*Really?* They said you'd been extremely helpful. They said you were a long-standing member of the Order."

"The Order?"

"Yes. But, well, what does it matter? You're here now. And —" she peered into the envelope — "may I?"

I nodded and she dipped her hand into the spores. And then she scattered them into the soil. They fell like talcum powder, sketching just a trace of dust into the humus. As she did so, I sprayed each square foot of soil with a hundred and fifty milligrams of potion — my alkaline mix.

And it was there and then, Peter — as we planted spores together — that she first told me the outline of her story. How her grandfather had been assassinated. How her family had been forced to flee for their lives. How Lenin's Russia had planned to take control of the Tuvan archipelago.

"*What!*" I must have looked surprised when she mentioned Lenin because she suddenly seemed slightly offended.

"Can't you see?" she said. "That's precisely why we couldn't go back. It was far too dangerous. There was a plot. I can tell you the whole story if you've got time. But not right now — I've got a few things that I really must get finished. But why don't you drop around tomorrow? I'd like nothing better. I must say, it's been a pleasure to bump into you. It's always good to meet a new face. And a young one, too." (*Young*, Peter, she thought I looked young.) "Yes. Do come tomorrow. Say you'll come."

And then, without waiting for my response, she explained how to get to her chamber. And her directions were faultless because I found my way quite easily on the following afternoon. And well — stone the sodding crows — where do I begin? The banqueting chamber: I've already described that, but that was only the beginning. Down in those quarries there was an entire palace on the scale of Versailles. No, it was bigger than Versailles. I was told there were more than five hundred rooms and several of them were as large as tennis courts. Drawing rooms, libraries, a billiard room, all linked by long wide corridors. I spotted a Rembrandt and a Velázquez. And then there was a white room and a powder-blue room — in fact, every single colour and size and shape of room you could imagine. There was a Chinese breakfast parlour with the most exquisite wallpaper; it was decorated with these delicate yellow flowers and little blue songbirds. And there was a Turkish salon all decked in Iznik tiles. That really made me blink. It was just like the harem in the Topkapi palace. Only thing missing was the topless slave girls.

And every single room was furnished with truly wonderful antiques. French. Dutch. Austrian. The finest I've seen in years. And yet what struck me the most — what really struck me — was the way it was lit. It was ingenious. You've got to remember that the entire complex was underground and there was no natural light. Or that's what I'd thought when I was first frogmarched through the service corridors. But here, in the main part of the quarries, the ceilings had been punctured by little apertures that let in shafts of light. It was brilliantly done; you had the impression that every room was lit by spotlights. And it was not at all dark or gloomy. The Chinese breakfast parlour was as light as any room in *your* house, Peter, and the light caught the gilded mouldings and made the whole thing sparkle like a Christmas bauble.

I knocked at Lola's door and she told me to come in. "I'm so glad you've come," she said as I entered the room. "I knew you would." And as I stepped inside, Peter, I blinked once, twice, three times.

"You look surprised," she said.

And yes, I *was* surprised. I was extremely bloody surprised. Her room was a veritable tropical paradise. It looked as if it had been scooped up from Tuva and transported to the depths of these quarries. There was a row of columns propping up the ceiling, except that they weren't columns, they were the trunks of long-dead palm trees. And there were stuffed birds hanging from the ceiling — parakeets and sea

135

eagles and rare Pacific owls, all in dozens of different colours. Some had their wings outstretched and looked as if they'd dropped dead in mid-flight. Others were perched on branches and seemed to be taking a snooze. And one even had a very dead-looking sea eel dangling from its beak.

"I've got the smallest rooms of the lot," said Lola. "But, then again, Tuva is one of the smallest countries in the world. The others have much bigger spaces. Ivan — he's got twenty rooms. Turkish Mehmet — that's what we all call him — he's got fifteen or so. And Mitterrand — he's also got fifteen. But he hardly ever comes. I guess it's difficult for him."

"Ivan? Turkish Mehmet? Mitterrand? What's this all about? Please. What the hell's going on? Who are all these people? Everyone talks in riddles. I get no sense from anyone. I've no idea what's going on. I feel like I'm trapped in a dream. Or going mad."

There were pressed flowers and fruits and dried seed pods the size of grapefruit. And there were fish that had been preserved in glass cases. And there were these huge eggs, pale green, that must have been produced by some monstrous great bird. And there was also a collection of shells that — well, I think it was the size of them that impressed me the most. Scallops the size of dinner plates, whelks the size of biscuit tins and a conch shell that was bigger than a bicycle wheel. Put that to your ear and it would probably bite your bloody head off.

"It was my papa's idea," said Lola. "He wanted to recreate Tuva in his own quarters here in Creux. He wanted to be reminded of home."

"It's extraordinary," I said. "It's completely extraordinary. Where did he get the palm trees?"

"From Tuva," she said. "They were shipped all the way from Tuva. It took months to get them here. And, here, look at this."

She handed me a tiny brush with an elegant bone handle and short curved bristles.

"What is it?" I asked.

"Just a brush," she said, "but it's very special. It belonged to my grandmamma and the bristles — feel them — they're so soft. They're made from the eyelashes of a sea cow."

I laughed, Peter. I think I actually snorted. *The eyelashes of a sea cow!*

"It's true," she said. And she showed me a photo of a sea cow. And, to my very great surprise and amazement, I saw that they do indeed have curvy eyelashes. They curve down over their eyes.

"And the handle is made of bone, the bone of a wild pig," she told me. "On Tuva we wrestle with them. It's an old sport.

"You'll soon learn everything about this place," she said. "Louis is going to explain it all now that you're one of us. But for the moment, well, all I can do is show you the Monarchs' Gallery."

"The what?"

She led me out of her room and along a corridor. And then we went down this impressive flight of double stairs, each one carved neatly out of the rock.

"Do you mean to say that the quarries are on several levels?"

"Oh yes," she said. "Hasn't anyone shown you around yet? That's terrible. People are so rude, don't you think? I suppose they're out of the habit. That's the problem with

137

spending too long here. There are three — no, four — different floors. Not across the entire area, of course. But there are heaps of rooms scattered around. You'll see. The Monarch's Gallery is very deep underground."

Down we went, Peter, and down some more. Fifty stairs. Sixty. I lost count. Perfectly sculpted from the rock and white like marble.

And then we found ourselves in front of a big door.

And Lola swings it open and not for the first time I'm pinching myself hard on my arm and blinking like there's no tomorrow. A room that's thirty or forty foot long. A ceiling as high as two double deckers. And every inch of wall space — every single bloody inch — covered with masterpieces.

"*Holy cow!*"

For once in my life, and for one time only, I was speechless. Struck dumb. They'd got paintings down there by every Old Master the world has ever known. Lost works. Missing works. And works that most art critics probably don't even know exist.

"*But — ?*"

"Oh, don't ask me," said Lola with a laugh. "I know nothing about art. You need to speak to Prince George. Of Hohenlohe-Langenburg. He's the one that looks after them."

And just as she said it, right on cue, he appeared. It was as if it had all been choreographed.

"You called?"

The voice came from behind us: clipped, precise, ripe as a plum.

"George, *mon cher*," said Lola in her light, tripping voice. "I was just talking about you. This is Mr Caesar, Arnold. The

138

mushroom man, the one Claude's been telling us about. He wants to see the paintings."

"*Ah!*"

I shook his hand. Prince George Louis August von Hohenlohe-Langenburg: that was his name. I later learned he was a descendant (on the matrilineal line) of Lieutenant-General August Wilhelm, the fifth duke, who vanquished Marshal Königsegg at Reichenberg.

And now — two centuries on — here was the old duke's great, great, great, great, great, great (or thereabouts) grandson. Tall. Erect as a pillar box. Half *mitteleurop*, half Royal Air Force. It was the moustache that did it; as lovingly clipped, I imagine, as the topiary bushes at his ancestral Hohenlohe.

I motioned around the room, still lost for words.

"*Oui, oui,*" he said, nodding. "It's quite extraordinary."

Now I'm the first one to admit that I'm not a world expert on art, Peter. But — well — I know a few things. Leonardo da Vinci's *Leda*. Hasn't been seen since the eighteenth century. And there it was, before my very eyes. A dirty great beast of a swan sticking its neck into a voluptuously distraught Leda. Two paintings further — *The Just Judges* by the Van Eycks. Missing since — well, I'm not quite sure when that one was lost. Michelangelo's David in *bronze*. Last seen during the French revolution. Four Vermeers that I can pretty much promise you the world has never clapped eyes on. Two Giottos. An exquisite Bellini with a green so luminescent it could make you weep. Three Masaccios and a triptych by Veronese. No fewer than six Canelettos. And —

"*How* did you acquire all this?"

I rubbed my eyes. And I rubbed them again. Yes, yes. I was wide awake and standing in front of Caravaggio's *Nativity with Saints Francis and Lawrence*, painted in the early seventeenth century. I knew something about this painting, Peter. I'd only recently read an article about it. It was stolen from the Oratorio di San Lorenzo in Palermo, ooh, some twenty or so years earlier. Whipped out one night. Whoever masterminded the robbery was never caught and the painting was never found. And here it was.

"You must never ask *too* many questions," cautioned the prince. "But, well, many have come from royal collections — from Nassau, Schwarzburg-Rudolstadt, Lauenburg — the last, when Hanoverian rule tragically came to an end. There are some from Baden, from Hesse-Homburg and Mecklenburg-Strelitz. They're not just from Germany, of course. We've had donations from Italy, from the Vatican, and from still extant royal collections around the world. This —" he pointed to Holbein's Anne of Cleves — "is from Windsor. A gift of your queen. And we have a couple from Buckingham Palace. The Dürers, for example."

Never in my life had I seen such a collection. It was the National Gallery and the Alte-Pinakothek rolled into one great pile of priceless paintings.

"Come," said Lola. She was getting impatient. "We must go back to my room. I'll make you a Tuvan lime juice. You can come back here whenever you want."

I thanked the prince. "We shall meet again," he said. "And *bonne chance* with the mushrooms. Did you know that my great-grandmother, the Princess Louisa, was a great expert on mushrooms? She also worked for the Order."

Lola and I climbed back up the stairs; she chatted all the way. She was as breezy as a bright spring day.

She'd lived a sheltered existence. Hadn't seen much of the world. She couldn't, you see. It was too dangerous for her. And she wanted to hear my stories. She wanted to hear everything.

"Tell me everything about mushrooms," she said to me on that first afternoon together. "I just love mushrooms."

And off I went — tales of the golden bootleg, the earthy powdercap and the edible blusher. Tales of the woods. Tales of days in Taplow Bottom with you, Peter. And I told her about the Soup Kitchen and about my research.

"And what about the magical ones?" she asked. "Have you ever tried them?"

"*Psilocybe semilanceata*. Once," I said, "when I was a boy."

"A boy!" She laughed. "What fun you've had. You're the —" she paused — "*le roi des champignons*. They're forever trying to pair me off with Prince Igor or Prince Ranwar or Count Aleksandr of Montenegro. But they're all so — well, you'll know what I mean when you see them."

And that was the point at which — bring out the violins, Peter, strike up a romantic melody — that was the moment we first kissed. A big one. It was she who kissed me. And afterwards, well, you'll have to use your imagination. All I can say is that the sun came out and the flowers burst into bloom and the birds started twittering and there was music playing and ripe clusters of grapes were hanging off the vines and, and —

"Tell me about Tuva," I said, during a long lazy afternoon spent in her bedroom.

141

"Well," she began, "for a start, hardly anyone in the world has heard of it. And the island has the distinction, along with a handful of other islands," (if I remember rightly, they were Nuku, Hiva, Tapuaemanu and Tabiteuea) "of never having been visited by any of the great explorers. Your Drake didn't get to Tuva. Nor Cook. Nor Darwin. Nor anyone like that."

"But what about Warlock?" I said. "I'm sure he went to Tuva."

Her eyes popped. "I'm impressed," she said. "And I'm very, very surprised. How did you know that? You're the first person I've ever met who has known anything about Tuva."

"It's all down to mushrooms," I said. "Warlock was an expert on mushrooms. And I know that he went to Tuva. He even wrote an account about his expedition, which I've been meaning to read for years."

We talked, Peter, and we chatted and we had long lazy afternoons that mutated into one long holiday of bliss. And then, one afternoon, we were walking along a corridor when we bumped into a man of middling years, dressed in a beautifully tailored suit.

"Ah," he says to me without a care in the world. "We meet at last. We'd been told to expect you."

We'd been told to expect you. Every bloody person in those quarries seemed to have been told to expect me.

"*We*? By whom?"

"By Claude de la Regnier, of course. He said it would be any day — and now you're here."

"And — you — are?"

"Apologies. Excuse my lack of *politesse*. Allow me to present myself. Louis. Louis Bourbon."

"Bourbon? Louis *Bourbon*!"

"Aha," he said. "A man with knowledge. *Un savant*. Yes, Bourbon. And pleased to meet you. *Oui, oui*. A lineal descendant of King Louis the sixteenth."

"But that," I blurted, "is not possible."

I know my history, Peter. It was *not* possible.

"If I remember correctly," I said, "Louis the sixteenth was executed in the winter of seventeen ninety-three. Guillotined. In the place de la Révolution in Paris. In front of a crowd of thousands. So — you — can't —"

"Please," he says, holding up his hand and stopping me in mid-sentence. "Allow me to tell you a little story. A story that will explain exactly what I'm doing here. Why this magnificent room is here. And why this entire complex is here, housing hundreds of people. And I will also explain why it has had to remain a secret for hundreds of years. You see, it all began with my direct forebear, Louis Quinze — the fifteenth — who foresaw the day."

He instructs me to be seated, Peter, and then he sits himself down opposite me. And he tells me a tale that helps to explain to you why I'm now living on the far side of the world and married to a queen peach and sitting in my study on the island of Tuva and looking out over a lagoon that's glittering like silver foil.

CHAPTER
ELEVEN

It was a sodden day in early January, two days after my dinner with Flora, and I was on my way to see Peter. He was business manager of the Strand Century Hotel, a careworn and anonymous sort of place close to King's College. I must have passed it countless times over the years and yet I'd never registered its existence. And now, entering through the main revolving doors, I felt as if I was back in the Intercontinental in Bucharest. It was the staleness of the air. It smelled of wet clothes and boiled eggs and coffee. But it was not good coffee. You could actually smell the light-brown cheapness of it.

"Tobias," said a voice from behind. "Did you get drenched, old chap?"

It was Peter, who shook my hand with golf-club heartiness and led me up to his office on the second floor.

"Tea? Coffee?" I plumped for the latter to see if my instincts were correct. They were. It dribbled slowly out of one of those plastic filters.

"Sandwiches to follow," said Peter. "I've ordered ham and cheese."

As we waited for them to arrive, he made it clear that he wanted to know every detail of what had happened during the course of my evening with Flora.

"She had duck," I said. "And I had venison."

"And for desserts?" he replied, placing just enough emphasis on the word "desserts" to make it sound lewd.

"A state secret," I said.

"Well, I'll report all of that back to Pipingtons," he said with a mock-serious sigh, "and —"

"Peter — there's not much more to add. But she did tell me a bit more about Arnold, if you're still interested in your oldest friend." I took a certain satisfaction in turning the tables; reminding him that the real reason why we were meeting — the *only* reason, in fact — was Arnold.

I'd come to Peter's office in order to listen to Arnold's latest tape. He'd originally suggested I spend another evening in Taplow Bottom, but I was busy most nights and so he invited me to his office instead.

"So, what does he say?"

Peter hit the play button and Arnold was there before us — larger than life and filling the room with his presence. *It was my second night alone and I was knocked sideways by it all.* We listened to the tape in its entirety, not pausing it or stopping it until it clicked itself off.

"Well?" I said to Peter, "what do you make of it?"

"Ninety per cent of me is screaming out: the man's a raving bloody lunatic. He's lost the plot. But there's a sneaking ten per cent that I can't quite shake off. You

145

see, I've known Arnold for thirty-six years and I long ago learned that with him, you must expect the unexpected. It's like the story of him losing his virginity to Grace Kelly."

"*What!*"

"Yes, you *did* hear correctly. And he did. He bloody well did. I didn't believe a word of it at first. He got back from America — this was years and years ago — and told me how he'd met her and had drinks with her and then she'd proposed that they jump into bed together."

"But how did he meet her in the first place?"

"He was working for ABC — you know? The American Broadcasting Corporation. It was a temporary job, a three-month placement. And he ended up working on a film. It was called — oh, it was something with the word poppies in the title. Funded by the UN. And the narrator of the film was Grace Kelly. And because Arnold was working with the sound recordists, well, he met her and she took a shine to him and before you know it — bang — they were in bed."

"That is news. And then?"

"Well that was it. It didn't happen again. But our dear friend Arnold, aged eighteen, was no longer a virgin, the lucky bastard."

"And did he ever tell Flora?"

"No bloody way," said Peter. "I don't think that would have gone down too well."

"Well," I said, "in one way you've helped me out by telling me that story. You've made what I'm about to tell you sound slightly less stupid."

"Oh, yes?" said Peter. "Go on then."

I told him what I'd overheard in the bathhouse in Bucharest and then I told him about a story that had been doing the rounds of all the foreign desks, a story that was quite strange. "There's this rumour — and I stress, it's nothing more than a rumour — that events in Eastern Europe may be being orchestrated by one central body. I've heard it from four or five different people in the last few days. They're saying there's some sort of conspiracy going on. They're claiming that everything that's happened in Germany, in Czechoslovakia, in Romania and elsewhere is being planned — organized — by one single group that's attempting to —"

"That's attempting to *what?*"

"Well, that's the problem. In fact, there are two major problems. A: could such an organization exist? And B: what's it trying to achieve? It sounds so ludicrous that it could have come straight out of a Hollywood film. But — I dunno — if there's one thing I've learned since starting out in journalism, it's that time and again these sorts of stories, these wild rumours, turn out to be based on a kernel of truth."

"But what the hell's it got to do with Arnold?" asked Peter. "How can he possibly be involved, for God's sake? He's six thousand miles away on Tuva."

"That's true enough. And I'm not saying for certain he's involved. He's probably got absolutely nothing to do with any of this. But I've got this suspicion — nothing more — that he's up to *something*. And, who knows, perhaps the queen and Prince Philip are also —"

"The queen! Prince Philip!" Peter spluttered into his tea. "Now you're away with the fairies."

"You're probably right," I said, "but there's one thing you ought to know. There have been stories about Prince Philip doing the rounds for years. Stories about him and Mountbatten. Stories about the two of them forging close ties with senior figures in the army. I've even heard talk of rumoured coups, that sort of thing. Ask anyone on Fleet Street and they'll tell you a similar story. Of course, no one can ever give you any more information. But Mountbatten's always been seen as a highly dubious character. And although I thought at first that Arnold was talking nonsense, the more I listen to what he has to say, the more I think that, well . . ."

I told Peter a little more about my time in Romania. And then I told him a bit more about my evening with Flora. And when I told him the fact that Arnold had not yet filed for divorce, he let out a long, low whistle.

"Wow. Now that *is* news. I just assumed — . Wait until I tell Pips *that*. And wait until I tell my mushroom-picking chums in the Red Lion. It'll cause a riot."

"If you want *my* opinion," I said, "Arnold wants to have his cake *and* eat it. On this particular issue, he's got everything he wants. He's escaped to his little island realm. He's got some tropical love queen who walks around topless most of the time. And he doesn't want to face the turmoil of divorce. He'd rather bury his head in the sand."

"But doesn't Lola mind? Isn't *she* bothered that he's still married to Flora?"

"Apparently not. You heard what she said to him. And, besides, polygamy's perfectly acceptable in the Tuvan archipelago. It sounds as if they've all got ten partners."

"Well, well, well," said Peter. "Makes me want to pack a gigantic great box of condoms and head for the sun. They must be at it like rabbits." He paused. "Er — you won't repeat that, will you?" he said. "Boys' joke and all that."

There was a knock on Peter's door and a platter of sandwiches appeared through the widening gap, followed by a hand, arm and then the rest of one of the hotel's waitresses.

"Ham and cheese," she said in a voice that was simultaneously young and old-fashioned. She smiled. "And tuna. And I've put you some ready-salted crisps, Mr Rushton. I know how you like crisps."

"Good girl, Deirdra," said Peter in a tone that was meant to be friendly but sounded distinctly patronizing.

She ducked out of the door and called to someone further down the corridor.

"I wouldn't mind sharing a packet of crisps with her, if you get my drift," said Peter as we launched into the sandwiches. While we ate, we replayed the section of the tape in which Lola was speaking: the part where she was reciting the poem about fishermen.

"She sounds rather — *tasty*," said Peter. "Rather — seductive. What do you make of her?"

And then he fell silent as we listened to Arnold resuming his story. Both of us looked blankly out of the window. It was still tipping with rain outside.

"Nice weather for ducks," said Peter.

I didn't respond. I was still thinking about Arnold.

"And fish."

CHAPTER
TWELVE

"Miss Rose, sir." It was Gilbertine speaking. "All skin and bones, don't you think?"

"Well," I answered, thinking aloud, "there are those who find skin and bones very attractive."

Gilbertine laughed. "My grandmamma used to say that a girl without flesh is like a pie without filling." She pulled at her belly. "You need stuffing, sir."

When I didn't respond (I wasn't at all sure what I should say, Peter), she asked, "Excuse my question, Mr King, but do you intend to marry Miss Rose?"

"I wasn't considering it," I said in all honesty. "I'm very happy with Queen Lola. And I'm not convinced by this idea of having ten wives."

"But you need a *few* more," she exclaimed, aghast at what I'd just said. "You're our king, sir." (I thought of you, Peter, when she said this. I only wish you'd been here to hear it.)

She looked thoughtful for a moment and then added with uncharacteristic hesitance. "Of course," pause, "Miss Rose would only count for one wife," pause, "whereas I'd count for at least two," pause, "if not more."

I asked what on earth she meant.

"Well," she said, "an average woman weighs, what, about seventy-seven okes." (An oke, Peter is the equivalent of about two pounds.) "Skinny Miss Rose, I imagine, must weigh only about fifty-five okes, whereas on a good day — after a really big meal — I tip the scales at one hundred and thirty okes. That's more than two Miss Roses! And if I manage to put on another forty or so okes, as I'm trying to do, then I'll be *three* times as heavy as her. So if you were to count her as one wife, then you'd have to count me as three."

"I'm not sure I underst —"

"Can't you see, Mr King?" she said. "It's a question of mathematics. If you want fewer wives, then you must choose the round ones. The big plump juicy pies. That way you get two, perhaps three, for the price of one."

I laughed. "Let me get back to you," I said. "I think I need to do my sums."

"Good," she said. "But you must bear in mind, sir, that me, plus Doris, plus Queen Lola, would almost certainly equal ten wives."

So there you have it, Peter. I live on an island where two plus one equals ten; where one wife counts as three and where my own chosen beauty considers polygamy not just acceptable but desirable.

Anyway, all this to tell you that last week I spent the entire day alone with Gilbertine. She said she had something she urgently wanted to show me on the northern flank of Mount Tuva.

We set off early for the mountain — it was before six — and the air was as close as it ever gets to being fresh. It was a beautiful morning. A real stunner. The sky was a pallid blue, glowing with luminosity, and the stars were holding out against the encroaching day: Sirius winking; Castor and Pollux flashing; and the Pleiades were this shimmering white mist, sprinkled across the sky like talcum powder.

We were wearing thick trousers and boots. Gilbertine was worried that it'd be tough going, what with the razor-sharp ngali palm and the thorny pagoda tree. You see, there's no trail leading to the north flank of the mountain. No one ever goes there and Gilbertine said she'd have to slash a path through the jungle with her machete.

"Tell me, Gilbertine. What is it you want to show me?"

"A little present, sir," she said. "All good things come to those who are waiting."

It was extraordinary how the jungle seemed to close in on us, its suckers and tentacles lurching towards us and trying to wrap us in a deathly embrace. It was claustrophobic. Oppressive. And hard to breathe. Towering trees, tangled creepers, dripping shrubs and palms. Tea trees with their willowy leaves, giant honeysuckles and saxifrage and lacebark shrubs with this oleaginous bark. Squelchy moss underfoot. We were traipsing across a giant sponge of green. It was springy, like walking on a mattress, except that each time you lifted your foot there was this long slurping sound — the sort of noise you get when you suck the liquid from a giant whelk.

Mushrooms, mushrooms, mushrooms. The moss was thicker than a pillow and we were hemmed in by knotted fuchsias so tangled they were almost impossible to push our way through. We were jostling through a thick crowd, elbows pushing and stabbing, except that the people in the crowd were dangling plants and obstinate branches and scratching, itching, vicious spines and thorns. I got one thorn in my foot and another pierced my elbow. "Bastards," I shouted as I pulled them out. "You're all bastards."

"This is not bastard, sir," said Gilbertine. "This — pagoda tree." She pointed towards a rambling succulent with pinkish flowers. "*This*," she said, "is the bastard tree."

The sky disappeared beneath the great green canopy, a gigantic umbrella of greenery. We knew the sun had come up, we knew it was now daylight, for the light filtered downwards in shafts. And the heat began to build — a thick, muggy, soupy, humid heat you could eat off a ladle.

Hack. Hack. Hack. Mushrooms, mushrooms, mushrooms. Gilbertine slashed at the fuchsias with her machete and each time a limb was lopped off there was this strong smell of sap. It was not altogether unpleasant, except for the fact that it was thick and strange and rather too pungent. Flowers were unnaturally bright. The blossom was unnaturally strong. It was like walking into a funeral parlour or crematorium. There was that same smell, sweet and sickly. An old lady's perfume.

Hack. Hack. Hack. As it grew hotter and more humid, a damp veil rose up from underfoot. It was as if the entire jungle was steaming and steaming — a kettle on the boil — and all the plants were glistening and dripping and sweating.

Great clusters of creamy-yellow flowers dangled from the mountain ribbonwood, looking for all the world like bridal bouquets. Gilbertine picked one and stuck it in my top pocket. And there was the hoary burn oak, with round hairy bits like balls of fluff. And the houhere bush, with its rasping leaves which had the feel of a dried-up old kitchen sponge. And the cabbage trees, clusters of green daggers that erupt from the soil.

"Don't touch, sir," warned Gilbertine. "Very poisonous."

It was still quite quiet in the jungle. All the animals were stretching and yawning and not quite wide awake. But then,

154

as we neared the northern side of the mountain which was in full sun, it was as if someone had flicked on the switch to a loudspeaker. Bang — there was birdsong — an orchestra of birdsong that was not quite in harmony, nor in tune, but, my God, giving the performance of its life.

Cwarck-cwarck-cwarck-Oola-Oola-Oola-
chick/chick/chick:chick/chick/chick-ik-ik:ik-
ik:ik-ik: WoooOOAH-WoooOOAH-WoooOOAH:
broooit-broooit-broooit.

And then we saw them, high up, in the canopy of the trees. Rainbow birds and king parrots and long-tailed cockatoos. There were lorikeets and fruit pigeons and oh, yes, most exhibitionist of all, the gilded parrot. There were two of them with these big red heads and green wings and yellow upper beaks. And they have a long blue tail and this great gilded tuft on the top of their heads. I'd been told that they were regular visitors to Tuva, but this was the first time I'd seen one.

We pressed on, hack, hack, hack, as we worked our way across the northern flank. Here the terrain was much more treacherous. There were great cliffs and bluffs of rock that seemed to rise sheer out of the jungle. That's what you see from far out to sea. They were dripping with water and festooned with creepers like telephone wires. At one point there was a crashing waterfall and we stopped to freshen up. Gilbertine stripped to the waist, exposing her breasts to the world and his wife. Blimey, Peter. Talk about pumpkins. That pair could have kept you going for years. She stood under the shower and beckoned me.

"Come in, sir," she said. "No need for clothes."

What would you have done, Peter? You'd probably have jumped in. You've always liked a pumpkin. But I certainly had no intention of taking my clothes off. And d'you know what she said next? "Is it because you're not well hung, sir?"

"*Sorry?*"

"Well hung. In the underpant department. How long is it, sir? When standing tall? Your manhood, sir."

Well, Peter, even as she said it, I was chuckling inwardly and thinking, "I can't wait to tell Peter about this."

"How *long* is it, sir!" She got full marks for persistence.

I erred on the small size in a desperate attempt to deter her advances.

"About three bilks," I said.

Gilbertine roared and roared. "That is indeed king-sized," she said. (I'd made a mistake, you see. One bilk is slightly longer than a metre.)

We sat on the bank for a while and Gilbertine sharpened her machete. The cutting edge was completely blunt.

"No mushrooms," I said, shaking my head.

"No mushrooms," she repeated. "But don't worry, sir. We'll soon be there."

Aieeeeeek. Aieeeeeek. There was this shrill shriek that came from somewhere to our left. And then again, but softer. *Aieeeeeek.* The echo seemed to bounce off the bluffs of rock — bing-bong — bouncing from one to the next. Gilbertine started moving forwards. "Ah, yes. We're almost there."

Hack. Hack. It was my turn to wield the machete and I attacked those plants with all the energy I could muster. We were enclosed in a maze of lancewood with a thousand branches which stretched across the ground like skipping

156

ropes. I sliced them in two — whack, whack — and then lopped off the top of a houhere bush.

"You have much muscle," said Gilbertine. "Look at the destruction."

It was true. I must have chopped down fifteen or twenty bushes.

And now, *sssh*, we're advancing slowly towards the shriek — *aieeeeeek, aieeeeeek* — and it's very close at hand. A final hack and we're out of the maze and find ourselves at the entrance to a partially roofed cave. The central section must have collapsed in on itself a century or two earlier and is covered in the same spongy moss. But the sides of the cave are completely intact and rearing to a height of perhaps fifty feet or more. And there on a ledge sits a lone male lemur, shrieking into the air.

But it's not that, Peter, which is exciting me. Nor is it the vaulted sides of the cave. It's the floor. And the ledges. And the nooks and crooks and crannies.

"Look, sir," says Gilbertine. "This is what I wanted to show you."

Everywhere, Peter, everywhere: mushrooms, mushrooms, mushrooms. Stinkhorns and jelly fungi and gargantuan organ pipes with those great fleshy-yellow tentacles. I'd never seen such huge ones. There were dozens of devil's tongues — they were glowing red, as if they actually had blood pumping around inside them. And in the darker corners of the cave there were little dots of light: it was the bioluminescent *Mycena chlorophos*. And right by my feet goblets and hairy goblets the size of teacups.

"And this, sir," said Gilbertine, "is what Warlock found when he came."

"*Warlock! Really?* He didn't mention it in his book."

"No, sir. He couldn't. The Order. They needed to keep it secret. Top secret."

I have to say, Peter, of all the surprises I'd had over the preceding months, few were more agreeable than this one. This was a sight that never, ever in my dreams could I have imagined. I felt that at last my cherished project might come true. When I left France — came to Tuva — I'd brought with me the spores of more than three dozen mushrooms: velvet shields, mealy bigfoots and deadly webcaps. And I also brought most of the agarics: the deathcap, the panthercap and, of course, caesars. Millions and millions of powder-dust spores. I'd already tried a few experiments, but all to no avail. It was either too hot or too humid. But now, I felt sure, I would succeed. For this cave — guarded by a lone male lemur — seemed to have everything necessary for spores to burst into life. Warmth, humidity, water, shade. In fact, this cave on the northern flank of Mount Tuva seemed to have its own peculiar micro-climate. All it needed was a little helping hand from my magic potion.

"Gilbertine," I said, as we stood dumbfounded in that cave, "we need to come back. We must come back. I need to bring my spores. Will you come back with me?"

"Nothing, sir, would give me more pleasure." And she winked.

CHAPTER
THIRTEEN

On 14 January, after a lot of persistence and more than a dozen phone calls, I finally managed to secure a telephone interview with the uncrowned King Leka of Albania. He'd been living in exile in South Africa for more than a decade and had not spoken publicly for several years. I wanted to know what he thought about recent events in the country of his birth.

Albania had not experienced the same degree of political turmoil as all the other countries in Eastern Europe. The hard-line Communist government was not under direct threat and there had been none of the mass demonstrations that had taken place in Berlin and Prague and Bucharest. But there had been small pockets of civil unrest — something unheard of in Albania. Several thousand protestors had demonstrated on the streets of Shkoder, a town in the north of the country. And there were rumours of demonstrations in Tirana, the capital.

King Leka told me of his hopes that these initial displays of dissatisfaction would be the prelude to something on a far grander scale. Indeed, he fervently believed that it would only be a matter of time before the regime of Ramiz Alia would be toppled, paving the way for him to take up his royal duties in a country that he had been forced to leave at the princely age of two days.

"You must surely know the story," he said to me over the phone. "The Italians invaded — they broke into the royal palace just hours after my birth. When they found all the sheets and towels still covered in my mother's blood, they were furious. 'The cub has flown.' That's what the Italian foreign minister was reputed to have said. I was that cub, the heir to the Albanian throne, and they were incensed that I'd escaped with my life."

I asked what he'd do if and when he got back to Albania. Would he try to form a political party?

"I am above party politics," he told me grandly. "I wish only to serve my country."

I asked him why he was so convinced that he would be able to take up his rightful place on the throne. Numerous difficulties seemed to lie on the road ahead, not least the fact that the present government had a very firm grip on power.

"You are straying into difficult areas," he told me. "I can tell you no more. But rest assured — I *will* return to Albania. Monarchy *will* be restored. Things *will* happen. The time is coming soon enough."

I pressed him further. Was he in contact with people inside Albania? Were Albanians in exile stoking the rebellion?

He was guarded in his answers. "I can say nothing. How do you expect me to respond to such questions? It is too dangerous."

160

I had one last question — I asked it half in seriousness and half in jest. "Were you," I said, "invited to Arnold Trevellyan's coronation?"

There was a lengthy pause. A really long pause. And then he said, "No."

And that was his final word because he hung up the phone immediately afterwards. Three, four, five times I tried to call him back, but there was never any answer. The interview had ended on an unsatisfactory note.

It was three days before the interview was published and it was a shorter piece than I'd hoped. But I was pleased it made it into the paper. It was one of the first about Albania to appear in any of the broadsheets since the troubles had begun a month or so earlier. Under the headline, "King Sets Sights on Throne", it recorded Leka's hopes for the future, just as he had recounted them to me. There was a side piece — much shorter — on Leka's father, King Zog, who'd been deposed in 1939. Zog had died in 1961, having never been allowed to return to his land. Leka had told me he was determined that history would not repeat itself.

It's said that today's newspapers are tomorrow's fish-and-chip wrappers but it's not always quite like that. My article about King Leka might have been the end of the story had it not been for a phone call that I received just two days after it was published. I was sitting at my desk when the phone rang.

"Mr Edwardes? This is Mr Lloshi speaking. Ministry of Foreign Affairs in Albania."

He spoke excellent English, albeit with an American accent, and was remarkably candid when talking about my article. How he'd managed to acquire a copy of the *Telegraph* in downtown Tirana remained a complete mystery, but he'd certainly read it and he wished to put the record straight.

"In short, Mr Edwardes, we wish to take the exceptional step of inviting you to Tirana. We wish to grant you an interview with our president, Ramiz Alia. He has a few — how do you say? — home truths that he would very much enjoy discussing with you."

It was an offer I could hardly turn down. I got the go-ahead from my editor, arranged tickets and, on 23 January, I found myself boarding a plane to Zagreb, followed by a second plane to Titograd, followed by a private transfer (state organized) that took me across the land border and into Albania. I'd left London at six a.m.; I arrived in Tirana after nine p.m. Fifteen hours to reach a city that was the same distance from London as Corfu.

Tirana by night: it was not exactly rocking. The streets were deserted and there wasn't a car on the road. We swung into Skanderbeg Square, a parade ground of dimly lit tarmac. In the centre of the square stood a gilded statue of the Beloved Leader, Enver Hoxha.

"Here. Your hotel," said the driver. "I will meet you in morning — at nine o'clock sharp — and take you to presidential palace."

My bag was taken to my room by one porter, my keys were carried by another. And when I requested something to eat, I was told that meatballs and rice would be served in the bar within twenty minutes. I was

162

impressed. Travelling on the invitation of those in power had its plus sides.

There was no one else in the bar when I returned downstairs. My meal was ready, as promised, and a waiter asked what I'd like to drink. But I scarcely had time to take my first mouthful of food before the maître d' appeared and told me that my driver needed a word.

I made my way back into the hotel lobby and there he was, smiling as before.

"There's been a change of plan," he said. "We must go now. The president wishes to see you straight away."

"*Now?* But — well — why? OK. But I must change."

"Five minutes," he said. "Or we'll be late. And in Albania we don't keep the president waiting."

I was thankful I'd already prepared my questions. I slipped my notebook into my suit pocket, checked the batteries on my dictaphone, then ran downstairs to the lobby.

"Let's go," said the driver.

It was a short drive to the presidential palace, taking us once again through empty streets.

Tirana was dreary; a hundred times worse than Bucharest. Dull streets, dull buildings, dull everything.

"Here — we've arrived."

The car stopped and the door was opened.

"Mr Edwardes? Good evening. I am Mr Lloshi. We spoke on the phone. Come — President Alia is awaiting you."

"Thank you, thank you. But why the change of plan?"

"Mr Alia is a very busy man," said Mr Lloshi. "He has several unavoidable meetings tomorrow. That's why he wished to see you tonight."

I was led through a series of atriums and corridors before we came to a large mahogany door. I was frisked and searched by a soldier, the fourth time since entering the building, and asked to take the batteries out of my dictaphone. Then, when this was done, Mr Lloshi knocked and a voice could be heard from inside.

"*Hyj?*"

"Come, we can go in."

The president was seated behind a desk, a thin-haired, middle-aged man with kind eyes. He had the air of a genial uncle.

"Mr Edwardes?" He got up and shook my hand. "You are very welcome in Albania."

I sensed that the interview was going to be tricky. Alia had been Enver Hoxha's right-hand man — and was now his successor — and he was up to his neck in Marxist-Leninist nonsense. Yet I found him disarmingly friendly, open-minded and apparently eager to engage.

I posed the questions; he had a ready answer for everything. He'd relaxed censorship; he'd released prisoners; he'd encouraged debate. He drummed his fingers on the desk, as if searching for all the other things of which I might approve. Ah yes — he'd reopened diplomatic relations with Greece, with Italy, with Turkey.

"But not with Britain," I said. "Nor America."

164

"It will come, it will come," he said with a smile, as though it was the most obvious thing in the world. In his capable hands, he seemed to suggest, Albania was on a swift path to modernity.

When I asked about the rioting and demonstrations — the troubles in Shkoder — he waved his hand nonchalantly through the air.

"Nothing serious," he said. "Nothing we cannot cope with. There are, you see, organizations — outside organizations — trying to destabilize us. But we know who they are. And we will —" he paused for a second before turning to me with a chill in his eyes — "*eliminate* them."

It was the first time I'd noticed any hint of menace. I realized that the kind uncle could, at the flick of a switch, become the wicked uncle.

I was about to ask another question, but he raised his arms as a conductor might do when he wishes to quieten an orchestra.

"No more. No more," he said. "I have a question for you."

"Please," I said. "Fire away."

"Why," he said, speaking slowly and deliberately, "did you interview the so-called King Leka? Did *he* contact you? Or did *you* contact him?"

I explained that I was interested to hear what he had to say about Albania. And whether he hoped to return as king.

"And he does," said Alia. "He's said so many times."

"Yes," I said. "He does."

"But he will not," said the president in a clipped tone. "We got rid of his father — the wastrel Zog, who plundered our country of riches; Zog, who sold us to the Italians; Zog, who was nothing more than a playboy. And now we shall get rid of the son."

"You mean you will —"

"I have said nothing. Your British press is famous for misquoting politicians, is it not? I say only this. Leka will never — not today, not tomorrow, nor at any other time — be king of Albania."

There was a pause. I was tempted — I was ever so close — to asking about Arnold Trevellyan. But I didn't dare. It seemed the wrong moment.

"Well, if you have no more questions."

I thanked the president for his time. He smiled and nodded. "We want the outside world to know," he said, "that while the rest of Europe is falling into turmoil, we Albanians — a proud race and a strong one — are very contented with the status quo."

"I shall make that point in my article," I said.

"Then I shall look forward to reading it," was the president's response.

I was escorted back to the car and then to the hotel. I was tired after the stress of the interview and it was well past midnight. But I knew I'd be unable to sleep — it always took an hour or more to wind down after an important interview — so I headed to the bar. And it was here that the evening took a whole new twist. Just a couple of hours earlier the place had been empty. But now there was quite a crowd. At least five or six of the tables were fully occupied and I scanned the room looking for somewhere to sit. And it was then — right at that point — that I saw a face I felt sure I recognized.

He was seated in the far corner of the bar, surrounded by three other men. And when I saw the left side of his face, well — that clinched it. He had the same dark red birthmark above his eye. It was an unmistakable sign. He looked slightly thinner than I remembered him, and less flushed, but he had the same throaty laugh. Here, less than five yards away from me, was the same member of the Securitate whom I'd first seen a couple of weeks earlier in the hot baths in Bucharest.

I knew he wouldn't recognize me — there was no question of that — so I seated myself at a nearby table. I wanted to be sure it was him.

I studied him and then his companions. There were three of them and they were all chatting away in what sounded like Russian. I couldn't understand a word they were saying, for they were talking fast and in a hushed tone, but it sounded conspiratorial.

At one point, one of them reached into a pile of papers and pulled out a map. I couldn't see it very clearly, for it was slanted at an angle, but I could swear that it was a map of the Tuvan archipelago.

I counted the islands — there appeared to be six or seven. And the man, the one with the birthmark, was pointing at Tuva. And their conversation became increasingly animated.

What were they saying? Were they discussing Arnold? I figured that they must have been. But I couldn't see how I could find out more. Besides, their evening was almost at an end. The fat one suddenly called for the bill and gathered up his papers. They all stood up and, after a round of laughter, made for the door.

It was when they'd gone that I realized how tired I was. I'd been up since dawn and now it was almost one-thirty. I was still wide awake and it took me at least half an hour to go to sleep. When I finally drifted off, I found myself dreaming about the events of the day, only this time I had Flora by my side. At one point, she turned to me in my sleep and said, "Arnold? Arnold, is that you?"

CHAPTER
FOURTEEN

I'd just bumped into Louis Bourbon — that's where I was. And he took me to his chamber and sat me down and then he began his tale.

You should really seat yourself in a darkened room, Peter. Wind back the old grandfather clock more than two centuries. You have to imagine yourself waking to a chill, wintry day in Paris. Ice cold. It's the year of our Lord seventeen hundred and ninety-three, Peter, and it is to prove a momentous one for France and for the world.

Listen. Can you hear the bugle? It breaks the dawn as a clean, clear note with an echo that sounds like mist. BroooooooOU; RrrooooooOU; RrrooooooOU; RrrooooooOU; R-oOU — R-oOU — R-oOU. Look! There's a large water rat scampering across the place de la Révolution. The icy breeze is tugging at the trees in the Tuileries gardens, pulling at the branches in just the same fashion that a puppeteer plays upon the strings of his mannequins. The breeze — it filters inside your cloak; it filters into your bones. You wrap the cloak close to your chest. Try to trap in some body warmth. In the centre of the square a shivering group of uniformed men are huddled around a brazier, amusing themselves by telling bawdy jokes. They've been awaiting the arrival of their commanding officer

— waiting for almost an hour. They want to know where, exactly, the guillotine is to be situated.

Less than two miles away, in his prison in the tower of the Temple, King Louis the sixteenth has just been woken by his grim-faced valets. This is the last time they will perform this ritual; the final time they will dress the king. For in less than four hours his sovereign majesty, the divinely ordained king of France, the great, great, great, grandson of the Sun King (the illustrious Louis Quatorze), is to have his head chopped off in front of a crowd of baying, jeering spectators.

"I slept well." These are the king's first words upon stirring that morning. "I needed it. Yesterday exhausted me." He might have continued in a similar fashion, but the pallid faces of his two valets suddenly awaken him to the stark and grim reality of the situation.

Their presence, if you like, provides him with his second awakening of the day. The moment when the awful, terrible horror of what is about to happen to him hits him in the back of the neck and leaves him shaking uncontrollably.

"Will it hurt?" he sobs. "It must be fast, surely? But how long will it take for the spirit to arise from my body? That's what troubles me the most." He sobs again. "Oh, my France! Oh, *mon dieu*! Oh, my faithful valets!"

Jean-Baptiste Cléry and Theodore Daumier exchange glances. They, too, have tears rolling down their cheeks. "It cannot be," they say to the king. "Surely the Lord Himself will intervene?"

It is important to set out the precise sequence of events on that January morning, Peter, for they are to prove of immense significance to everything that will follow. The king is dressed by his valets long before it is light and then he attends Mass.

170

It is a little after six o'clock. At seven he returns to his study and asks Cléry to bring him some scissors. He wishes to cut his hair in the privacy of his prison, rather than having to go through the indignity of having it cut on the scaffold. *Non!* The request for scissors is denied by the council of guards. They fear that their prisoner will attempt to take his own life. The king is insulted. He would never commit suicide.

The order for execution is planned as follows. At eight-thirty, the king will be led down into the street. He will be taken to the place de la Révolution in the coach that belongs to Paris's mayor. He will be accompanied by two senior military guards and his faithful Irish confessor, the Catholic priest Henry Essex Edgeworth de Firmont. He and the king will read penitential prayers and psalms on the one-and-a-half hour rattle-ride through the capital's boulevards.

The coach will take him to the very foot of the scaffold. The door will be opened from outside. And, from this point on, he is on is own. He must mount the steps, face the indignity of having his hair chopped in public by the executioner, and then listen to the roll of the drums as he shuffles — leaden footstep after leaden footstep — towards the guillotine. He will kneel. Place his head on the wooden block. He will feel the hard chill of the wood pressing on the bumpy knot of his Adam's apple. This will become uncomfortable — it may even hurt — when the stout oak beam is clumsily brought down around his neck, yoking him to the machine that is to take his life.

He will be shaking; he will have a burning acid in his throat; he may lose control of his bladder and bowels. And as he tries to focus on his prayers — he will be desperately reciting the Creed and the Notre Père — he will hear the crowd chanting, baying, screaming over and above the roll of the drums. And then he will hear a sudden little clink, followed by Zzzzzrrrr — a split second, no more — faster — faster — rrrzzzrr. And then.

Nothing. No pain. No feeling. No sense that anything has changed. Just a vague abstract sensation that he is looking at a crowd which is growing misty and blurry and hazy and the sound of shouting is melting, melting and drifting and —

And at that point Sanson, the executioner, will contemptuously toss the head that he's been displaying to the crowd into a wicker basket. And the men and women and children will surge forwards in order to dip their kerchiefs into the dead king's blood.

That, at any rate, is how the revolutionary council and officers and soldiers and executioners have imagined the morning's events to unfold. But unbeknown to them, it's not going to happen like that. Because a most unexpected turn of events is taking place right now in the king's study.

Once again, Peter, the exact unfolding of events is of critical importance. Look, the king is seated behind his desk, writing a final letter to his wife. In front of him stand Cléry and Daumier, his valets. The king is pale, as pale as a winding sheet, but Daumier is paler by far. He is shaking slightly, his mouth is dry. He has something to say, but he's uncertain how to begin.

Daumier, it should be noted, has been the king's ever-faithful valet for more than two decades. He has the same temperament as the king, which is perhaps why he understands his master's agony. He is similarly adipose in the middle regions. His belly has been well catered for by the royal kitchens.

He coughs. Attracts the king's attention.

"Your majesty," he begins. "Your noble majesty. Allow me to speak. For more than one and twenty years, I have served you to the best of my ability. I have dressed you; brought you your victuals, your meats, your fruits, I have striven to be a loyal servant — a faithful and diligent one. And now I ask you one favour in return."

The king looks at Daumier; he wonders where this is leading. Can it really be so important right now, when he is about to die?

"I ask that you give me your ring. Your watch chains. Your waistcoat. Your lorgnette. I ask that you remove your clothes — immediately — and hand all of them to me. In short, majesty, I humbly ask and beg you — yes — to let me give my life for you. I am willing, and God only knows I am ready, to take your place. To sacrifice myself on the scaffold so that you may escape."

There is a long pause before the king gives his answer.

"But how?" he says. "The place is surrounded."

"It is all arranged," replies Daumier. "Edgeworth has it organized. Your escape. Safe houses to stay in. A horse. You will be taken to the quarries in Burgundy and there you will lie low until this — this blasted infernal revolution is blown away."

"You are willing to —" The king lets out a nervous little laugh.

"Yes," says Daumier. "It is my duty, my duty to your majesty. And it is my duty to France."

Less than three minutes later Daumier is dressed as the king and the king is dressed as Daumier. Even Cléry has to admit that the subterfuge is remarkable. Daumier's belly. His

173

jowls. His pronounced nose. His sagging eyes. All are so remarkably like the king's that when Edgeworth enters the room a few minutes later, he turns to Daumier and addresses him as "your majesty".

Only after a few seconds does he do a double-take, smile and take Daumier by the hand.

"Brilliant," he whispers. "Daumier, you are a genius of disguise. And if you do this for your king and country, you are destined to become the greatest martyr of this whole terrible revolution."

Daumier falters for a second, bites his fingernail and clutches Edgeworth's hand.

"You will be with me? You'll be there to the end?"

"Yes," replies Edgeworth. "I am charged with taking the king to the scaffold. I will be there to the end."

An hour passes. The deception is complete. Daumier even manages to mimic the king's lilting speech.

"I defy anyone to challenge your identity," says Edgeworth. "Besides, once we are outside the confines of the tower, no one we meet will ever have seen the king face to face. With God's will, and God *does* will it, this plan will succeed."

There is nevertheless a moment of tension when there's a rap at the door and in walks Santerre, commandant of the Paris National Guard. He's the one man who might see through the deception. But he scarcely even looks at the faux-king.

"It is time to go," he announces in his usual peremptory fashion. And then he sweeps back out of the room with the expectation that his prisoner will be following him.

174

"It is time to go," repeats Daumier in a faint voice. "Farewell, Jean-Baptiste. And farewell, Daumier. May God protect you."

The king smiles weakly and embraces the real Daumier.

"One day, we will meet again," he says. "One day."

He embraces Daumier for a second time and watches him descend the stairwell.

"Come, your majesty," says Cléry to the king in an urgent tone. "We have no time to lose. We must also go down; we must head to rue de la Madeleine. There will be horses waiting for us in the courtyard of La Madeleine. We will be going to the Abbaye de la Pierre near Vincennes and then heading for Sens. We will be joined by Edgeworth as soon as he can get away. If God wills it, we will succeed."

And that, Peter, is exactly what happened. The king reached Vincennes in the company of Cléry and then rode on to Sens, Troyes and Auxerre before eventually arriving at Creux. I'm told that an account of the escape, written in Edgeworth's own hand, is kept in the London Library. It's bound together with a number of other printed volumes, all under the title, *Annals of the French Revolution*. It shouldn't be there, of course. It was inadvertently bequeathed to the library, along with several essays by Burke and Lacretelle, when one of Edgeworth's descendants popped his clogs in the early sixties. The Order is intent on getting it back. So if you want to read it, Peter — and you must — you'd better go and look at it now, while it's still there.

Anyway, digressions, digressions. The operation to save the king went like clockwork, with the only hitch occurring when Edgeworth tried to rescue Marie Antoinette and the dauphin. This proved impossible and Marie Antoinette lost her head on the scaffold and the dauphin died of some hideous disease in the prison of the Temple.

But.

     But.

          But.

I can almost picture you, Peter, jumping up and down in your living room with impatience. So many blanks. That's what you're saying to yourself. So much he hasn't explained.

Well, believe me. I shall try to explain. I *have* to explain, otherwise nothing's going to make any sense at all. I think I've already told you that it was King Louis who'd instructed Soufflot to excavate the quarries at Creux. Did I tell you that? He wanted a royal bolt-hole for times of trouble. The quarries were on land belonging to the de la Regnier family, who were related to the house of Bourbon through numerous different bloodlines. They were a family whom King Louis could trust implicitly.

But Louis was not alone in showing concern for his throne. Across the Channel in our beloved Albion, King George the third had also been growing wobbly. Think about it. America. Seventeen seventy-six. The year when the Americans stripped George of his crown and declared themselves a republic. And it shocked the king to the marrow of his bones. He suddenly realized that monarchies could be toppled: goodbye and goodnight. He realized that divinely ordained kings could have their heads chopped off without so much as a by your leave. He realized that the kings of Europe needed to fight back. They needed to defend their power. And, after much to-ing and fro-ing between England and France, he and Louis founded an organization which soon became known as the Order of Monarchy. Its motto was "The earth is my kingdom."

Its purpose? To defend monarchies, pure and simple. To provide protection to kings in trouble. To restore deposed monarchs to their thrones, not just in Europe but right around the globe. The Order believed in the aristocratic hierarchy — the principle of purple blood — and it drew support and wealth from all the dynasties that had close links with the reigning monarchs.

And this is how the Order managed to keep everything so secret. They were centred in an underground quarry at Creux, on the private estate of the de la Regnier family, in the heart of the Morvan, which just so happens to be one of the least populated areas in the whole of France. The few local inhabitants were gently evicted from their houses (they were paid off so handsomely by the de la Regniers that the family received not even a scratch during the revolution). And no one even got the merest whiff of an idea that the quarries were there. No one stumbled across them. No one set foot inside them. No one, that is, until yours truly came along and couldn't help poking his inquisitive fat nose into other people's business.

At first, Louis the sixteenth was alone in the quarries, attended by Edgeworth and his one remaining valet. He had a few visitors, of course — dukes, princes and nobles whose lives were in danger. But it wasn't long before the king found himself joined by other deposed monarchs — kings, queens and heirs whose lives were in danger and who'd been whisked to safety by the Order of Monarchy. There was Wilhelm von Hessen of Hanau. Ludwig Karl Franz Leopold of Hohenlohe-Bartenstein. Maximilian the first, Duke of Palatinate-Zweibrucken-Birkenfeld. He lost his throne in seventeen ninety-nine, when Bavaria annexed his lands. Stanislaus the second, king of

Poland, came here in seventeen ninety-five, I think I'm right in saying, and Ercole d'Este of Modena arrived in the following year. And before long they were arriving from further afield. King Takitaki-malohi of Vava'u arrived in seventeen ninety-nine, Shah Zaiman of Afghanistan in eighteen-o-one and Emperor Demetrios of Ethiopia later in the same year. (He died shortly after, of consumption.)

I was shown the quarries' visitors' book; I actually held it in my hands. All their names were there. It kept me occupied for hours, trying to work out who they all were. Half of them were illegible and half I'd never heard of. The king of Vava'u's entry was the most spectacular — an entire page of squiggles and stamps. A big entry for a small kingdom.

One of the Order's most pressing tasks was to find a new wife for King Louis the sixteenth. Someone of royal blood, with whom he could produce a new heir. But there was no one available. They had to wait nine whole years before a suitable candidate arrived. Yes, it was in eighteen-o-three when the Princess-Abbess of Essen, a pious and by all accounts rather dumpy lady whose real name was Maria Kunigunde von Sachsen, was ignominiously deposed by the Prussian infantry who'd marched into her territories. She might have been imprisoned — or even killed — had she not been whisked to safety by the Order. Within an hour of her arrival in Creux, she was presented to King Louis.

The king and the Order both agreed she was suitable material to bear the king's children. Not *too* ugly, I suppose, (although perhaps a little sweaty after her long ride). And her father was King Frederick Augustus the second, king of Poland.

But there were two major hiccups to this little matrimonial union. Number one: Maria was fifty-three years of age when she met Louis. Number two: she'd taken a lifelong vow of chastity. She'd put a big fat padlock on the important bits. Well, well, well. The Order quickly managed to persuade her to unlock the padlock and drop the chastity vow. They informed her that producing an heir was a duty before God. But they could do very little about her withered-up womb. The king launched himself into Maria with all the gusto at his command, rumping and pumping his way into the princess until she must have been aching in every ligament in her body. But all to no avail. Plenty of regal little spermlets — but not an egg in sight.

And it was at this point that Maria herself was struck by a rather brilliant idea. You must be able to guess, Peter! Yes, mushrooms. It had long, long been a custom among the Habsburgs to consume serious quantities of mushrooms. I'm sure you remember the stories. They loved their mushrooms. Not any old mushrooms, mind; let's be quite clear about that. They ate caesars — and *only* caesars, the food of kings and queens ever since the time of, well, of Julius Caesar. But caesars were not just exquisite to eat. They were also renowned for their aphrodisiac qualities. They boosted libido. They got the juices flowing. They cleared out the tubes. (They really do, Peter. It's one of the chemical compounds that does it.) They'd certainly enabled Maria's mother, a Habsburg, to pop out sprogs on an annual basis. Maria was child number thirteen.

After several weeks of bedroom acrobatics — and no sign of Maria falling pregnant — she commanded a week of feasting. The principal dish of every bloody meal was to be composed of caesar mushrooms.

Well, Peter, you can only imagine the panic this caused the Order. Scouts were sent into the forest, the earth was scoured and not a leaf left unturned. It was most fortunate that all of this took place in a damp and uncommonly warm September, the ideal conditions for the pernickety amanita caesar. Every morning the scouts left the quarries. And every evening they returned with overflowing panniers.

And then — . Miracle of miracles! Holy of holies! Sound the trumpets! And bring on the band! The menopause must have gone into dramatic reverse. There were eggs everywhere. Boiled. Fried. Scrambled. And at an age when most women where either dead or grandparents, the chaste, pious Abbess Maria gave birth to a baby boy. Out he popped, healthy, fresh faced and with more purple blood pumping through his little heart than half the royals of Europe. He was named Ferdinand Philippe, the rightful claimant to the throne of France. And although it says in all the history books that his father was Louis Philippe, this was not at all the case. His real father was Louis the sixteenth.

It was a triumph. It was unprecedented. It went against Nature. And in celebration of the achievement, a new custom came into being in the quarries of Creux. Once every seven years all the crowned and not-so-crowned heads of every bloody kingdom in the world would gather to celebrate, to feast and to consume enormous quantities of caesar mushrooms. And —

CHAPTER
FIFTEEN

Peter hit the stop button.

"Preposterous," he said. "He's bonkers. Now he's talking nonsense. Ridiculous nonsense."

Ridiculous nonsense it may have been, but it was curiously compelling and Peter soon enough pressed the play button once again so we could listen to the rest of the tape. Arnold recounted how Louis Philippe picked up the crown of France in 1830; how he lost it again in 1848; how the family once again retreated into the quarries of Creux. And then came his maddest claim of all. He said that France's president, François Mitterrand, was also a lineal descendant of King Louis the sixteenth — through Ferdinand Philippe — and that he intended to hold on to power until his dying day.

Mitterrand's royal bloodline (he said) was the reason why he had showed so little enthusiasm for the bicentenary celebrations of the French revolution. (This had, I remember, raised eyebrows at the time.)

And he had one other thing to say of Mitterrand. The Grand Arch that had been inaugurated earlier in the year — and the president's brainchild — was apparently intended as a riposte to the Arc de

Triomphe, which Napoleon had erected to commemorate his victory at Austerlitz. Mitterrand wanted to outdo Napoleon's architectural legacy. Build things bigger and leave a whole set of royal monuments scattered around Paris. The glass pyramid. A new national library. And a whole host of other buildings.

And that was where Arnold's tape came to the end of its spool. It left many gaps and unanswered questions but it had kept us entertained for the better part of half an hour.

And there it might have ended. Amusing, entertaining, but also — as Peter had said — preposterous. Indeed, I might have thought nothing more of Arnold's claims about Mitterrand, had it not been for a report about the French president which appeared on the Reuters' wires just a few days later. I printed it out — I've still got it stuck on the wall in front of my desk. "Mitterrand in funding scandal. Deputies' demands for enquiry into missing millions refused." There it was in black and white. A scandal — and a bank-load of French francs that had vanished. Mitterrand stood accused of diverting substantial amounts of state funds to the Morvan, where he had served in several senior political posts before the presidential election in 1981. It was said that these funds, which amounted to the tune of several tens of millions of francs, had disappeared into thin air. They had sunk, said the article, into *un creux*. It actually used that word. A hole in the ground. No one could account for them. And no one could say where the money had gone.

No one, perhaps, except for Peter and I. And Arnold.

CHAPTER
SIXTEEN

The phone rang. I was at work and expecting a call from one of our reporters in Berlin.

"So, why haven't you phoned?" said the voice at the other end. "I thought you'd want to meet up again." It was Flora.

"I was intending to. I promise. But things have been so busy since I got back and —"

I flicked idly through the pages of my diary, already aware that I had nothing whatsoever lined up for the next few evenings.

"How about tonight?"

"You're as busy as me," she said with a laugh. "I think I can squeeze you in." We agreed to meet at my flat in Bayswater at 7.30p.m. I said that we'd either go out or — if I had time — that I'd cook something.

The bell rang, I opened the door and there stood a smiling Flora. She looked much more relaxed than when I'd first met her at Peter and Philippa's.

"Mmmm." That was her very first word. "Smells wonderful. What is it?"

"Chef's special," I replied. "His signature dish. Beef stroganoff. You said you were a carnivore."

It would, I knew, be delicious. I'd tipped half a bottle of brandy into the sauce.

We ate, we drank, and Flora told me more about her two visits to Taplow Bottom. Philippa, she said, had been a pillar of strength, but her motherly habits were driving her "absolutely stir-crazy". I dared to ask her what she *really* thought about Peter and Philippa. She winced slightly. "I shouldn't say this," she said. "He means well — and she means well. And yet, I don't know, they make me feel as if I'm a teenager. And — no, no — it's worse than that. They make me feel as if the world is a very small place indeed; that its perimeter doesn't stretch much further than Taplow Bottom. I like them, I *do* like them, but I hated seeing them with Arnold. He became like them. They hemmed him in. And that's why I wanted to get him away. From them, from his work, from his routine."

She'd lost me. I'd found Peter and Philippa welcoming and friendly, if a little bizarre.

"Has Peter told you about —?" I didn't have to finish my phrase.

"The new tape? Yes, he told me."

"And — what do you think?"

"I don't know. I really don't. But let me tell you something about Arnold. I'd not intended to talk about him tonight. I really didn't want to. And I'm sure that you've had quite enough of him. But let me tell you one thing about him.

"Arnold has a theatre that's forever playing in his head. Characters walk on and off the stage. They shout, laugh, sing, dance. And when things happen to him, they happen in superlatives.

"I always thought it must be odd to see the world through his eyes. Once, we were in the forest, there was this thick carpet of bluebells. And I turned to Arnold and I noticed he was laughing to himself. 'What's up?' I said. 'What's so funny?' He looked puzzled. He couldn't see how I could be so matter of fact. 'That blue,' he said, 'is the bluest blue in the world. And it makes me laugh. Can't you see?'

"I couldn't. I really couldn't see things the way he saw things.

"'It's a primary colour,' he said. 'You can't invent a colour like that. You're either born with it or you're not. You've either got it or you haven't.'

"I still didn't understand him. But I thought it was wonderful."

The evening passed quickly and it was nearly midnight when Flora said she ought to be going.

"Do you have to?" I said. "I can offer you —"

"A bed for the night?"

She'd taken the words out of my mouth. "Yes. Exactly," I said. "I can offer you a bed for the night. If you'd like —"

And so it was that I found myself in bed with Arnold Trevellyan's wife, who was — in a very short space of time — naked from head to foot. And I couldn't help thinking to myself: Arnold was a fool.

The phone rang at work: it was Peter.

"Soufflot," he said in an uncharacteristically breathless tone. "The French architect. The quarries. It's all true."

"What's all true?" I asked. "What have you discovered?"

"The Panthéon — you know, the big church in Paris. Cross between a temple and a wedding cake."

I did know it. I'd been inside a few years earlier.

"Well, wait for this, old chap. The stone used to build it — guess where it came from. Guess. Guess."

He didn't give me the chance to answer.

"The stone came from Burgundy. From the Morvan. It was quarried there. It came from the famous quarries of Creux. Yes. Best limestone in France, apparently. They brought it all the way to bloody Paris from Creux."

I asked Peter where he'd discovered all this.

"In the library," he said. "I went at lunchtime. Did a spot of research into the buildings of Paris — and the architects. I checked out Soufflot — Jacques-Germain Soufflot. He was in charge of all the royal buildings in Paris. And he was also the architect of the Panthéon. The big church in Paris. Of course it wasn't called the Panthéon back then. It was the church of Sainte Geneviève, I think. But that's by the by. It was built by Soufflot, whose home village was wait-for-this-wait-for-this right next to the quarries of Creux. And he insisted that all his buildings, every single one of them, should be built with stone from those quarries."

"Which means —" I was thinking aloud — "that the quarrying would have been taking place on a massive scale. And *that* means — that — the hole — in the ground —"

186

"— would be absolutely bloody ginormous," said Peter, finishing my thought. "And wait for this. One of Soufflot's more secretive assignments — ordered by none other than King Louis the fifteenth — was to design a bolt-hole — yes, a place for all the royals and their hangers-on to flee in times of trouble. Somewhere to hide in times of civil unrest. There's a whole page about it in one of the biographies. They got the idea from the Habsburgs, apparently. They'd constructed something similar."

"And? This is actually getting interesting."

"Well, this bolt-hole was long believed to be in Paris," said Peter. "Somewhere underground. Under one of the royal palaces. If it existed at all, of course. But now, having heard Arnold — well — I'm not so sure."

"You're thinking —?"

"I don't know what I'm thinking. But you don't have to be a genius to realize that Arnold might actually be trying to tell us something."

CHAPTER
SEVENTEEN

Lola wanted it. Gilbertine certainly wanted it. Every sodding person on the island seemed to want it. And so, Peter: *DER-der-derder. Here comes the bride!* Yes, I've just taken my second trip down the aisle. Wife number two (or three, if you count Flora in all of this). It was like I was living in déjà vu. Same little chapel. Same baking sunshine. Same vicar. Only this time, there was one big difference.

"Do you, Arnold Trevellyan, take these four women . . ."

Four! I gulped. Gilbertine had so plumped herself up for the occasion that she was now being considered as four brides' worth of wife. They always weigh the bride before the wedding, you see, and she'd tipped the scale at over two hundred okes.

"To have and to hold —

"To have and to hold — ." She winked.

"To love and to cherish —"

"To love and to cherish —"

"To feed and to fatten —"

"To feed and to fatten —"

"And to enjoy and share with the Anglican vicar of Vanu whenever he's on his own and feeling lonely and in need of company." I swear, Peter, that that's what was going through his head. He was looking at her with these leery, hungry eyes

188

and dreaming, dreaming, dreaming. But his dreams were to lead him to even richer pastures. It was at the reception, you see, and he sidles up to me and says, "See that woman over there?" He's looking directly towards Doris and he's clearly very excited.

"Yes," I say.

"She's just proposed to me."

And those five words, Peter, made me uncontrollably happy. With those five words, I'd escaped the Gilbertine-Doris double whammy that everyone on the island seemed to be hoping for. I was so relieved that I couldn't stop myself from planting a big fat kiss on the reverend's forehead.

"Oh no, no, no, Mr King, sir," says Gilbertine, coming up to me and frowning and getting totally the wrong end of the stick. "No, no, no. Wives have to be female on Tuva. And just because the Reverend Taupu is from Vanu, where they do things differently from us, and just because you like him very much — it doesn't mean you can take him to be your lawful wedded wife."

So there we are, Peter. How about all that for news! I'm now married to Lola *and* Gilbertine and I find myself living in a *ménage à cinq* with the prospect of five more wives to come. If that doesn't keep me young, I don't know what will.

And later that evening: — well, well. I've seen a few women naked in my time, Peter, but she was one hell of a magnificent specimen. She was big — statuesque — but without an ounce of fat. Muscle in her arms. Muscle in her legs. You could see it even when she was standing quite still. And if I could only begin to give you a picture of her breasts. I'd seen them once before, of course, when she'd taken that shower under the waterfall. But I hadn't had a chance to study them in great detail. And, well, holy bananas. Think big, then double it.

She comes towards me. You've got to picture it in your head. Swaying bosoms — swaying like there's no tomorrow. A generous grin. Unbuttons my shirt. Off with the trousers. Off with everything. And then she stops in her tracks. Has a good look. "But Mr King, sir," she says, "we can have much fun with this."

And then she kind of straddles my lap and the next thing I know, Peter, I've got helium balloons in my face and a grinning Gilbertine telling me that life's a mushroom.

And jiggly-jog and up and down and side to side and before we know it, it's all going fast and furious and we're sweating like drainpipes and we're falling, falling off the bed.

And then a great triumphant cry: "*Aieehalimotuo, Mr King, sir!*" It's all over. She's done, I'm certainly done (I've been done for some time) and, once a couple of joints have clicked back into place, everything's more or less gone back to normal.

"Thank you, Gilbertine," I said. "That was — I can honestly say that was quite an experience."

"No, no. Thank *you*, sir. And a big thank you to Lola. We must be grateful to her."

"We must," I said, nodding sagely. "I must remember to thank her."

And all the way I was thinking to myself, "Arnold Trevellyan, that was the most surreal jiggly-jog encounter you're ever likely to experience in your life." And later, when I was settled into my study, I still had this pair of helium balloons swinging before my eyes.

"So," said Lola the next morning, "I heard it all went well. At least from Gilbertine's point of view."

"It was like making love to a monsoon," I said. "Next time, remind me to take some sea-sickness pills."

"Well, thank you," said Lola. "It was very kind of you. Did anyone ever tell you you're a very wonderful person?" And she kissed me.

And a few hours later, off we go, me and Gilbertine: back to the mountain, back to the cave. I was going to transform it into my secret laboratory and research centre. My scientific hub. My Faustian den.

We trekked through the jungle, more or less retracing our steps. It was extraordinary how the suckers and creepers had closed in on themselves, scarcely leaving a hint of a trail. We'd hacked that path out just three days earlier. Now, it was all but grown over.

We began by clearing the floor of the cave — cutting away the mottlegills and inkcaps. I kept all of the yellowing knights, for I intended to cook them when we got back. But I discarded all the others as I wasn't sure if they were edible.

Gilbertine passed me my bag, which was filled with amanita spores. Thousands upon thousands of microscopic bits of dust. But not just any old dust, Peter. They were the very building blocks of life. Crumble, crumble, crumble. I crumbled all the dried caps into the soil, scattering the spores. We sowed the deathcaps in one corner, the panther-caps in another. And we reserved one whole side of the cave for the caesars. And then I sprayed the soil with my potion — one hundred and fifty milligrams per square foot. Not a drop more, not a drop less. And it was as I sprayed the liquid and watched it soak into the nougat-smelling humus that I suddenly felt a delicious crest of excitement. It began as a ripple in my legs — and then it tingled up through my groin and into my spine. And by the time it reached my neck, I was covered from head to toe in goose pimples.

"Cold, sir?" asked Gilbertine.

"No," I said. "Just excited."

She nodded. "And me, sir. I'll always be excited to be with my husband."

Now you of all people, Peter, must understand how I felt. Because I knew, as you would have done, that these spores were certain to burst into life. I had six weeks, perhaps seven, to wait.

"And these, Mr King Husband, sir?"

Gilbertine handed me an envelope.

"Yes," I said. "And these." This was the most exciting bit of all. You see, I was not only interested in planting mushrooms, Peter. I had something else to sow — a very common plant, a weed — that had first come to my attention a few months earlier. I'd realized one day, when I was out walking in the forest of Creux, that there's one plant among the billions in the plant kingdom which always grows alongside amanitas. It's as if they have a symbiotic relationship. Think stinging nettles and dock leaves. It's as if they were meant for one another. It's as if they're friends. And when you get plants growing together like that, well, they usually share something *significant*.

And now it's raining. It's pouring. No, allow me to rephrase that. It is absolutely *pissing* it down. Cats and sodding dogs. There are sheets of slanting rain lashing against the roof and walls of the old chapel. It's coming in these pumping, blasting waves that are being driven in from the ocean by a howling, buffeting gale. Thub-bang. Thub-bang. You can probably hear it. Imagine thwacking a frying pan hard against a cushion. Thub-bang. That's the sound it's making.

And the water is sluicing into the snow gutters and then emptying itself into the sandy soil, gouging a little watery trench all around the outside of the building. And there's a miniature moat that's formed.

And as for the lagoon: it's usually a lapis colour or turquoise or topaz-green, but now it's the colour of a good mushroom soup — it takes me right back to the Soup Kitchen. And the spray's hanging over the reef like a big white smudge and the wind's a hairdryer on high speed.

We knew the storm was coming. We knew because the storks and razorbills rose up from the treetops and began circling round and round in the thermals. But it didn't stop our illustrious visitor — he wasn't going to be put off by a bit of wind and rain. If only you could have been here to see it, Peter. It was a sight I'll never forget. Fifteen pirogues being rowed through the crashing surf. And there was this hollow beating of drums — boom, boom, boom — over and above the slurping of the waves.

Boom. That was the first we knew of their arrival. Boom. Boom. There's this sea mist that's glued to the sky like some sort of celestial net curtain and it's blurring everything that lies behind it. Long before you saw anything, it was the boom that announced them.

And then the colours — orange, green, red, mauve. Stains on the curtains, smudges in the spray. And that, Peter — well, *you* wear glasses so you'll know what I mean. You know how when you take them off there's a split second when everything's out of focus? And then everything just slides into vision. A little flotilla all decked with streamers and pennants and coloured bunting. Fifteen bloody Christmas trees coming through the mist.

And then we caught sight of him: King Taufa'ahau Tupou the fourth of Tonga. Try saying that when you've had a few. Taa. Faa. Haa. Too. Poo. The fourth. That's it. It was his first visit to Tuva in more than twelve years. *AaileeeEAlmooo!* "Hoorah!" *AaileeeEAlmooo!* You should have heard the roar.

The rowers didn't stop. They rowed the king from his ship to the shallows — they kept up the same frantic pace. And when they were only ten feet from the shore: whoooosh, They stood up, thrust their oars in the waters — they're these big flat pizza shovels — and lean into them with all their might. A loud gurgle, a surge of water from beneath each oar and the pirogues grind to a halt. Br-rrr-rrr-rrr. A roll of drums. The blast of a conch shell. And out steps the king — all this happened just a few hours ago — and he wades through the warm shallows.

"What a pleasure," he says to Lola. "It's been far too long."

And then he turns to me. "Welcome to kingship," he says. "You're going to save the world. I've heard many good things about you. I'm told you made yourself very popular in the quarries."

You'll want to know why he'd come. Well, it's all tied up with the Order, you see. They've arranged everything. It's they who brokered the deals. It's they who've negotiated the weaponry. And they also raised all of the funds. And, I have to say, they did it in quite spectacular fashion. The money came from Oman, Morocco, Denmark and the Saudis. Those were the first to step in. And even our own queen. I was told, in the strictest confidence, that she stumped up several million. "One must do one's bit to help." That's apparently what she said. "One never knows when we all might be grateful that such a place exists."

The government of Tonga tied up the deal. It was done behind the scenes, of course. The Order had to use a bona fide country, you see, to confer legitimacy on the whole thing. It was a cover, if you like. And now — well, they've been one hundred per cent successful, as was inevitable. They planned it all to perfection, just as they plan *everything* to perfection. I do believe they could tackle any bloody disaster in the world and come through it with flying colours. And now they've achieved the unthinkable. We are — are you ready for this? — the proud owners of sixteen shining, gleaming pieces of technology that'll protect us from attack by land and sea. Sixteen defensive shields brought here all the way from France, with a little spot of behind-the-scenes help from dear old President Mitterrand. Sixteen missiles, Peter. Sixteen RBS-15s! That's what we've just taken delivery of! At a cost of quite a number of millions.

But why the king of Tonga? And what's his role in all of this? That's what you'll want to know. Well, he wanted to be here when the weapons were actually delivered. And he's also offered thirty of his paramilitary guard — trained in Sweden — to help with the building of the depot. And they're going to be staying here on a semi-permanent basis, living at the depot. That's the place where the missiles will be housed and serviced and — if they're ever needed, God help us — fired.

It doesn't take too much of a military brain to fire them, or that's what the experts have been telling us. All you need to do, if you want to send them scooting into the sky, is activate the computer. It's already been programmed for every conceivable scenario. Fighter jets. Destroyers. Anything. You simply select your target. Aim. Press a few keys on the keyboard. And bang, whooooosh. They next thing you know, you're looking at a gigantic bloody great fireball.

The defence experts came here weeks ago to select the best place to base the weapons. That was probably their most difficult decision. They hummed and haaed and eventually they chose Katu-Waitu island, principally because it's tiny and isolated. It sits just outside the main reef — which they said was important — and it's little more than a blob in the ocean, a coral-coloured rock that sticks out of the sea like a chunk of crumbling Parmesan. Just enough room for thirty soldiers and sixteen missiles. And if you stand at the edge, as I did yesterday morning, you can see the sea bottom dropping almost vertically away from the rock — down, down, down into nowhere land — and you notice these amazing flashes of silver and gold and orange and green. It's these shoals of fishes; the parrot fish and ribbontails and spotted pomfreys. Round they go and round — an endless merry-go-round of fishes.

Our first task, once this hulk of a storm has died down, will be to head back across to Katu-Waitu. We'll go with the Swedish engineers and the Tongan soldiers and help build the housing for the generator. That's step number one. It's a concrete and steel contraption — it's all been brought from Tonga. And once that's done — and the new generator's up and running — the soldiers will start working on the missile bunker.

196

But the storm, the storm. It's ripping through the archipelago like a juggernaut and slowing everything down. That's the trouble here — we get so many storms. Can you hear the noise in the background? A wind so powerful it's shredding the trees on the top of Mount Tuva. The trunks are left standing like thick black telegraph poles, with their leafy canopies torn and tattered and ripped into thin strips. And as I look at it right now, it's as if the peak's been decked in bunting.

CHAPTER
EIGHTEEN

"I'm leaving."

These were the first words that Flora said to me after our night together.

"*Leaving?* Who? Me?"

She let out a cheerful laugh. "I didn't know we were together," she said. "But — no — what I mean is, I'm leaving Lambourn Road. I'm packing up shop. I'm getting out. I can't spend another day in the old house."

"Where will you go? Not to your friend Simon's, I hope?"

"No," she said. "Not in a million years. I'm hoping to spend a few days in a friend's flat. Just a few days, while I look for a new place."

"Oh? And —"

"If he doesn't mind, of course."

"*He?*"

"Yes. He's kind. And generous. And although I've not known him for very long, I think he's warm-hearted and —"

It clicked.

"Phew," she said with a smile. "I was beginning to think I'd never get through."

"Well, you just said we weren't together and I'd put two and two together. I assumed that you wanted this to be, well, for one night only."

"Two and two makes one," said Flora. She looked upset.

"No. Not at all. It came out wrong."

"Well, that's good," she said. "And, by the way, I didn't say we were *not* together. You're a very bad listener, Mr Journalist. I said that I hadn't realized we *were* together. You mustn't forget I'm still married, for what it's worth. And, no, I certainly hadn't intended for it to be for one night only unless —"

"I'd love you to stay," I said, interrupting her. "Nothing would make me happier. Move in tomorrow. Today. Make yourself at home."

"*Really?* But do you mean it? Don't you want to think about it? Take your time. I've got other places I can stay. It's just, well, I'd very much like to be here. Life hasn't seemed this bright for many months and I feel about ready to — to enjoy myself. I want to recover some normality."

"Oh, I see," I said with a laugh, "you're accusing me of being normal again."

She looked at me and smiled. "You're as paranoid as me," she said.

Flora moved in on the following morning — two suitcases, two overnight bags and a case of wine.

"Hello, landlord," she said, on arriving at the door. "When would you like your first instalment of rent?"

Peter and I spent that lunchtime together, listening to Arnold's new tape. It left us more bemused than ever.

199

"Missiles," said Peter as he began to count off a list on his fingers. "And conspiracies. And international finance. And bunkers on deserted islands —"

"And let's not forget the queen — *our* queen — and the king of Tonga. And a whole lot of mushrooms."

"Yes," said Peter. "A lot of mushrooms. But then again, Nature's a strange old beast. Only last week, I was reading about a group of American scientists who'd found some untouched valley — in Uruguay, I think it was — that contained dozens of new species. And this cave that Arnold's found — well, if the temperature and humidity are right, and there's the right sort of soil — then there's no reason why mushrooms wouldn't burst into life, just as he said. That much, I'm willing to credit him with. If there are mushrooms on Tuva, you can trust Arnold to sniff them out."

"And not Warlock?"

"I'd trust Arnold over Warlock," said Peter. "Any day. But these missiles — these RBS-15s — . I mean, could it *really* be? It's such a mad story and, well, those things can sink a bloody aircraft carrier. Look at the damage they did in the Falklands. Could an organization, independent of any government, acquire sixteen of them? Just like that?"

"If I remember rightly," I said, "he didn't say it was independent of any government. He said that the Order — whatever it is — bought them through the good offices of the government of Tonga. *It was the government of Tonga who tied up the deal.* That's what he said. Or words to that effect."

"You're right," said Peter. "He did. And he also mentioned Mitterrand. And not for the first time. But what I want to know is whether or not you can buy a state-of-the-art missile just like that."

"Of course," I said. "*Anyone*, so long as they've enough money, could lay their hands on sixteen missiles. Every government in the world is corrupt. One of my work colleagues got back from Yemen recently and was telling us that there were surface-to-air missiles on sale in the gun souk. And that was in Sana'a, the capital."

Peter nodded, but his thoughts were clearly elsewhere. "I was going to tell you something about the quarries," he said. "I've managed to find out a little bit more information. Something of interest."

"Oh?"

"Yes," said Peter. "The architect, Soufflot, he was living in Paris for much of the time it took to build the Panthéon. It was in one of the books I found in the library. But as soon as the Panthéon was finished, Soufflot returned to Burgundy — to the Morvan — and stayed there for more than two years. And it's not entirely clear as to what he was doing."

"So you're saying that if he really *was* supervising the king's bolt-hole — this underground safe haven — it must have been then."

"Absolutely. The chronology fits. And I'd love nothing better than to go to Paris; I'd love to check the manuscript, but I can't afford the time. I really can't. I'm up to my neck in the conference season."

"Well, I certainly haven't got time to go back to Creux," I said. "Not with everything boiling over in Eastern Europe. But if I was offered a trip to Tuva, on the other hand —"

"Now you're talking," said Peter. "If you get sent there, I'm coming with you." He paused for a second, deep in thought. "But, seriously, what do you make of it all? Is it possible that Arnold really *is* caught up in some huge conspiracy?"

I shrugged. "Let me get back to you on that," I said.

I was chatting to Flora on her first evening in my flat and I'd just asked her if she'd ever consider going back to Creux. "Aren't you tempted to find out if something really was going on?"

"No," she said. "I've no wish to see that place ever again in my life. In fact, I don't think I even want to hear that word again."

She paused and looked at me. "Why — ? Do you?"

"No," I said. "Besides, I've got far too much on at the moment. But —" I stopped in mid-sentence, unsure how to phrase my next question. "But I've got something else to ask. On a different matter."

"Fire away."

"Well, I was wondering if you're going to divorce Arnold. How long will you allow him to carry on like this?"

"I don't know," she said. "I don't know what's going on. I don't know anything. But I can't divorce him straight away. Not without seeing him. It would be the strangest divorce in history. Wife divorces husband but doesn't quite know why. So, well, the answer is: I don't know."

"What *will* you do then?" I ventured. "Will you go to Tuva? Go and see him there? He doesn't exactly show many signs of coming back to see you."

"Maybe," she said, "but I've got even less desire to go there than to Creux. Why should I have to chase after him for answers?"

She glanced down at the floor. "Oh, I don't know — Arnold's infuriating and Arnold's impossible. But Arnold's also Arnold. And he's — ." She let out a long sigh. "Oh, I might as well tell you. For more than seven years now — more than seven years — I've wanted to start a family. Have children. I so very much wanted to have children. But every time I tried to broach the subject — discuss it with Arnold — and persuade him it was a good thing, well, he refused point-blank to talk about it. He wouldn't even entertain the idea. He wouldn't have anything to do with it. Even though he knew it would make me the happiest person in the world —"

"So what's his problem? Just selfishness?"

"No, not really. I don't believe so. You see, he's had to confront some difficult things in his life. His parents died when he was still quite young. Not quite twenty. First his mother and then his dad. And that — imagine — was quite a thing to deal with."

"Is he an only child?"

"Yes — yes. I thought you knew that. So, yes, he had to arrange everything. Two funerals. Two emotional hurdles. Two —"

"Did you know him at the time?"

"No, no. This was before I was on the scene. But I'm sure he'd have got over it on his own. I'm sure he'd have coped. But it was when they read the will, that's when it hit him."

"Why? What happened?"

"They left everything — every last penny, their house and all their possessions — to some bloody charity in Africa. Ethiopia or something like that. Can't remember the exact details. Clean water. New village school. That sort of thing. Imagine, Arnold must have felt totally and utterly betrayed — as well as being left penniless. He was never close to his parents — they were quite old when they had him — but this I guess was something that never in his wildest nightmares was he expecting. And he must have felt a complete sense of rejection."

"So how did he cope?" I asked. "Being left with nothing."

"Well, that's where Peter stepped in. He'd known Arnold for many years. They'd been at school together. And Peter was already earning money. He helped out — kept Arnold afloat. Indeed, it was thanks to Peter that Arnold was able to go off to America for a few months. He wanted to work in film — at least, that was one of his many ideas — and he did actually succeed in working on a film out there."

I asked if she thought all of this was why he didn't want children.

"Yes," she said. "I think it probably is. And I think it's why he ended up clinging to things. And I'm sure that's why he was so obsessed with the house. And his job. And it may even have had something to do with why he wanted to set up the Soup Kitchen. He clung to all the routines — it was as if they gave him some sort of security in life. And I wanted him to rise above it and let go of his fears. I thought it would be the making of him. And that's also why I wanted him — us — to have children."

She threw her hands into the air. "And, well, with you I guess I can come clean now and admit that children was one of the reasons why I wanted to go abroad. And why I wanted to get away from London. I thought that a complete change of scene — I thought it would help him change his mind. It was my last chance, if you like. My last throw of the dice. I gambled and managed to lose absolutely everything. All I succeeded in doing was to push him even more onto the defensive. And it exasperated me. I didn't know what else I could do. And that's why I felt I had very little option but to walk out. And then, well, you know the rest."

I arrived late for work the next morning. It was after ten by the time I was at my desk. I'd been struck by a thought on my way into the office and now I acted on it. I picked up the phone and called the press office at Buckingham Palace.

A woman answered the phone; she sounded bored in the way that press officers always sound bored. I asked if the queen and Prince Philip had visited the Morvan at any point over the last twelve months.

"The where?"

"The Morvan. Burgundy. France."

There was a long silence as she checked her files.

"Well — yes, actually." I detected a certain hesitation. "But it was not an official visit. A private engagement."

"But can you tell me where they went?"

"I'm afraid not, Mr Edwardes," she said. "I couldn't tell you even if I had the information to hand. Her Majesty is entitled to a little privacy, you know. Besides, I don't have the information. Now, may I quickly ask the reason for your enquiry?"

"Nothing," I said. "Nothing. Just something I'm looking into." And I hung up the phone before she had the chance to ask any more questions.

I got back to working on an article about events in Prague and it wasn't until after lunch that I had the chance to ask Charlotte Stanhope, the paper's royal correspondent, if she had any idea as to why the queen and Prince Philip might have gone on a private engagement to Burgundy.

"Burgundy?" She shook her head. "But — are you around later? I might know a birdie who does."

She did indeed know a little birdie. An hour or so later she appeared at my desk, flourishing a piece of paper.

"Here," she said. "A present." On it, she had written the words, "de la Regnier".

"It's a family who live in Burgundy. A big old family. And Philip's godfather to one of the sons. They've been several times over the last ten years or so."

I asked her why Philip had been chosen as godfather.

"They're a rather illustrious family," said Charlotte. "Descendants of the house of Bourbon. Louis the sixteenth and all that. Not direct descendants. They're cousins of uncles of — you get my drift. They're listed in my *Almanach de Gotha*. Kept a low profile during the French revolution. And kept their heads. From what I read, not a single one was executed. And look — this is their shield."

It depicted some sort of duke wearing a purple cloak. The motto, which Charlotte translated from the Latin, was "The earth is my kingdom".

"And," she continued, "they live in a big house in a place called the Morvan. Miles from anywhere, it would seem."

"I know," I said. "I've been there."

"Clever clogs you. How come?"

I reminded Charlotte of the story of Arnold Trevellyan — one that I suspected she'd wanted to cover herself. I explained that he'd lived very close by; how I'd passed the de la Regnier family house on the way to his rather more modest home.

"How funny," she said in a tone that was suddenly rather clipped. "So why all the interest in the queen? I hope you're not straying onto my patch. You might just find me proposing foreign correspondent articles on Hungary or Poland if you're not careful."

"Just curious," I said. "Does the name Soufflot mean anything to you?

"Soufflot? Soufflot?" She hummed and haaaed. "No. Who's he?"

"Just someone."

"A friend?"

"Sort of."

"You get more and more cryptic with every day that passes," said Charlotte. "It's ever since you met that new girl."

And she headed back to her desk.

CHAPTER
NINETEEN

One. Two. Three. Four. Barefoot I go and the sand is rasping and scratching and tickling at the jelly-soft soles of my feet. Twentyoneandtwoandthreeand — keep it rhythmic, Arnold, that's the trick. What's that! A stone or what? Andfiveandsixandsevenandeight; stoop down; tug it from the sand. It's a monster. A clam shell. So huge it could snap off your arm. Lean down, Arnold. *Careful!* Mind your ears. That's it. Listen. SsssshhHH. Sound of the sea.

Each step brings me closer to the starting point. And the wave comes in.

CccraashsHshSH.

And the wave laps out.

SsHhloooluoee.

Sixtyfiveandsix —

CccraashsHshSH.

Sixtysevenandeightand —

SsHhloooluoee.

Gives a pleasing rhythm to my circuit of the island along the strand of the beach of the powdery sand. And each three steps there's the draw of the sea and each three steps that follow there's a long unwinding slurp. Sucking through a straw at an empty glass.

The sun. Dazzling. The sky. It hurts. And on my left — always on my left — a shaggy stage curtain of thick velvety green. And behind its steaming drapes, a botanist's reverie. Warlock.

Aaah. Yawn, yawn, yawn. Hope I'm making sense, Peter, my tutti-fruity cake. Take two before bedtime, with a glass of water. That's the instructions. "With a glass of water." I like that. As if you'd take them without. All a bit of a blur now, mind. But I can't sleep, you see. The heat. So I take two. Before bedtime. With a glass of water. And then I drift.

Fine things, Mogadon. They take thirty minutes, or so they say. Time enough for a chat. And you come and you go. One minute you're here. And then you're there. Away with the fairies. The airy fairies.

And back. And forth. Until one moment — you're not even aware it's happened — there's everything neatly slipped under the sheet and you're snug and you're warm and you're drifting drifting drifting into nowhere land.

But I wanted to tell you — yes, yes, before I sleep — I must tell you — in case I don't even survive the night — yes, yes. I must tell you about this walk I made. You see, I might not survive. They might come and get me. Grab me and kill me. Stab. Slit. And then it'll be curtains. And I want you to know.

The walk. Ah, yes. Around Tuva. On the beach. With the sound of the ocean slurping its way up and down the beach. Counting my steps and a fiery sun and a damp sponge of a breeze hanging out of the veg. *Veg?* I mean vegetation. Not vegetables. Tropical vegetation. Plants.

So there I am — onethousandandfifteen, onethousandand-sixteen, and there's this pissing-pissing-pissing. It's the northern point of the island and a waterfall's tipping off the rock.

210

There's a great green umbrella and a torrent of water pissing out from underneath. And a kind of cove — a hollowed-out, almost hidden cove. Black as black. Watery. And the water — oh, Peter — it was so achingly cool.

Inch forward into the dark. *Mind your step, Arnold.* Don't want to get trapped in a cave when the waves crash in and smother you in bubbly, foamy surf. In the head goes, into the darkness. And. My God, Peter. My God! That's when I got the shock of my life. Yes. And just thinking of it now — reliving it — has injected my heart and quickened my pulse. And it's set me racing. Panic. Panic. Panic. There, you see. That's the trouble with being here. That's all it takes and I'm fully awake again.

A boat. A *foreign* boat. Single engine. Outboard motor. And it did not belong on Tuva. And nor did it belong to anyone on any other island. (No one could have afforded such a thing.)

You've got to realize, Peter, that no one turns up unnoticed on Tuva. No one just chugs into the archipelago without people knowing of their arrival. They've got eyes like telescopes. They can look at the horizon, where you and I will see only sea and sky, and they'll tell you that a fishing boat is approaching and will be here in an hour and a half. Gilbertine can spot a whale that's over a mile away. And yet no one — *no one* — had seen this boat. No one had mentioned it. And no one had seen its owners.

I stepped into the cove and placed my hands on the fibreglass hull. I wanted to check it was real. Oh, yes, it was real all right. And yet there were no clues as to why it was there or where it had come from. I climbed inside. I opened every bloody nook and cranny of that vessel. But apart from some shoes, an almost empty whisky bottle (Caol Ila — they had taste) and an old packet of Stimorol chewing gum, there was nothing.

Could you cross an ocean in such a boat? Could you cross from Tonga to Tuva? I certainly wouldn't want to risk it, but that's what they must have done. I can't see where else they could have come from, but there were no other clues. Even the footprints in the sand (they *must* have left footprints) had been erased by the last high tide.

I continued with my circuit of the island, deeply unsettled. Onethousandandseventeen. Onethousandandeighteen. And on. And on. Round the headland. There's Oloua in the distance. And that smudge over there; that must be Tu'unoho. And there are two basking whales, what, some two hundred feet from the shore. Oh, Philippa, Philippa, where art thou? We could get married. Ha. Whales. Sharks. Dolphins. And for all I know, sea cows, with their funny curved-up eyelashes. Yes, waddling around in the water like puffed-up blubbery balloons. And the water. Sucking. Slurping. Sucking. Slurping. CraassSH — slooooaaAH. CraassSH. SlooooaaAH. CraassSH. SlooooaaAH. Craasssshhhhhhhhhhhhhhhhhh

That was good. Ah, yes. That was indeed good. I'm lying here in my bed, my tape recorder on the table beside me and it's a new dawn and I slept like a hippopotamus. For weeks, Peter, I've suffered this crushing insomnia. Sleeplessness. Tossing and turning. No rest. And now — Mogadon. Two before bedtime and you're out like a light.

I don't know why it started. Six, seven weeks ago, I went to bed, fell asleep in seconds and then — ding-dong — it's two in the morning and I'm smack-bang awake. It's like being plugged into an electric socket. It takes two seconds to be fully awake. Just two. In the first second, you're thinking, "Oh, no — no, please. Please don't let me wake." And in the second second, you're already awake and analysing everything that's happened in the day. And your mind is whirring-whirring-whirring like a machine that never shuts down. I try to switch off. I repeat to myself in my head, "Sleep, sleep, sleep, sleep." Try to block all other thoughts from drilling themselves into my brain. Sleep, sleep, sleep. But it's impossible. Everything that's happened over the last few months comes flooding in — a tidal wave of thoughts.

I dreamed of Flora last night. For the first time I slept and dreamed and dreamed and slept. She'd not entered my thoughts since I arrived on Tuva. Not as a tangible presence, at any rate. And yet there she was last night, talking to me, asking me questions. She wanted to know what was going on. She was visibly there, Peter. She was in front of me. She was two feet away. I could have reached out and touched her. Her arms. Her cheeks. And so I did. And her flesh was warm and her nose — it was all so very real. And she asked me what I was doing and she asked me if I was happy and she posed so many questions and I said I don't know I don't know I don't know.

And it was only when I woke up that she finally left and was no longer there. And yet — this is what's strange, Peter — *it's as if she's still here*. That's how absolutely real the dream was. And so I was wondering — I wanted to ask — just because I want to know — how is she? Is she coping? She's still on her own? And what's happened to the house? Yes — what's happened to our house? And what news from Clapham? You must tell me because I'm hungry for news.

News is what I need more than anything. I've only received one of your letters and I'm feeling very cut off from it all. And now, what with all this thing with the boat and all that, well, I'd like to know the news and what's going on with you and Philippa and with Flora and with everyone, but especially with Flora —

And then I must have fallen asleep again, but I was so restless. And then I was awake for the next two hours and tossing and turning. And then — at just after six — that's when you hear them. Faint at first, and then slightly louder. Eeeeeiek. Eeeeeeiek. Eeeeeiek. It's the spoonbills in the lagoon. They've woken. They sing. They sing their hearts out. And it's then that I know that dawn is about to burst into the sky. And suddenly there's relief. The night is over. And how lucky, I think to myself, for the sun to have a chorus of birds singing her passage from sea to sky.

Because, before you know it, the solo's become a quartet. And then a quintet. And then, spectacularly, an entire orchestra bursts into music. All the birds of the jungle are letting rip for all they're worth — singing, squawking, shrieking — and it all adds up to a harmony that's not of this world.

And I jump from my bed (taking care not to awaken Lola) and make my way to the window. I want to be alone. I have to be alone. And there, Peter, is the most glorious sight that ever a man can be witness to. Above and beyond the sky is like ink. But in front of me — on the horizon — a burning bulb of gold is rising slowly, spectacularly, from the water. It's dripping with fire. And the birdsong crescendoes and I swear you half-expect the heavens to open and some epic great cathedral organ to crash into twenty octaves of music.

214

And this alone is enough to make you forget that you haven't slept in eight nights. And — roll up! roll up! — you thank God that you've been privileged to be granted a front-row seat in the very best musical in the world, starring the biggest diva of them all — the machinery of Nature. And when you hear those birdies singing their hearts out, you think to yourself: they must have been practising for ten thousand years or more.

And now I must turn to the quarries — tell you what happened — otherwise I'm going to find myself with no tapes left. There's the mushrooms. There's the tales of the kings and queens. There's the — yes, yes, I was telling you the story of how Louis the sixteenth cheated the guillotine. And yet, as I stood there deep inside those cool, hollowed-out quarries, I still couldn't quite believe what was taking place. It was a hive of activity, Peter. As many as three hundred people, perhaps more, spent virtually every bloody hour of their lives down there.

Lola told me there were over three miles of corridors. There were six or seven hundred rooms. Not all of it had been part of the original construction, of course. And, by the way, I meant to tell you that if you ever get to Paris you really should check out the plans. You'll see that the bolt-hole, as first drawn up by Soufflot, was actually quite small. Twenty rooms, perhaps a few more. But as more and more monarchs were brought there — whisked to safety — the quarries were extended. Room after room hacked out of the rock.

Who did I meet? Well, that's a story in itself. You could write a book about it. Descendants of King Mwanga of Buganda. (He was deposed in the late eighteen eighties.)

Descendants of Queen Ba-cong-chua of Cambodia. And of Karl Albrecht the third of — wait for this — Hohenlohe-Waldenburg-Schillingfurst. And I also met the great, great granddaughter of Queen Ranavalona of Madagascar. She had the hugest thighs I've ever clapped eyes on. A real Gilbertine. And all these people were either living here, or staying here, or paying brief visits here — and they'd all left children and grandchildren who hoped, one day, to reclaim their thrones.

It reminded me of that place in Turkey. Somewhere in Cappadocia. There's an entire underground city — medieval — hewn out of the rock. On eight different levels. And all the people, the whole local community, used to move there and bury themselves away during times of unrest. And that's *exactly* what this place was like, except for the fact that this was only for royalty. And they came and they went, depending on the level of threat to their lives. I was told that the old emperor of China, Pu-Yi, had lived out the rest of his days in these quarries. He never left. It was too dangerous for him to be seen in the world at large. Others — King Michael of Romania, for example — were free to come and go. He wasn't in danger. In fact, he was fast becoming something of a hero. And that made the Order clap their hands with glee.

Who was financing the place? Who was backing the whole operation? Now there's a million-dollar question. No one would give me a clear answer at the time, not even Lola; although she hinted that the money was coming from our own royal family and from the French state, along with some two dozen other countries. And then I began to realize that the Order had tentacles — secretive ones — that spread out across the globe. Their resources seemed endless: there were deep pockets all round. You only had to look at the security that surrounded the place. Holy bloody Moses! The closed-circuit television cameras — which were *everywhere* — were backed up by a massive bank of computers inside the quarries. The entire complex was covered. No one could get in or out without being monitored. And when I realized all of this, it made me wonder why I'd been allowed to move in. And then — of course — it suddenly dawned on me. Mushrooms. They knew exactly who I was. They had done from the very beginning. They even showed me my two papers on the amanita genus. They'd read them. The knew about my potion. And so it was no accident that they'd agreed to me living in that funny old house. And it was no accident that our lives were turned belly upside-down soon after we moved in. That's exactly how they wanted it and it's exactly how they'd planned it.

And I now know that it was all part of their plan to get rid of Flora. She was superfluous to their needs. They were not sure she could be trusted. And you've got to remember, Peter, that we're not talking about some tin-pot little organization. This place was like the bloody Politburo. They specialized in psychological weirdness — that was their way of frightening people. And they were masters at it. And now — I'm talking about the first few weeks of the New Year — they were convinced their hour had come.

What got to me, time and again, was the scale of the whole thing. They were manipulating *everything*; everything that was occurring in those last few days of 1989. They had agents everywhere, Peter: Romania, Serbia, Czechoslovakia. They were all over the place and they were operating at the most senior levels. They were actively trying to destabilize the Soviet Union as well. They'd been operating undercover for decades, of course, but the end of the Cold War had led to a huge expansion of their activities. And now, well, it was as if all their dreams were coming true.

This is their plan: I'll spell it out for you in plain English. They intend to reinstall monarchs on the thrones of countries all around the world. Everywhere. Europe. Africa. Asia. But their first goal is Eastern Europe. Just wait. And mark my words. They're going to start them off as constitutional monarchies — that's all part of the plan. But it's only stage one. Stage two is to destabilize the new democracies, undermine their parliaments, and then call for the monarch — newly installed as head of state — to step in and reverse the country's woes. I'm over-simplifying it all, of course. Each country has its own team of operatives. The Order has people working in over one hundred and fifty countries around the globe. There's been meticulous planning and meticulous espionage and meticulous bloody undercover agents working absolutely everywhere. And they're convinced it'll work. They're convinced that one day soon it'll be bingo. Before you know it, you'll find yourself with ten or twelve countries — countries in *Europe* — governed by absolute monarchs who are fully in control of their armies.

There's one thing that amused me, Peter, one thing that made me laugh like a drain. It was the whole thing about the mushrooms. So much importance had been attached to the mushrooms. It was drummed into me on numerous occasions that it was absolutely one hundred per cent imperative that the caesars grew. "Your life depends on it." That's what they said to me. It was of vital importance that these people, these would-be royals, had their fifty-five pounds at the end of seven weeks.

But why? It's priceless, Peter. Absolutely bloody priceless. Symbolism and tradition. That's what it's all about. For hundreds of years the royal heads of Europe have been accustomed to eat, once every seven years, a meal that's centred around the rarest of mushrooms. It's a custom that pre-dates the construction of the quarries. Yes, it stretches way back into antiquity. In fact, it goes back to the Roman emperors. They used to have a feast every seven years in their palaces on the Palatine hill — a feast at which every single dish was composed around caesars. You can read about it in Gibbon, he's got half a page on it. And this tradition had continued throughout the Dark Ages. And it continued throughout the Middle Ages. Handed down from king to king like the bloody Apostolic succession. There were caesars on the table at Queen Elizabeth the first's coronation. And there were even more caesars on the table — *roasted!* — when Charles the second was restored to his throne. And when dear old Maria Kunigunde Herzogin von Sachsen managed to unblock her tubes at the ripe old age of fifty-three after eating a bucket-sized dollop of caesars, well, the mushroom's status was forever confirmed. And so, you see, it all makes some sort of sense. When Queen Elizabeth and Prince Philip arrive at the quarries every seven years for the Order's ceremonial banquet — accompanied by half the crowned and not-so-crowned royals of the world — caesars are always top of the agenda. How stark raving bonkers is that? And after nineteen eighty-eight — what with the wet summer and dry-as-a-bone autumn — finding wild caesars was a very tall order. What they needed was someone who could cultivate them.

The mushrooms — they grew. They burst into life. They were exactly the colour of egg yolks. Luminous orange. The colour of a traffic light. "Arnold," I said to myself, "you are a prize bloody genius. You're Einstein and Wittgenstein rolled into one." With my fair hands — and a little help from my magic potion — I had managed to propagate the rarest mushroom in the world. And no one in the whole history of the world has ever managed to do that. And so you must tell Flora, you really must. I'd like her to know.

CHAPTER
TWENTY

"Have you heard the news?" was Charlotte Stanhope's opening line when I arrived at work on the following morning.

"Tell me."

"Romania — King Michael — he wants to go back. Reclaim his gilded throne."

"*Really?*" This was news indeed. "How do you know?"

"It's on the wires. A few minutes ago. But it seems unlikely the government will allow him to."

I checked the wire report. Charlotte was right; the king did want to return. And it took me straight back to Arnold's crazy stories. It made me wonder if all the events taking place in Eastern Europe were indeed being manipulated by one central organization.

I told Flora everything that Arnold had recounted on his tape when I arrived home from work that evening.

"*What!*" She let out a cry and then a whimper. "No — that's too much. Now he's gone too far." She studied the floor for a moment and her voice fell to a whisper. "What's happening to him?" she said. "He'll fall apart — that's what will happen — and then —"

"Well, let's go and find out the truth about all his stories."

"How? Where?"

"We're going to Paris. I've got to go for work. In a couple of days. Come for the ride and we'll make a weekend of it."

"Well, how could I possibly refuse an offer like that?" she said. "I'll start packing right away."

Forty-eight hours later we were sitting in the Brasserie St Paul in the Marais and I was watching Flora plough her way through a dozen snails.

"You have to forget what they are," she said, as she offered me one on the end of a spike. "If you think of them as innocent little things with eyes on stalks then it's tricky to swallow them. But if you think of them as pests that've just destroyed all the basil you planted last spring, then it's perfectly easy to eat them. It's revenge food."

"Did you know they come from Burgundy?" I said, taking advantage of her good humour to risk a joke.

"Oh no," groaned Flora. "Next you'll be telling me they're in a royalist snail plot to take over the world."

"You don't believe Arnold?"

She shrugged her shoulders. "I've never said that," she said.

"But you think he's having fun at Peter's expense?"

She shrugged her shoulders a second time. "It's an expensive way to have fun," she said. There was a pause; her voice dropped a tone. "It's cost him — and me — our entire world."

She played with the snail shells on her plate before speaking again. "I've not listened to a single tape and I have no desire to listen to them. But it doesn't exactly sound, from what you've told me, as if he's having the time of his life with these new women of his."

It took hours to get a reading pass to Paris's Bibliothèque Nationale. In fact, if it hadn't been for my press pass, I wouldn't have got in at all. But I did, eventually, negotiate my way around the complexities of French bureaucracy and gain access to the manuscript collection. The male librarian graciously allowed Flora to accompany me. That's Gallic gallantry for you.

We ordered the manuscript and waited. Half an hour. Forty minutes. Fifty-five minutes. And then a librarian reappeared with a scroll of documents. Cartes de la France: Ms.C3512.OE. It was the one that Arnold had mentioned.

I was surprised to discover that the manuscript existed at all. Despite everything Peter had told me about Soufflot, I was expecting to be told that the reference number, the shelf mark, didn't exist. But it *did* exist and this discovery made me feel uneasy. I was struck by the possibility that the quarries, as described by Arnold, might exist as well. And if *they* existed —

"So," said Flora with uncharacteristic impatience. She looked visibly agitated; I remember being struck by the fact that she looked nervous as I prepared to open the scroll. She was paler than usual and fiddling with her hair, spooling it round and round on her fingers.

"Well, here we go." I untied the ribbon that was holding it all together and wrestled with the three sheets of paper.

It was not at all easy to work out what was what. The ink was very faint — in places there were only vague traces of lines — and the writing was all in French. But it was immediately apparent that these drawings, or architectural plans, were of underground quarries on a grand scale.

"You're not going to like this," I said to Flora, "but it's them all right. It — is — *them*."

She looked at them closely; she was biting her bottom lip.

One drawing was a general plan of the area. The hamlet of Creux was clearly marked, as was the property belonging to the de la Regnier family (I noticed that it was described as a manoir, not a chateau).

A second drawing seemed to be a floor plan of the interior of the quarries. It looked a great deal smaller than the labyrinth of Arnold's description. The third and final manuscript was by far the most interesting. It appeared to depict the actual banqueting room that Arnold had described. At the top of the page were the words: "Salle Louis XVI", and below them a perspective drawing that showed the banqueting table and two glass chandeliers.

"You said there were three," said Flora.

"No — *he* said there were three."

She was lost in thought for a minute or more, half-looking at the plans and half-staring into space.

She, like me, was trying to take in the fact that once again Arnold had been proved right.

"It's still like that," she said at length. "The little hamlet . . . the chateau. It hasn't changed a bit in two centuries."

She allowed the manuscripts to roll back into themselves, then threw up her hands in a sign of surrender.

"Maybe I was too quick to judge," she said. "It's here. They're original. It's even bloody well signed by Soufflot. I don't know what I'm supposed to say. It's extraordinary. To think that here in France there's a place like this. It's in the public archives, in the national library, and yet no one knows about it. And no one's ever visited the place. Except Arnold."

I sat back in my chair and thought for a moment. "Let's look at it from another point of view," I said. "Is it really *that* extraordinary? Imagine what things are hidden in England. Bolt-holes for the government. Nuclear shelters. Underground bunkers. They all exist. You only have to talk to our security correspondent. Apparently there's a tunnel that runs from underneath Number Ten to a deep bunker somewhere under Whitehall. All governments have such places — shelters and such-like — they have to, to enable them to continue governing the country even in the middle of a nuclear meltdown."

"Yes," she said, "but this is completely different. Can't you see? This is two hundred years old. And people have apparently been living in it for much of that time. And — and —"

"And what? I asked.

Her face twisted into a strange expression — half concern, half despair. "I'm coming round to the idea that Arnold is —"

"Is what?"

"In some sort of trouble," she said.

CHAPTER
TWENTY-ONE

"Oh, Flora, my darling," Philippa as she let out an excited little gasp. "Flora, Flora, Flora. How glad we are to see you again. And to see you both together. Ah, yes. Hope springs eternal."

"Hello, old boy," said Peter, slapping me on the shoulder. "Have a bottle." And he presented me with what looked like a rather fine Margaux.

Two days after our return from Paris — and for the first time since we'd originally met in Taplow Bottom in early December — I'd invited Peter and Philippa around for dinner.

"So," said Philippa, as she settled herself into the sofa and allowed the cushions to embrace her ample bottom, "what news? How was Paris? And how —" she turned to Flora — "is he behaving?"

"Ding dong ding dong," sang Peter, a not-so-subtle reference to wedding bells.

"Potsy, darling. She's not yet divorced."

"'Thrift, thrift, Horatio. The funeral bak'd meats did coldly furnish forth the marriage tables.' It's *Hamlet*," said Peter, evidently rather pleased with himself.

"Oh, per-lease," said Flora in a tone of suppressed frustration. "Can we please change the subject. And

Tobias — can we have some drinks? Please, no more of this. We're fine. We had a lovely time in Paris. And we're happy to see you. But not this."

"There," soothed Philippa. "Never you mind. We'll not say another word, My lips, my dear, are sealed."

"You'd need iron bolts to seal those lips," chortled Peter. "And even then you'd squeak."

After an initially bad start, the rest of the evening found itself steering a safer course through pleasantry, politeness and a few items of interest. The subject of our weekend in Paris was not raised again until after the main course and it was Philippa, as ever, who asked the questions.

"Was it lovely?" she said. "Romantic? Oh, Peter, why can't you whisk me off to Paris? Just because we've been married for —"

"Seventeen years and four months."

"Yes. It doesn't mean we can't have romantic breaks, you know."

Peter took a large gulp of wine. "You wouldn't know romance, darling, even if it jumped on you and shook you by the ears," he said, half in jest and half in earnest. "Anyway, I didn't come here tonight to hear about romance. I want to hear about maps. Did you get to the library? Did you find it? Come on, old chap. That's what I want to know."

"We did get there," I replied. "And we found the plans. And it was most revealing."

I went on to explain how they depicted the quarries much as Arnold had described them. Not as large, perhaps, but complete with banqueting chamber.

228

"*No!*" was Peter's response. "Then the old bugger's telling the truth. It's for real. They're there. They do exist. It's what I suspected all along. I told you so."

"The plans actually showed the layout of the banqueting hall. And there was a pencil sketch of the inside of the room. Just as he described it."

"You believe it then?" asked Philippa, turning to Flora. "Our dear, beloved Arnold — let me rephrase that — *your* dear, beloved Arnold — is not telling porkies after all? This is for real?"

"I really don't know what to say," Flora replied. "More yes than no, I suppose — and it makes me wonder if . . ." Her voice trailed away.

"I've been thinking about it," I said, breaking the silence, "and I just don't think that it's necessarily so surprising. We're talking about a quarry, an underground quarry, that's been used —"

"Not surprising!" spluttered Peter. "Banqueting halls and kings and queens and you say that's not surprising."

"Well the kings and queens are another matter," I said. "Let's put them to one side for the moment. What I'm trying to say is that it's entirely possibly that this Order of Monarchy that he keeps talking about — it's entirely possible that it was operating in the seventeen nineties. There were loads of semi-secret organizations, monarchist and republican, working in England and France at the time. It's also possible that the Order was still active in the nineteenth century and managed to save the lives of several other monarchs."

I told them I'd spent quite a lot of time thinking back through all the events that had recently unfolded in Eastern Europe. Everyone on the newspaper — all the correspondents I'd spoken to — was saying how strange it was that the whole Soviet bloc was folding in on itself like a pack of cards. I remember an old quote from my history teacher — I think it was said by Castlereagh or Peel: "Only rotten doors are kicked in." But the Soviet bloc was most definitely not a rotten door. The centre was still strong and the army was still loyal. There *had* to be some other force working inside these countries and destabilizing them from within. And perhaps there was indeed an organization that was attempting to restore monarchs to their thrones. It all made some sort of sense.

"No!" exclaimed Philippa. "Oh, that's priceless, Peter. But it can't be. Surely?"

"Go on," said Peter. He clearly thought I was on to something.

I explained how I'd been investigating two monarchs who'd lost their crowns in the current century.

"Did you ever see *The Last Emperor*?" I asked them. "The Bertolucci film? Came out a couple of years ago?"

They hadn't.

"Well, it tells the story of Emperor Pu-Yi — the emperor of China. He was kicked out of Beijing in nineteen twenty-four and was eventually installed on the throne of Manchuria as a Japanese puppet. But in nineteen forty-five he was captured by the Red Army and taken to Moscow."

"And then?"

"Well, if you believe the history books, he was repatriated to China by Stalin in nineteen fifty and thereafter spent a decade in some sort of re-education camp —"

"But?"

"But I spoke to our Beijing correspondent the other day and he told me that there had always been some doubt as to whether it really was Pu-Yi who'd been repatriated. There were rumours of a rescue operation. Of a bid to snatch the emperor from his quarters in Moscow. And that Stalin was too embarrassed to admit that he'd let a prisoner slip through his fingers."

"No proof?" said Peter.

"No proof," I agreed. "But it's intriguing. And there's also the case of Mehmet the sixth, the last Ottoman sultan. He was kicked out of Constantinople in nineteen twenty-two by the new nationalist government. He was whisked to safety by the British. He eventually died in San Remo — in Italy — but there were many months when he disappeared without trace. No one spotted him at all."

"And you're saying?"

"I'm not saying anything at all. I'm merely suggesting that — look, take Romania or Bulgaria or Serbia. Or even Albania, for that matter. All of them have monarchs clamouring to reclaim their thrones. All of them see this as a unique opportunity. And who's to say that this whole thing — this collapse in Eastern Europe — hasn't in some way been engineered by one organization? It's successfully restored Lola to her throne — along with her new husband. Now, they're going for the big ones. Romania. Bulgaria. Perhaps even Russia."

CHAPTER
TWENTY-TWO

I went to the London Library, as Arnold had suggested, in order to look at the account of the French king's escape — the one supposedly written by Henry Essex Edgeworth de Firmont.

I looked for it in the old printed catalogue under Edgeworth de Firmont. There was nothing. I looked under Firmont. Still nothing. And then I remembered that Arnold had said it was bound together with two other volumes by Charles Lacretelle and Edmund Burke.

There were dozens of entries for Burke but none that included a work by Henry Essex Edgeworth de Firmont. And then I checked Lacretelle, but to no avail. I was about to abandon my quest when I remembered Arnold said the book had been bequeathed to the library some fifteen or twenty years ago. If this was the case, it would have been acquired too recently to be in the old printed catalogue. I needed to check the card catalogue.

And there it was. Three books bound together in one volume and, according to the catalogue, "acquired by the library in 1963". It more or less fitted with what Arnold had said.

It was not shelved under history. Nor was it in the ten feet of books about the French revolution. Instead, it had been placed in political science and was to be found under L for Lacretelle. It had the title *Annals of the French Revolution: Three Treatises* on the cover. And inside were three accounts: one by Lacretelle, one by Burke, one by Henry Essex Edgeworth de Firmont.

I turned to the last section and started reading it immediately. It was exactly as Arnold had told it: Edgeworth's account of the king's flight from Paris. He related how Daumier had offered to sacrifice his life in order to save the king's. He described how he'd helped Daumier into the carriage without raising the suspicions of anyone, not even Santerre. And he said that Daumier had almost been sick in the carriage — "puked" — as it rumbled through the streets towards the place de la Révolution.

Edgeworth's greatest fear had been that of discovery. He was terrified their ruse would come unstuck. And yet at no point did anyone suspect anything, and by the time they reached the guillotine he knew they were safe. He knew that the king would have left his tower prison and already be on the far side of Paris. He knew that his life would have been secured. Yet still Edgeworth remained anxious: "I could not slacken my nerves until Daumier had been executed." That's what he wrote. It was imperative that Daumier didn't falter; essential that he didn't betray his true identity. Daumier *had* to die if the king's long-term safety was to be assured.

Edgeworth need not have worried. Daumier, though half-sick to death with fear, mounted the scaffold and placed his head on the block and the blade came down. And Edgeworth said that at that moment he knew the deception was complete.

It was a grisly account of the execution and what followed was even more fantastic. Edgeworth described in considerable detail how he headed to La Madeleine, picked up a horse from Abbaye de la Pierre and learned from him that "SM" (*sa majesté*) and Cléry were safe. He then set out for Vincennes, Sens and Troyes, before finally catching up with the king at the abbey of Pontigny. Once here, they were on safer ground. They were in Bourgogne, where there was a small network of priests, monks and royalists who were only too willing to help them.

They still had to take care. The countryside was being scoured by revolutionary officers whose task was to track down anyone with royalist sympathies. The king and Edgeworth stayed in Pontigny for two nights before making their way, under the blackness of a new moon, to the quarries of Creux.

I had been there once before some Three years previously, at the outbreak of the revolution. Henri-Auguste Jean de la Regnier — at that time the *chef de la famille* — had led me down into the Quarries and showed me the chambers. He wished to know if everything was satisfactory for the King's comfort, if ever he might need to spend time here. I must confess, I was taken aback by the lavishness of Soufflot's work. The King's bedchamber resembled his private quarters in Versailles and his private chapel had been furnished according to His taste. There was even a little diptych by Pietro Lorenzetti, a gift of the pope. But, for sheer exuberance, nothing could match the Banqueting Room. I told Henri-Auguste that the Sun King Himself would have been agreeably surprised by such a hideaway.

Edgeworth's account stopped at the point where the king arrived at the quarries. There was nothing about him living here. And there was no mention of the arrival, some years later, of the chaste, pious and apparently "sweaty" princess who was to bear him a son.

I flicked through the rest of the book. The two other accounts were rather dull and very different: I couldn't see why they were bound together in the same volume. In the frontispiece, there was a library issue-plate bearing the stamps of everyone who had taken out the book since it had first been acquired in 1963. NOVEMBER 17, 1963; MARCH 4, 1968; JANUARY 22, 1979; SEPTEMBER 1, 1984; OCTOBER 18, 1988.

October 18, 1988. It was with considerable surprise that I discovered the book had been taken out no fewer than five times since 1963 and that it had last been returned to the library some eighteen months earlier. In his tape, Arnold had said that the volume had been bequeathed to the library by accident. All other known copies had been destroyed, presumably by the Order, and the existence of this little volume was supposed to be a secret.

I made my way downstairs to the issue hall and approached one of the librarians, an elderly lady with a light moustache on her upper lip. It was she who'd helped me on my previous visit.

I explained to her that I needed advice and asked if it was in any way possible to find out who had last taken out the book.

"Gracious," she said, "what a question. Well. We may still have the slips, but they'll be in the offices. And, well, I can't do it straightaway. But if you could give me — if you wouldn't mind — if I could take your details . . ."

I gave her my number, returned home, and shortly after six o'clock she called to tell me that the last person to take out the book was a Mr Armistead Jones of Queen's Close, St Albans.

I wrote it down. "And would you by any chance have his number?"

"Oh yes, my dear," she said. "Just one moment."

I heard her rummaging around in the background for a few minutes before she picked up the receiver once again.

"Yes, dear," she said. "Here we go." And she gave me the number of Mr Armistead Jones.

"So why don't you call him?" said Flora later that evening. "Find out what he knows."

I dialled the number and it rang eight times before anyone answered.

The conversation that followed had little coherence and not much logic.

"Could I speak to Mr Jones, please."

"By Jove, that's me."

"Mr Jones, my name's Tobias Edwardes."

"Good, good. You're the plumbing fellow."

"No. I'm —"

"Jolly good. Tomorrow at eleven. That'll suit me just fine. Yes, yes. Thanking you kindly."

And he hung up.

I called back and explained why I was calling before he had the chance to cut me off for a second time.

"The French *revoluuuution*?" he queried, as if it was something he'd never heard of. "Essex Edgeworth de Thingummy. No, no. Not my bag. Magnifying glasses. That's my game. And telescopes. And helioscopes. Optics, you see. Not whiskies. Visual. If your Edgeworth had written about optics, why, there's every chance I'd have borrowed his books. But the French revolution? No, sir. Not at all."

It struck me as strange. The only possible explanation was that the librarian had made an error. But librarians don't make errors.

CHAPTER
TWENTY-THREE

"Isn't it all mad?" I said to Lola one morning while we were walking in the forest. "To think that this entire operation — everything taking place in these quarries — is for the sole purpose of preserving royal bloodlines."

"Well, I see it rather differently," said Lola. "I need this place. Much, much against my will, I'm caught up in a whole network of international intrigue — and without these quarries I might very well be dead by now."

She explained that the Soviet Union had long taken a keen interest in the Tuvan archipelago. She told me about rumours of any number of plots.

"But why?" I asked. "Why on earth would the Soviet Union be interested in Tuva? What possible use could it serve? And what's really going on down here?"

"But can't you see?" she said. "They want to stop the Order. They want to prevent Tuva from . . ." She paused. "No, but of course," she said. "Of course you can't see. You don't know the background, and without the background none of this will make any sense. I think it's time you met Ivan of Russia."

"Ivan?"

"Tsar Ivan. The grandson of Tsar Nicholas."

"Who was executed in 1917?"

"I'm surprised that you, of all people, believe *that*," she said. "Come, we'll go and see him right now. See if he's got time."

We set off down one of the corridors — left, right, right, left — until we reached a solid door adorned with a small Romanov eagle, a beautifully executed piece.

Knock, knock —

"Enter."

He was as cordial as could be. And he told me the history of his family — the story of what *actually* happened. For decades, Peter, people have come up with theories about the Romanovs. Stories of how Anastasia escaped. Of how she moved to Paris. Of how other members of the family also got away.

But it wasn't like that. It wasn't like that at all.

You need a spot of background, otherwise it will make no sense. Just a few of the facts. The Romanovs, you remember, had been under house arrest since March 1917. They were held in Tsarskoe Selo — one of their palaces — while the new government deliberated on what to do with them. And then, in April 1918, they were moved to Ekaterinburg, on the far side of the Ural Mountains. A Bolshevik strong-hold. The Red Urals, that's what they were called.

"I'd go anywhere," was what the tsar said to his wife, "only not to the Urals." But he didn't have a lot of choice. For the next three months the family was guarded and monitored by Bolsheviks — an uncouth band, according to Ivan's version of events. They told coarse jokes, made obscene gestures at the tsar's daughters and scratched lewd graffiti into the garden swing where the children were allowed to play. And several of the guards tried to rape one of the girls — Olga, I think it was.

Nicholas and Alexandra awaited their fate with increasing despair. (It's a feeling I'm getting used to, Peter. It's terrible when you're not in control.) They hoped and prayed they'd be rescued. And they had some reason for optimism, for there were scores of rumours about rescue missions. Grand Duke So-and-So was supposedly coming with a carriage. Prince So-and-So was on his way with a battalion of loyalist infantry. General So-and-So was about to appear with an armoured vehicle. There were even stories that the British intelligence service was behind a rescue plan. But what no one knew was that in the quarries of Creux, Prince Mikhail and the Duke of Palma — who were, at this point, the driving force behind the Order — had been putting the finishing touches to a most audacious rescue plan. Its success was dependent upon the Czechoslovak Legion, a band of fighters who (for reasons too long-winded to explain here) had long been fiercely and personally loyal to the Russian tsar. But now — post-revolution and all that — they found themselves stranded in Russia and their only way out of the country was to cross Siberia and leave from the eastern port of Vladivostok. And this would take them right past the gates of Ekaterinburg.

But — ah — too many facts and too much information. I'm boring you, Peter. You need to picture the scene. You need to imagine yourself there. Otherwise, you won't understand how on earth events could have unfolded in the way they did.

* * *

A big white house. A fin-de-siécle pile of a place with enough stucco to decorate a wedding cake. Domes and architraves, cupolas and denticles. It's a former governor's mansion, you see: opulent, ostentatious, dripping with excess. That, at any rate, was how the red-as-blood Bolsheviks of Ekaterinburg had long viewed the building when they shuffled past in their beaver-skin boots and knitted woollen hats.

But not any longer. Now, we're in the summer of nineteen eighteen and the governor's mansion has been converted into a house of detention. Now, when downtrodden Mikhail and half-starved Dimitri and militant-minded Larissa (and every other member of the local proletariat) shuffle by, they see little more than a twelve-foot-high fence constructed from old railway sleepers.

"Blood sucker." That's Mikhail shouting over the fence as he heads home from the lignite mine.

"Long live Lenin," shrills Larissa. She's tempted to hurl a turnip over the fence — smash a window. But, no, that's supper.

"*Tsaria russkogo Nikolu, za khui sdernuli s prestolu*," sings Dimitri at the top of his voice. "Our Russian tsar called Nick was dragged off the throne by his prick."

The Romanov family has grown used to such taunts. It's July, it's sultry and they spend as much time as their guards allow in the small garden that surrounds the house. There are three birch trees. A solitary pine. And some sort of Russian camellia that is covered in scabies. But the family see only the fence. It separates them from the outside world. It separates them from freedom.

Try to think, Peter, how you'd behave in such a situation. Just imagine: you, Philippa, your children, all kept under house arrest and knowing full well that your brutal guards *and* the people outside *and* the cynics in charge of your country are all itching to spill your blood. At any day, any hour, any minute, they could come and lead you down into the cellars or to some other part of the house where no one ever goes — and kill you. Not just you, Peter, but your wife and your precious children — the dearest things that you have in the whole wide world. Snatched from you and gunned down by murderous thugs who don't understand that — *really* — you are not to blame. For you are not an evil man, you see, nor even a bad man. Just the wrong man in the wrong place at the wrong time.

Tap, tap. There's a knock at the door to your private chamber. It's Yakov Mikhailovich Yurovsky your guard. At least he still knocks — you can be thankful for small mercies. The others just walk in. Walk in when you're shaving; when you're getting dressed; when you're eating. Just two days ago they burst in when your wife was wearing only her corset. The indignity of it all.

"A new guard," snaps Yurovsky. "Colonel Aleksandr Aleksandrovich Voeikov. From now on, you will answer to him. You will do what he says."

The ex-tsar nods. And his wife nods. "Yes," says Nicholas in the same despondent tone that has characterized his speech for the last four months. He's weary. Tired. It's the pressure and strain, you see. The uncertainty.

Somewhere in the distance, a little carriage clock chimes six. It makes a lovely little ting. It's cheery. Reminds him of happier times.

"Six o'clock already," yawns Nicholas. "Another day slips by."

The new guard, Aleksandr, is as rude as the rest. At least, he's rude for a day or two. But on the third day he approaches Nicholas as he sips at his soup. He coughs to attract his attention and then begins speaking in a whisper. He has something of great importance to say.

"Your imperial highness —"

Nicholas drops his spoon into the bowl, splashing soup onto the tablecloth. And Alexandra spills salt from the salt cellar. Her husband hasn't been addressed like this for many months. Indeed, she can't remember the last time —

"Tonight. In the early hours. Two o'clock. Maybe three. They will arrive — the Legion. The Czechoslovak Legion. They're heading for Vladivostok. They will take you. All of you."

Nicholas glances at Alexandra. They both look at Aleksandr Aleksandrovich.

"How — can — I — trust —?"

"Just trust," comes the reply. "Time is short. There are rumours that Lenin has already given the order. That *it* will happen — and happen soon."

He stresses the word "it". He does not want to use the word execution — not in front of the tsarina. "This may prove your very last chance."

Aleksandr explains the plan. The family are to go to bed fully dressed. They are to conceal all their remaining jewels in their corsets and undergarments — stitch them into any possible place where they won't be detected. There will be one short blast on a cornet. Just one, mind. And they must creep outside, to the south gate, which Aleksandr himself will have unlocked, They will slip out undetected.

This, Peter, was the rescue plan. I was given it in much greater detail, of course, but these are the bare bones — this is all that you really need to know. You see, the plan didn't quite work out as Aleksandr Aleksandrovich had envisaged.

To cut to the chase, we must wind forward the clock fully eight hours. There: it's now two o'clock in the morning and there's not a sound to be heard. Not a light. Nothing stirs. The tsar and tsarina are in bed, both fully clothed. Their children — Olga, Tatiana, Maria, Anastasia and the boy, Aleksei — are also fully clothed. All are wide awake. All are waiting. Waiting. Waiting. Waiting.

Is that the blast of a cornet?

No.

Is *that*?

No.

"Ssh," whispers Anastasia. "Or we won't hear it."

She's hot in her clothes and is feeling decidedly uncomfortable. She has eight diamond necklaces in her corset.

Aleksei, too, is feeling only bumps and lumps. Five fob watches (gold); six necklaces; four ruby-drop brooches; a purse filled with gold roubles; a dozen or more rings.

No one in the family is aware that the men of the Czechoslovak Legion are still three miles away. Nor do they know that here and now, in this very house, there is movement in the basement. Yurovsky and his senior henchmen are passing from room to room, looking for the most suitable place.

They enter the small side chamber that adjoins the pantry. Yurovsky taps the walls and his face betrays a smile. "Here," he says. "Perfect."

He gets a quizzical look from his companions and realizes he needs to explain. "It's plaster-covered wood," he says. "The bullets won't ricochet."

"So — are we ready?" asks one of the men.

Yurovsky opens his fob watch; checks the time; snaps it shut.

"We are ready," he says. "I shall wake them. Bring them downstairs. Is the detachment ready?"

The detachment. That's the execution squad. Twelve men who are under orders to shoot the tsar and his family.

"Shoot at their hearts." That's Yurovsky's order. It leaves less mess, you see. Less blood to clear up.

Yurovsky climbs the great stairway and paces slowly along the north corridor, counting his steps as he goes. He's wondering how they will die. Will they scream? Or go quietly? He can't wait to kill the tsar. Bang. He pictures the scene in his head. "I'll pop it through his heart," he thinks, "as if he's a wild boar."

He knocks on the bedroom door and enters before he hears an answer. "Up," he barks. "Everyone up."

The tsar and tsarina experience three emotions in as many seconds. Surprise. Excitement. And fear. And then fear again. It was not meant to be like this. Where was the blast from the cornet? And what's *he* doing in their room in the middle of the night? And then they realize that the game is up. The rescue mission's been uncovered. Someone's informed on them. It must have been treachery on the part of Aleksandr Aleksandrovich? Or some sort of plot to incriminate them.

In fact, it's neither of these. It is pure unhappy coincidence that the order to execute them has been given on the very same night that they are due to be rescued.

Yurovsky immediately notices the clothes.

"Aha," he says. He fumbles at the tsar's lapel. At his collar. At his polished buttons.

"Mama — Mama — will we be safe?" It's little Aleksei, the family's only son. He's entered the room because he's overheard the commotion.

"Yes, yes. Don't you worry, *ma biche*. Everything will be fine."

Yurovsky enters the children's room and tells the girls to get up. Then he leads them all along the corridor, down the grand staircase and into the basement: Nicholas and Alexandra (Aleksei is in his father's arms); Olga, Tatiana, Maria and Anastasia. They're soon joined by the rest of the household: Dr Botkin; Trupp the footman; Kharitonov the cook; and Anna Demidova, the tsarina's maid. All of them. Woken up. Ordered downstairs. They'd all been fast asleep.

They are led into the small basement room, which has been emptied of furniture. "Not even a chair?" says the tsarina. Yurovsky asks for one to be brought, but doesn't allow her to sit down. He's quietly pleased with himself. That, he thinks, is a refinement of cruelty.

He orders them all into a row — all eleven of them. And then he turns to address them, speaking in a clear voice.

"The Ural Executive Committee," he says, "has grown increasingly alarmed by the fact that the tsar's family in Europe continue to aggress Russia. It has therefore been decreed that you are all to be shot."

"What?" splutters Nicholas. "*What?*"

We must change the scene for a moment, Peter; we must turn our spotlights on the Czechoslovak Legion, who are now just

246

three miles from Ekaterinburg. There are eight of them, the advance column of a band that numbers nearly nine hundred.

"We'll take the southern road," says Tomas, the leader, as they approach a muddy crossroads in the hollow of a field. Even in the middle of a long hot summer, the ground is marshy and wet. "Yes, the southern. It'll bring us closer to the house."

One of the men takes a swig of water. The night is indeed hot and all of them are sweating heavily. "We'll be there in half an hour. Maybe less. Need to load our guns."

They swing round their horses and nudge their bellies. All eight start trotting in unison.

"What?" splutters the tsar. "*What?*"

Yurovsky repeats his words; tells the assembled group that they are to be shot. As he says this, the twelve-strong detachment — the execution squad — enter the room.

"*Oh, my God.*"

"No — it can't be."

"Papa — save us. Papa."

"Mama. Mama. Mama. *Mama. Mama.* Help us. Oh, please. No. Oh, God. No. Not this."

It's a terrible scene, Peter. Brutal beyond belief. And pitiful. Yurovsky nods; he nods at the detachment. They raise their guns. But they know that they are not to fire just yet. Yurovsky, you see, has been waiting for this moment for many months and he wants to savour it.

"Help — oh, please."

   "No."

     "Oh, God, no."

       "No. Not this."

Yurovsky draws out his pistol and points it at the tsar. He places his finger on the trigger. He feels his skin flush against it. The fleshy fat of his finger is squeezing against the metal trigger. Squeezing, squeezing, squeezing. And then, surely, there is no more to give. One more tiny squeeze — tiny, tiny, tiny — BANG.

The tsar falls into a crumpled heap. Shot through the heart. And then, a split second later, bang-bang-bang-bang-bang-bang.

Mayhem. Bullets flying, whizzing, ricocheting. Bang-bang-bang-bang-bang. One bullet leaps back across the room like a piece of hail. Zzzzzzzz. It narrowly misses Yurovsky. He ducks. Zzzzzzzz. Another. He orders the men to stop.

But, instead of silence, there's crying and wailing. Three of the children are still alive. And so is the maid. And Dr Botkin. Bang. Bang. Bang. Another tirade of bullets — bang, bang — and then —

Silence.

Yurovsky kicks the tsar's crumpled body. He kicks the tsarina. He scratches his head. Wonders why the bullets ricocheted. He specifically chose this room for its plaster-covered walls.

"Load them up," he orders. "Into the cart. We need to get going for the mine."

And that's where it might have ended, Peter. That could have been the final act. Curtains for the Romanovs. But what Yurovsky and his fellow killers in the execution squad had failed to realize was that it's not over until the fat lady sings. And on this particular occasion, the big fat Russian prima donna had not yet opened her mouth.

It's the Czechoslovak Legion, you see. They were entering the outskirts of the town — riding along the streets — approaching the Ipatiev house in the shadow of the night. And it was then, when they were still several hundred yards away, that they saw the flickering of a torch. And a cart being loaded. The corpses. And the soldiers.

"*Whoa*." Tomas brings his horse to an abrupt halt. For a minute or more, he stares at the gruesome scene taking place. And then, slackening the reins of his horse, he addresses his men in a hoarse whisper. "We are too late. Too late. They are dead."

He pauses for a moment, as if deep in thought. "But our mission is not quite over. We must follow them. Follow them into the forest. We must be witnesses."

And so it was that twenty minutes later they found themselves shadowing Yurovsky and his men, following — at a very discreet distance — a cart that was laden with a cargo of human meat and rattling its way towards a disused mine in the forest on the outskirts of town. Tomas and his men were not noticed by Yurovsky. They were not seen by the guards. And why should they be? It was dark, they were lagging far behind and they were professionals.

"Halt," commands Tomas. "They're stopping. You wait here. You. And you. All of you. Except Stefan. Stefan and I will go and investigate."

They *were* professionals, Peter. They knew exactly how *not* to be seen. And their task was made easier by the distractions of the men in front. Yurovsky arguing with his men; his men arguing with each other. There's a quarrel about the mineshaft. Is it deep enough? Should they burn the bodies? Who's forgotten the sulphuric acid?

At length a fire is lit. A vodka bottle produced. And the men wait for the wood to catch before preparing to dump the bodies on the flames.

And it was then, Peter, at that very moment, that it happened. Tomas, who was by now less than fifteen feet from the cart, saw it first. A twitch. A convulsion. One of the bodies moved.

"*Stefan*," he whispers hoarsely.

"Sir?"

"Did you see? Look — look there."

It twitched again.

"Holy —"

And right then — at that very moment — while Yurovsky and his men are stoking the fire and swigging the vodka and boasting and bragging about the basement slaughter, Tomas and Stefan start crawling on their bellies, inching themselves forwards. And then, ever so quietly, they pull themselves into the grim charnel cart, which is thick with blood and stinks of intestines and death.

The body twitches. "Take him down. Here — take his legs." With great care — and in absolute silence — the young boy is lowered onto the mud.

"Check the others," hisses Tomas. "Quick. We've got no time."

They're all dead. Each and every one. Only Aleksei — tsarevich until an hour ago, and now the tsar of all Russia — is still alive. He is breathing, he is conscious; miraculously, he is not even wounded. Five fob watches, six necklaces, four ruby-drop brooches, a purse filled with gold roubles and a dozen or more rings have saved his life.

"Take his arms. I'll take his legs. Don't bruise him. Remember, we've no Rasputin to care for him now."

The fire burns, the men drink, the corpses lie in the cart. And Tomas and Stefan whisk Aleksei from the clutches of death; carry him to their horses; ride off into the night. And within hours they are on their way to Vladivostok — a two-thousand-mile ride across mile upon mile of forest and grassland.

Yurovsky doesn't realize there's a body missing on the evening itself. He's had a lot of vodka and he's exhilarated by the killing and his pulse is beating overtime. "I shot the tsar," he brags to himself gleefully. "I shot the bloody prick of a tsar."

The bodies are burned; the bones are broken. Then the whole mangled lot of fat and grime and bone and teeth is tipped down the mine. And then acid — gallons of the stuff — is tipped down after it.

"They've gone," says Yurovsky to his men. "We did it." And they all do a little dance.

And it is only when he awakes on the following morning — sore of head and in a state of fuzzy dislocation from reality — that he begins counting on his fingers. Tsar. And tsarina. That's two. A girl. A second girl. A third girl. And a fourth girl. Six. The doctor. The footman. A cook. A maid. Ten. He has a niggling feeling that he's forgotten one. And then the feeling grows. Even with his roaring head, it grows. He has a suspicion. That. Something. Is. Not. Quite. Right.

Holy shit. Holy-shit-holy-shit. The son. The son was not there. He was not — no — . *He was not there.* Yurovsky delves into his brain, thinks back through the vodka and the firelight and the cadavers on the cart. Yes, he remembers the boy being put on the cart. Yes, he remembers seeing his lifeless arm. And yes, he remembers — . But no. In fact, he does *not* remember — he absolutely does not remember — taking the body off the cart. And it is at this point that he lifts himself out of bed — *agh, my head, agh, my head* — and summons two of his most faithful guards.

I'm sure you've guessed what happened next, Peter. I'm sure you can piece it together. The Legion made it to Vladivostok, narrowly avoiding capture on several occasions. And once they reached the port, they managed to get passage on a ship bound for Kagoshima. Then they went to Naha and to Sapain and to Pohnpei and Kosrae and Orana. And finally, many days later, they arrive in the little tropical paradise of Tuva, which the king — a loyal member of the Order of Monarchy — had always offered as a place of refuge.

Yurovsky had long since given up the chase. But his two henchmen, Federov and Vatutin, were still in pursuit. They, too, managed to get aboard ships. They, too, finally got to Tuva. And it was here that Aleksei's two protectors, Tomas and Stefan, made their first mistake. You see, they genuinely believed they'd be safe on Tuva. They genuinely thought that no one could arrive undetected, that any approaching boat would be spotted long before it actually reached the island. But Federov and Vatutin had served in the Russian special forces and they'd been trained by the Cheka. They knew what they were doing. Somehow — almost certainly under the cover of darkness — they got ashore. Somehow, they crept undetected into Lipoku village. And there, seated around a table lit by a small paraffin lamp, they saw their quarry —

Aleksei, the uncrowned tsar of Russia. He was sitting with his two protectors and the king of Tuva — Lola's grandfather.

And it was at that very moment, Peter, just when the Russians were about to pull their triggers, that Tomas spotted a movement outside. He realized that something sinister was afoot. Quick as a flash, he whipped out his pistol. Bang. Vatutin was shot through the heart. But Federov was still alive and he was determined to finished the job. He burst into the room firing, firing, firing. Three, four, five bullets sank deep into the walls. And Tomas was firing as well. And Stefan. Bang. Bang. Bang. Bang-bang-bang-bang.

And then silence.

The shoot-out had claimed two lives. At the head of the table, slumped onto his dinner plate, was the plump and previously rather jolly king of Tuva. A bullet had passed straight through his brain. And by the door, lying in a pool of blood, was Federov, the second assassin. But Aleksei himself was safe. He had thrown himself to the floor (he was becoming something of an expert at surviving assassinations) and escaped unscathed.

And when the dust settled and the corpses had been taken away, Tomas and Stefan found themselves in agreement about young Aleksei's future; indeed, they'd answered the greatest question facing the Order: whether or not to move the entire operational control of the organization to Tuva. They'd been thinking along these lines for many years. The quarries of Creux — it was felt — were too exposed, too risky. The Order believed it could only be a matter of time before they were discovered. It had been easy enough to stay hidden in the nineteenth century: the Morvan was completely isolated and as wild as a jungle. No one lived for miles around and no one went there. Besides, all the surrounding land was owned by the de la Regnier family. But two roads had been built just before the First World War — the highway to Lyon and another to Clermont Ferrand — and there were those in the Order who felt it was time to move somewhere even more remote.

There was never any doubt as to where they'd move to. For several decades the king of Tuva had been suggesting that they use his archipelago as a refuge. And, in many ways, it seemed the perfect place. After all, it was already teeming with monarchs. Oloua, Tu'unoho, Kitu and Ta'ula — and, of course, Tonga — and the archipelago was about as remote as it gets. The only big question mark (and I'm not kidding you, Peter) was whether or not mushrooms could be grown. Yes! This was actually one of their principal concerns. Mushrooms, for God's sake. It was when I heard that — well — I realized just how ludicrously important mushrooms had become to the entire operation. It was all bound up in ceremony and ritual, of course, like so many things in their lives. Mushrooms had acquired so much mystical value that I really got the feeling that the assembled kings and queens in Creux couldn't live without them. It reminded me of that long line of Byzantine emperors who were unable to rule unless they had possession of the miracle-working icon of St Stephen.

But where was I? Ah, yes — as you can imagine, Peter, a tropical climate is not exactly convivial to the humble mushroom. And that's why Warlock had been sent: to see if it would be possible to grow caesars in the Tuvan archipelago, where the temperature hovers around the hundred mark and there's so much humidity that you lose about six pints of water a day. And that's also where Gilbertine enters the story. It was her grandmother who knew of the existence of the cave on the northern slopes of the mountain — the same bloody cave which was full of mushrooms in 1918 and is still full of mushrooms and which has now become my laboratory and workshop.

Warlock didn't put any of this in his book. Indeed, he actually wrote his whole account in an attempt to prove to the world that there were no mushrooms whatsoever on Tuva. That's the one you copied for me. But it was a big fat whopper of a lie, of course. There were mushrooms — and plenty of them.

So what happened next? Well, the year was nineteen eighteen. The Order was ready to move. They had everything in place. But then — bang-bang — the king of Tuva is assassinated. And with one giant crash all their plans had to be abandoned. Young Aleksei Romanov was whisked back to Europe and the Order decided to remain for a little while longer in Creux.

But how history repeats itself. Now, once again, they're all getting itchy feet. There's a feeling that danger lies ahead. There's a feeling that they need a bolt-hole; a place to escape if everything should go wrong. *Everyone* feels it — even monarchs who are comfortably ensconced on their thrones. Even the queen and Prince Philip are supporting the project, to the extent of putting in their own money. And that's why we've been so busy on Tuva. We're getting everything ready. We're leaving nothing to chance. Nothing will be able to go wrong. It's one giant monster of a master plan. And if the Order pulls it off, it will have been a work of rare genius.

CHAPTER
TWENTY-FOUR

It started snowing as I returned home from the *Telegraph*. Snowing hard. "There'll be traffic chaos in the morning," predicted the owner of the corner shop close to my flat. "Just you wait."

Snow or no snow, I was sure he'd be proved right. When I'd left work, the news team were busily preparing an article on blizzard conditions sweeping in from the Arctic.

Flora arrived home just a few moments after me. I'd grown used to the sound of the key in the door and her cheery hello. But on this particular evening she looked pale and tired and I sensed that something was not quite right.

"I've got two bits of news," she said. Her voice was more restrained than usual and drained of any brightness. "One is good and one is bad. Which do you want first?"

"The good," I said, trying to inject a note of cheer into the room. "Definitely the good."

She sat down in the least comfortable chair in the room (even at the time I remember noting that she seemed to have chosen quite consciously that particular chair) and slowly repeated my words. "The good news.

Well — OK. Here goes. I've got a job. At Hobby House — a children's publishers. You know — ? I hadn't told you before but, well, I'd applied to six or seven. No, not applied. Written. And Hobby Horse called me up and asked me to come in. They loved the work I'd done at Foxtree and — the long and the short of it is they've hired me. On a temporary basis."

"Well, that *is* news," I said.

And it really *was* news. She hadn't told me anything — not about applying for jobs nor about the fact that she even wanted a job. All I knew was that she'd given up at Foxtree more than three years earlier.

"When do you start? And why didn't you tell me any of this? Why all the secrecy?"

"Well, I'm allowed a few secrets," she said. Her restrained voice was suddenly framed with sarcasm and I could sense (for reasons that were as yet obscure) that I was about to become an object of attack. Our first argument was in the offing.

"I want to earn my keep," she said. "And I don't like being a charity; I don't like it at all. You're very generous. And I'm very grateful. But — well — I just don't feel very comfortable with the way things are at the moment."

I nodded as if to make it clear that I agreed with what she was saying. I didn't feel like an argument. I took a quick mental decision to agree with whatever she said.

"So what'll you do there? Will it be the same sort of thing as at Foxtree?"

"It's in the art department. For illustrated books. Five-six-seven year olds. Exactly like I used to do at Foxtree. Until I stupidly, stupidly, stupidly gave it up."

"Well, that's —"

I stopped myself in mid-sentence. I suddenly realized that I was in two minds about this piece of news. In one way, it was great. And in another way, it was not great at all.

"It's great," I said. "It's great. We must have a glass of something. We must celebrate. But you didn't have to — you know — you absolutely didn't have to do this on my account. You didn't have to do it because of me. I'm very happy. I'm more than happy with the arrangement."

"Oh, I'm sure you are," she said. The smouldering sarcasm had developed into a full broadside. "Oh, yes, and so was Arnold. More than happy to have a wife at home not doing much. Always there. Always smiling. Dinner cooked. Dinner served. Dinner ready. Washing done. Ironing done. Knickers off. *A job? Why do you want a job?* Yes. No. Yes. No. Well, Tobias, I'm sick of it. I've had enough of it and I don't want to fall into the same trap again, thank you very much. Before I know it I'll be ironing your shirts and cooking your dinner. And that's something I'm not pre —"

"OK. Stop."

I actually shouted. I hadn't shouted at her before. And then I held up my hands. "Just stop. I think you've made your point. I haven't asked you to iron my shirts. And I've never asked you to cook my dinner. In fact, it's almost always me that cooks the dinner. And I haven't tried to stop you from getting a job. I didn't even know you were trying to get a job. And as for 'knickers off'. That really is — if you get my drift — below the belt. But the job is good news. No. It's better than good. It's great. Let's have a drink. Let's celebrate your new job."

There was a moment's silence. She didn't say anything more, so I stood up and was about to go into the kitchen when I remembered her opening words.

"That was the *good* news. You said there was bad news. You'd better tell me the bad news before I get a drink."

There was a long pause.

"I'm pregnant," she said.

"*What!*"

"I'm pregnant. Well — I'm ninety-nine per cent certain I'm pregnant."

"But how? When? How do you —?"

"I think a woman can tell when she's pregnant," she snapped, cutting my question in two.

Pregnant. My brain was processing the information, trying to calculate how bad this news was. In one sense, it was very bad. We had not planned this and our relationship was still in its early days. We had not — until tonight — had a single row. This was going to change everything, our friendship and our future. And I would be a father.

Yet it was only much later that night that this last thought — and the baby itself — entered my head. At that moment it was not even a part of the equation. My only thought was one of quiet triumph. It had slowly been dawning on me that I liked Flora — I liked her a lot. And this would surely drive Arnold out of her life forever.

"I know what you're thinking," said Flora. "I know exactly what you're thinking."

Her voice startled me. Neither of us had spoken for almost a minute.

"What?" I asked. "You're not a mind reader."

But she was.

"You're thinking that it'll drive me to divorce. That it'll at long last be the end of the road for Arnold and me. Officially over. Paperwork done. All sealed and delivered."

I was amazed at the way she'd read my thoughts.

"I hate you," she said. "All of you. You haven't even thought about the child. I can tell that he — or she — hasn't even entered the equation. It's true, isn't it? Admit it. You're thinking of yourself. And it's just so typical. You men are all the same. You're so predictable. And you're so bound up in yourselves. Just look at how you reacted to the news that I had a job."

"*What!*" I said. "I was delighted. What more could I have said? What did you want me to say?"

"Huh," was her response. "I don't think you were delighted. I think you were annoyed. You had to conceal it. Hide it. Because you were embarrassed at being annoyed."

"Nonsense. In *your* head I was annoyed. But in *my* head I didn't have a problem with it."

"*Didn't have a problem.*" She repeated in an even more sarcastic tone. "That's hardly a ringing

260

endorsement, is it? That's hardly 'Oh, Flora, that's fantastic, brilliant, wonderful.'"

"You're upset and you want to take everything out on me."

There was a moment of silence. A car alarm sounded in the street outside. And Flora glared at me furiously.

"So," I said in the calmest voice I could muster, "I've told you how *I* feel about you being — pregnant. But how do *you* feel. Why is this bad news for *you*. Only the other day you were telling me how —"

"It's terrible," she said. "It's a disaster. And it's awful."

She began crying and ranting at the same time. Her face looked suddenly drawn.

"It's the single worst piece of news that I've had in years. I hate it, hate it, hate it. And I wish I could wake up and discover it was all a dream. Only it's not and it never will be. It's for real."

Another pause. She pushed her hand through her hair, then wiped her eyes clumsily. It struck me that perhaps I was missing something. In all honesty, I couldn't work out why it was such bad news for her. After everything she'd told me — after the whole story of how she wanted to start a family.

And then I realized.

"Of course," I said, "it's the job. You're worried that —"

She sneered. "If you really think it's *that*, then we're living on different planets. A job's a job."

"Mmn."

"Mmn, nothing," was her response. "There's nothing — absolutely nothing — you can tell me that will make me feel better or make me change my mind. It's terrible and that's that."

"But I thought you wanted children. I thought you were desperate —"

"Yes!" She shouted and sobbed at the same time. "For years I wanted to have children. For years I tried to persuade Arnold, but —" She took a deep breath. "I'm going out," she said.

"What, now? Where?"

"I just want to go out. Get some fresh air."

"D'you want me to come with you?"

"No," she said. "I want a few minutes to myself. I haven't had time to think all day."

Her arms dropped to her sides as if they — and all the rest of her — had suddenly calmed. The anger was subsiding and now she looked only sad.

"As you wish," I said. "I'll see you later."

"Yes," she said. And she put on her coat and left the flat.

I waited an hour and then another.

I cooked supper, but couldn't face eating. I watched television but only half-listened. And I watched the minute hand of the wall clock slowly make a circuit of the dial. It felt like the end of a chapter. Things were no longer quite the same.

And then a whole hour had passed and the clock began repeating its circuit. And it started to dawn on me that it was no longer *when* she'd come back, but *if*. What if that was it? Once upon a time, two people met

262

each other and then they separated. The end. It was not the happiest of stories.

It was then that I started to worry that something was seriously wrong. It was 8.20p.m. and I'd convinced myself that Flora was in trouble. I wanted to ring someone, but couldn't think who to call. The obvious person was Peter, but what was the point in ringing Peter? Besides, he'd tell Philippa and then she'd try to contact Flora. And that would make matters even worse.

I turned off the television and the room fell silent. I walked over to the windows in the hope that I might glimpse Flora in the street. The snow had stopped, leaving the streets wet and gleaming. At one point I saw a woman who looked like Flora and I was about to dash downstairs when I realized it wasn't Flora at all.

Nine o'clock. Nine thirty. And it was then — two hours and ten minutes after she left — that the telephone rang.

Please God, I thought, let it be Flora.

"Hello?" said a man's voice. "Mr Edwardes —?"

CHAPTER
TWENTY-FIVE

It was five days ago. Gilbertine and I — chop-chop-hack-hack — made our way back up to the cave. Same steaming jungle, same tangle of creepers. The only difference was that on this occasion I was literally trembling with excitement. Would the deathcaps have sprouted? Would I find a carpet of caesars? You know the answer. Of course you do.

Oh, Peter, what sight for the eyes. Even Gilbertine dropped to her knees. There were hundreds of them — hundreds and hundreds and hundreds: deathcaps, panther-caps, destroying angels. And alongside them — along one entire wall of the cave — were caesars. I counted sixty-four in full fruit and a further one hundred and twenty poking their bald little heads through the soil. You, of all people, Peter, can imagine the heart-skip of excitement I got when I saw those shiny orange egg yolks pushing up through the humus.

Gilbertine took my hand and shook it vigorously.

"Well done, Mr Husband, sir," she said.

"No," I replied, "well done to you. It was you that found it. And it was you that got us here."

We picked them. Not all of them — just the deathcaps and caesars. We levered them ever so carefully out of the soil, taking care to preserve the thick root bulb. And there's one other thing we picked, Peter. A plant that's of key importance in everything I'm about to tell you. Do you remember what I told you in my earlier tape? Do you remember how I said I'd sowed some seeds of the blessed milk thistle? Well these beautiful little buggers had also poked their sweet noses through the soil and were in full and magnificent bloom. Little purple balls of fluff — that's what they looked like — with these needle-sharp spines pointing out in every direction. I snapped them at the base of their stems — crunch. It sounded like treading on a snail. And they exuded a strong and slightly bitter smell — a mixture of old yoghurt, stale fridges and bleach.

"Shall we cut them all?" asked Gilbertine.

"Each and every little last beauty," I said. "These may well prove my life-savers."

All this took place last Tuesday and I would have told you earlier, but I've been so busy and everything's got so exciting that I've been rushed off my feet for the first time since I arrived here. But now — sound the trumpets — I'm in a position to tell you every last jot. But, first, I must warn you. I'm going to have to get technical. I'm going to get all scientific. It will interest you, Peter, I know it will, but I'm not convinced about Philippa — *Philippa? Are you there —* ? This might prove a little tedious. Unless, of course, you harbour a fascination for the innermost workings of a mushroom. The secret bits. The hidden parts. The toxic juices and fibroid poisons. If you do, then even the ugliest, spotiest, wartiest mushroom on this planet of ours can be an object of fascination. And beauty.

Alpha-amanitin. That's the deadly toxin in the deathcap. That's what weevils its treacherous passage into your liver, obliterating everything in its path. For the first ten hours —

nothing. You don't even know you're ill. Another ten hours pass. You still don't realize anything's wrong. Good night, sleep tight. In fact, it's not until the second or third day that you have any inkling that something might be wrong. And if only you knew the whole horror of it all. The red lights should be flashing. The alarm should be ringing. There should be a deafening cacophony of bells and sirens. The toxins, you see, have burrowed their way deep into your liver. The alpha-amanitin is nibbling, nibbling, nibbling into your cells. It's causing a cytolysis of hepatocytes — that's the technical term — a devastating destruction of the cells that make up your liver.

Kidney failure. Liver failure. And then your breathing starts to go. The hepatic coma comes as a blessed relief. At least you don't know you're on the threshold of death. One more day. That's all you have. And then it's curtains.

Alpha-amanitin. That's what finishes you off. And it's fascinated me for years. It's a polypeptide, you see: a linear polymer with two amino-acid chains. *Two* — imagine! They plough through the membranes of all the cells in your liver. It's like using a combine harvester to cut the hair of a bald man. It's Goliath against David and this time Goliath is guaranteed to win.

Are you still with me? Do you need a pause? Well, let's leave the deathcaps to one side for a moment. What about the blessed milk thistle, then, with its spiky prickles and its smell and its bitter juices? That, Peter, is what really got me going. I sliced the flower heads with a scalpel — all of them — and carefully extracted the seeds. And then I made a pin prick in each and every seed. It took hours because they're microscopic. Like grains of dust. And then I warmed them up to eighty-six degrees, ever so gently. No hotter, or you'll destroy them. And then — equally carefully — I squeezed them between glass. Two thick and spotlessly clean sheets of glass. And what came out? A translucent liquid: pure silymarin. The distillation of the plant. The essence. The holy juice. And this, Peter, was liquid gold to me. Because silymarin, if correctly ingested, acts as a powerful block on the liver membranes. It's like closing the shutters, pulling down the blinds. Silymarin has the power to stop a hepatic coma. You will not die. At least, that was my theory.

But how the hell do you get the silymarin into the very places where the amanitin has gone? How do you work it into all the nooks and crannies of your liver? This is where I had a stroke of genius, Peter. It was staring me in the face and I could have kicked myself for not having thought of it earlier. Use an extract of amanita to do the work for you. Link the silymarin to the active ingredients of a caesar — couple them together like a horse and cart — and you're ninety per cent there. The caesars are ingested in exactly the same way as deathcaps, you see. They pass through the same bits of the body. They're processed in precisely the same way. Precisely. They, too, pass through your liver. But they do so harmlessly. And I felt sure that these yolk-coloured caps would provide me with a fast track to all the cell membranes under attack.

Of course, I'm leaving out a lot of the technical detail. I've made it sound much easier than it was. And a lot less scientific. Well, the science can wait for the academic paper I'm going to write. But I can tell you that I had an absolute nightmare trying to extract all the active juices of the caesar. They account for a tiny percentage of the fluid in the mushroom and it took me twenty, perhaps thirty, attempts before I finally met with success. But those few drops, Peter — well, they were as precious to me as the tape recorder on my desk. They were life-savers. For I had high hopes that when they were harnessed to the silymarin, they'd enable me to bring people back from certain death. I could play God, using God's own tools to do so.

It will work, Peter; I absolutely know it'll work. I know more about silymarin than any other mortal soul on this planet. I've peered into it down microscopes. I've examined its molecular structure. I've read everything that's ever been written about the stuff. And now it's time to put it to the test.

What's the use of an antidote without testing it first? What's the use of science if we're not prepared to experiment and take risks? Didn't Thomas Harriot conduct experiments on his own cancerous nose. We need a guinea pig; we need someone to step forward in the interests of science and for the good of mankind. *Arnold? Arnold!*

In short, Peter, this very evening — less than twenty-five minutes ago — I ate three whole deathcaps. Cap. Stalk. And root bulb. The lot. Gulp. I cooked them. Gulp. And ate them. Gulp. Every little bit of them. Gulp. With a spot of tarote root to make them palatable. And tomorrow evening — exactly twenty-four hours after eating them — I shall take my silymarin anti-toxin. My life-saver. It will work, Peter. Believe me, it will work. I'm three thousand per cent confident that those toxins will pass harmlessly through my body. And if I'm wrong — well, you'll have to explain what happened. Explain everything to — . Well, it'll be too late. Too late.

I'm waiting and waiting and waiting. Two hours. Three hours. And while I'm waiting, let me tell you more about the quarries. The quarries at Creux. This might be the very last time I ever speak to you. To think, this might be my swansong.

Each day I went to check my caesars. And each day Lola would meet me and then invite me back to her chambers. She made all the running, Peter; she just ran with it. And it was all a light breeze compared to the gale I'd grown used to with Flora.

Flora and I were two high-pressure fronts rumbling in from the east and west. Rumble, rumble. And then — well, you know how it was. A giant crash of cymbals and a sky that's ripped in two. I couldn't see how it could be any different. I mean, if you think about it, it's quite odd to be living in each other's pocket.

And yet here's the thing — to be with her virtually every hour of the day, to know all her habits, to understand her so well that there are evenings, yes, entire evenings, when you sit there in complete silence. And then there are other times — bang, bang. It was never about anything at all. Not in the great scheme of things.

"You're funny." That's what Lola said when I praised her calmness. "I'd prefer to be like you. You're a spark after all the dull people in this place. You're like an English brass band."

What struck me, Peter, was how different she was. With Flora, I felt she was constantly disappointed. And she was. She told me so. And — oh — why am I musing aloud in this fashion? Must be the heat. All I really wanted to say is that Lola and I got along famously. I told her about mushrooms and history. And she told me about Tuva, an island she'd never visited and knew only from the stories her father had told her. She was very good at evoking the place. I could already picture it in my head. I could already see the steamy peak of Mount Tuva.

"We'll go there together," she said. "When it's safe."

About three weeks after we'd first met, she asked me if we were a couple.

I thought for a moment. "I'm forty-two," I said, "and you're twenty-nine."

"Thirty," she said. "Well, almost."

"That's thirteen years. And that's a lot."

"Is it?" she said. "It's not a lot for me. Besides, I prefer older men."

"And I'm married," I said. She laughed. "That doesn't bother me," she said. "Monogamy's never been part of life on Tuva. My grandfather had six wives. He could have had ten, but he said six was enough. One for every day of the week and a long rest on Sundays."

One evening she asked what Flora was like. "You tell me about every subject under the sun, but you've never once spoken of her, except to tell me she'd left."

Flora. I repeated the word slowly. It suddenly struck me that I hadn't heard a single word from her in four weeks. *Four whole weeks*. My God — they'd passed like a flash. I don't think I'd ever *not* seen her for four weeks. What had become of her? And where was she? A great bubble of nostalgia welled up inside. And I can confess to you now, Peter, I had to keep it under wraps.

"*Arnold!*" It was Lola. "Wake up, dreamer. I was asking you —"

"*Eh?* Oh, yes — Flora."

For once, I didn't know what to say.

"She's fiery," I said. "She's the very opposite of you."

"Fiery? I'd like to meet her."

"No you wouldn't," I said in all honesty. "There'd be blood on the carpet."

"Did she like mushrooms?" Her question made me laugh.

"Yes," I said. "She liked hedgehog fungi lightly sautéed in olive oil and then simmered in crème fraîche and Dijon mustard. And served with a grand cru Chablis."

"How sophisticated. Would you cook it for *me*?"

"Perhaps," I said. But I knew that I wouldn't.

The caesars grew. Thirty-eight days. Yes, and seventy-one hours before the royal dinner their caps opened themselves up like magical parasols. Their flesh was firm and compact, like a piece of Edam. You prod it and it gives slightly. They were the finest caesars I'd ever seen — and what made it all the more exciting was the fact that they were the first ones I'd ever managed to propagate.

"How will you cook them?" asked Lola. "I'm hungry already."

"*Cook them?* I'm not going to cook them. Caesars must be eaten raw."

It was Lola's turn to be surprised. She told me that in previous years they'd always been cooked.

"Well, this year they're raw," I said. "As raw as a steak tartare. But without the egg."

They're better raw, Peter, they really are. You must remember when we ate them raw at your fortieth. They were delicious. And quite simple to prepare. You turn them onto their big bald heads, parasol down, and slice them with the sharpest possible knife. One millimetre slices. Not a fraction more. They must be wafer thin. Arrange them in a single layer

— a porcelain plate is best — and then melt the butter. Demi-sel. It *must* be demi-sel. Brush this onto the caesars, just enough to glisten them, and then squeeze the juice of a lemon. A sprinkle of salt (sel de Guérande), a dusting of pepper, a whisper of nutmeg, a few flakes of parsley. Leave them to steep for five minutes, perhaps ten. And then brace yourself for one of the world's greatest culinary pleasures.

Discord and harmony in each and every slice of mushroom. Six ingredients — five of which you can find in every kitchen cupboard in the land — and yet each of them has an explosive effect on its culinary companions. The mushrooms are the bedrock. They hold the savour of the forest. It's vegetal decay, Peter, that's been transmuted into something altogether more splendid. Think about it. You are eating the organic building block of creation.

It takes a second or two — you must be patient — and then the adagio begins. A second layer of flavours will slowly start to trickle onto your tongue. It's the butter, you see, the rich molten butter. A milky sweetness, a caramel richness that infuses itself with the vegetal decay. And then the citrus: the joyful little citrus comes tripping and skipping into your mouth like a coquettish ballet dancer. It brings a tang of sharpness to modify the butter, to balance the oil. They're starting to work in harmony; a symphony by virtuoso musicians. And the musical chord expands in complexity with each new ingredient that's added. What *is* that chord, Peter? Listen to it plucking at your musical tastebuds. Is it something by Rachmaninov? A Lenten Kastalsky? Or shall we keep it simple? Yes, let's make it a dominant seventh. Harmony — but unresolved. You're tipping towards completion. You're rushing towards satisfaction. But you're clinging to that state of near ecstasy. And it's not until the nutmeg explodes onto your tongue that the chord finally crashes its way to completion. Play it on the piano, Peter. Play it. You'll see what I mean.

On the thirteenth of March they started to arrive: royals and would-be royals from across the globe. King Carl the sixteenth of Sweden and Queen Beatrix of the Netherlands were the first to pitch up. You should have seen her hat. Then came King Jameson Tampo, who's the rightful heir to the throne of Malawi. He was accompanied by King Birendra Bir Bikram Shah Dev (or something like that). Most of them arrived at night. They were set down at the de la Regniers' house — they all came by car — and had to make the last stage of the journey by foot. Pedro Henriques, the uncrowned monarch of Angola, came (if you please) in lama-skin boots. And Emperor Amha Selassie of Ethiopia brought fourteen bodyguards decked in lion pelts. Lion pelts! And they sang and beat drums all the way through the forest. We could hear them from inside the quarry: bang-bang-bang, Waaalua-waaalua-lua-lua-ayeee. It was like being in Africa.

And then came our very own queen, Peter, in the company of Prince Philip and three barking, snivelling corgis, which insisted on peeing all over the place, including my shoes. *Our own bloody queen!* She was smiling at everyone. Oh, yes, looking very regal indeed. And she chatted with Lola, who'd met her on numerous occasions.

It's so odd to see her in the flesh. You know the face so well — you've seen it in a thousand photos — and that makes it even more bizarre when you find yourself standing in front of her.

"And you are — ?" she said, turning to me. She was facing me, Peter, she was less than two bloody feet away from me. And I was gawping like some stupid Cheshire cat.

"Arnold Trevellyan," I said. "I'm in charge of the caesars." I couldn't think of anything else to say.

She emitted a short sort of snort. "King of the caesars," she said, turning to Philip and then back to me. "That makes you top dog." And everyone standing around laughed politely at her joke.

"I hope to take him back with me to Tuva," explained Lola. "If and when it happens."

"Oh, it *will* happen," said the queen. "And soon. Everything's in place."

The banquet had been set for the fifteenth of March at seven-thirty sharp and the preparations had been under way for much longer than that. Waiters, chefs, footmen, butlers, had all appeared from nowhere. I could never work out where all the staff came from: there was an army of people down in the quarries. And now, in the days preceding the banquet, even more people seemed to have arrived. There was constant activity and noise and bustle. A clatter of trays, the jingle-jangle of crockery. Cutlery being polished and glasses being cleaned. Lola took me down to the kitchens, where Jean-Claude presided like an autocrat over the stoves and the pans. "*J'insiste — oui. Oui! Et ça . . . c'est un ordre!*" He fired the words out with staccato clarity.

The kitchens, Peter, the kitchens. They were half country house (all Agas and pans) and half high-tech wizardry. The pans were hanging from a rack like a row of gleaming discs: two dozen copper sunsets, each one bigger than its neighbour. And there were onions frying and sauces bubbling

274

and garlic being chopped and toast being grilled and someone's uncorking wine and someone's splashing brandy and there's a sizzling pan with almonds and pine nuts and there's the thick smell of parsley and fresh mint and rosemary and sherry that's steaming in a pan and there are shallots that are sweating in butter and there's a bowl that's filled with cream and there's a bowl that's filled with raspberries and one of apricots and one of spliced figs that are all purple and ripe and I looked around and I'm feeling so achingly empty and hungry.

And Jean-Claude passes me a spoon that's brimming with sauce and it's clinging to the rim with an ever-so-fragile skin. And I put it into my mouth and it touches my palate and dribbles down onto my tongue and then it's all wine and shellfish and it's butter and it's pepper and there's a hint of fennel and a touch of mace and it melts into my mouth and then — slowly, slowly — it fades, fades, until there's only a shadow that's left.

"My bisque," says Jean-Claude, "took four years to perfect."

It took me three hours to chop the mushrooms and a further hour to dress them. I timed it, Peter, to perfection. On the stroke of eight the footmen appeared and carried them into the banqueting hall. And then we waited. We were standing in the kitchen — I had Jean-Claude at my side — and waiting to hear their verdict. Five minutes. Then ten. And then a waiter burst in with a scrap of paper. It was a note from Lola. "You're a triumph." That's what it said. And then, in smaller letters underneath: "Will you marry me?"

And I don't know if it was the sheer exhilaration of it all, Peter, or if it was the wine, or if it was the fact of being here,

surrounded by all these royal oddities. But before I knew it —
without even thinking about it — I'd written the word "Yes",
and asked for it to be delivered back to Lola.

Yes, Peter. Even though I was already married.

Yes. Even though — if I'm honest — I hardly knew her.

Yes. Even though there was every possible reason in the
world for saying no.

Yes, Peter. I said yes. I bloody well said yes. I think it must
have been the strangest moment of my entire life.

And then there's the memory of later that night. The
memory of her undressing before me. Like a professional, she
was.

She kicks off her shoes. She inches her top over her head
— squeezes it ever-so-ever-so-gently-over-her-ears-and-nose.
Cascading hair — like a shower of water. And suddenly
she's topless. And she's a pomegranate. Or is it a mango?
Oooh-la-la. And you find yourself watching the most
innocent striptease in the world.

"And won't you," she says, "come to bed?"

That's exactly what she says, Peter. Those were her very
words. "And won't you come to bed?" Well, you're not
exactly going to say no, are you? Of course you're bloody well
not. So you jump out of your clothes, quick as a flash and
slide into bed. And later that night — when you lie awake in
the darkness — you think to yourself. "Life's a mushroom.
It's a great, big, delicious mushroom."

CHAPTER
TWENTY-SIX

It was the publican on the other end of the phone, the owner of the Hope and Anchor on the corner of North Street and Amos Grove.

"Mr Andrewes? I have a Flora —"

"Trevellyan."

"Yes. A Flora Trevellyan here. She wants you to pick her up. She's had a few too many, if you get my drift. She's a bit the worse for — well, you know what I mean."

"I'll be there," I said, fumbling to reach for my coat. "Give me two minutes."

Flora was sitting at a bar stool with a half-finished pint of lager in front of her. She had her back turned to me; she didn't see me approach. I noticed an empty shot glass on the bar beside her. And then she turned around, alerted to my presence by the barman's knowing glance.

"Let's go home," I said.

"Yes," she agreed. "I want to go home. There is nowhere I would rather be than at home."

I helped her to her feet and noticed that she was unsteady. I had no need to ask how much she'd drunk, for the barman helpfully supplied me with the information, pointing at the pint glass and holding up four fingers and then the shot glass and displaying two. Flora must have known what I was thinking: that she was pregnant and she was drunk.

I wanted to say something; I *had* to say something. My panic about her whereabouts had changed almost immediately into anger. But I couldn't say anything now, as we pushed our way to the door of the pub.

The icy wind provided a welcome jolt. It acted on Flora as well, sobering her head and steadying her feet.

"It's cold," she said. "Will it snow?"

When we were back inside my flat, I asked her if she wanted some food. She shook her head and settled into an armchair.

"You should. It'll do you good. Otherwise you're going to feel like a disaster tomorrow morning."

She shook her head again but then seemed to change her mind. "OK," she said. "Why not? Whatever you say, A little."

Both of us seemed aware where our conversation was heading and both of us knew that it was up to me to make the opening shot. But I didn't want confrontation.

"Good soup," she said quietly. "Did anyone ever tell you you're a very good cook. An excellent cook. A chef, no less."

She had — on numerous occasions.

"I shall eat five bowls and then —" she took a deep intake of breath — "and then I shall be fine tomorrow."

"*Flora?*"

But before I could say anything more, she stopped me by raising her hand.

"Please don't," she said. "I beg you not to. Just leave me — let me be in my little space. You can say a thousand things. You can shout at me. You can be furious. Of course you can. You've got every right to be. I know it, God, don't I know it? And I regret — but please, don't. Please."

She suddenly appeared sober. She took another spoonful of soup. I got up from my chair and kissed her. "OK," I said. "I won't mention it again. I promise. Not now. Not in the morning."

"You won't need to mention it in the morning," said Flora, "because my head's going to be screaming at me all day."

She put down her spoon and sat back in her chair. "I can't eat five bowls of soup," she said. "I can't even eat this one. I need to go to bed."

She got up from her chair and stumbled slightly on the rug. And when she went to brush her teeth, I heard the clatter of the toothpaste on the floor, followed by the clatter of her toothbrush.

"Oops," she said to herself. And then I heard her brushing her teeth.

She was still asleep when I left in the morning and I decided not to disturb her. I left a note in the kitchen instead. "Hope your head doesn't scream," I wrote. "Give me a call later."

I'd forgotten that I was going to be out for much of the day — first at a meeting with the foreign minister of Poland and then at a lunch with Peter and Tim Burton. I'd suggested to Peter that we ask Tim what he made of Arnold's story about the fate of the Romanovs. He, after all, had spent the better part of two years researching the subject. "I've got three weeks before the book goes to press," he told me. "So if you've got any last-minute changes . . ."

We met in La Giaconda, the little Italian place behind the Royal Opera House. I knew Peter liked it and I was always well treated there because the owner's brother, Marco, had spent a few months working as a courier at the *Telegraph*. The dish of the day — how could I forget it! — was tagliatelle with giant whelks. Peter and I both laughed when Paolo told us. "Crunch, crunch," said Peter.

"They're from the Adriatic," said Paolo, throwing his hands in the air in a gesture of mock offence. "If you want the really big ones, you'll need to go to the tropics. There you find — how you say? — *whoppers*."

We told Tim the gist of Arnold's story about the tsar and he listened attentively, stopping us once or twice to ask questions. Even when we'd finished speaking, it was a few seconds before he said anything.

"There are lots of stories along those lines," he told us, "but almost all of them concern the survival of Anastasia. Indeed there are several people still alive who claim to be her. I interviewed one of them — a lady called Anna Anderson, who lived in Charlottesville. In Virginia. Mad as a hatter, even though her story sounded plausible enough. She was the right age and she could tell you any number of stories about 'her family'. She makes it into my book — chapter fourteen — but only as a curiosity.

"But this story of the tsarevich — this is very interesting. You see, there's never been any mention of *him* surviving. At least, not for a long, long time. It was probably ten years ago — more perhaps — when, out of the blue, a very elderly man was sighted in the Russian church of St Serge in Paris. It's a bastion of the old times — all aristocrats and émigrés, white Russians, that sort of thing. And this rumour started. A few elderly babushkas started telling people they'd seen Aleksei."

"And then?"

"And that was it. He was never seen again. He, whoever he was, never returned to St Serge. And the story died a death. There was a short piece about it in *Le Figaro* and that was all. I didn't even think it worth including in my book."

"And do you now?" I asked

"I'm wondering if I shouldn't at least mention it. Just a passing reference. Just to acknowledge the story. Cover my back."

"Nothing more?" asked Peter.

Tim smiled. "I'm hoping and praying that your Arnold Trevellyan is talking nonsense," he said. "Otherwise I'm going to look like a prize prick. But I can't rewrite my book now. I've just spent two years researching it and we found nothing about this in the Moscow archives."

He drained off his wine and looked at his watch. "Have we got time for another glass?"

Two news conferences later and I finally arrived back at the *Telegraph*. It was almost five o'clock.

"You're lover's been trying to get hold of you," said Charlotte Stanhope. "She must have rung six or seven times. It's definitely love, Tobias."

"Did you speak to her?"

Charlotte shook her head. "Evelyn did. She took a message. Apparently, she wants you to call her back."

"Well, thank you for your concern," I said, aware that every sentence Charlotte said contained a commentary on my relationship with Flora.

"A pleasure," replied Charlotte. "No thanks required. You owe me a drink, that's all. But not tonight. I'm busy."

I dialled my home number as soon as I was at my desk. It answered immediately. It was Flora.

"What's wrong?" I asked. "You've been trying to get hold of me."

There was a long silence.

"Flora?"

"It's — well —"

There was another pause, time enough to brace myself.

"Tobias — I've had a miscarriage. I've lost the baby. This morning."

A chill shot through my body.

"How —?"

"*How?* Well, do you really want to know?"

"No," I said. "No. Not now. But — well — are you *sure?*"

282

"I *wasn't* sure. But now I've been to the doctor's. And there's nothing more to be done. It happens. That's what the doctor said. She told me it's not unusual. It's not a symptom of anything wrong. She said that it happens to one in four pregnancies. And —"

"Yes?"

"Well, Tobias, I told her what happened last night. The pub. The drinking. I was completely honest. And she said — she *assured* me — that it was not that. But she told me to take more care of myself."

"You should," I said.

"I should," she replied. "And I will. And — oh — when are you coming home? I want you to be here. Right now."

"I'm coming. I'm literally leaving my desk right now. I'll be back by seven."

"Tobias."

"Yes."

"I'm sorry. I can't say anything more. But I'm sorry."

"You don't have to be," I said. And I placed the receiver back on the base.

CHAPTER
TWENTY-SEVEN

Ladies and gentlemen, we regret to inform you that Arnold Trevellyan is dead. Struck down in the prime of life by a deathcap mushroom. How tragic — how ironic — for a mycologist to be hoisted by his own petard.

Ha! Not true, Peter, not true. It's me — Arnold — and I'm alive and kicking and if only you could see me. I'm running round like a wild warthog. I've got more energy than ever before. It's been a week — seven whole days, one hundred and sixty-eight hours — since I sat down to eat a heaped dinner plate of freshly cooked deathcaps. And? Well, truth is I feel bloody marvellous. Not an ache in my liver. No pains in my tubes. No hepatic coma. In short, I've neutralized the toxins. The blessed milk thistle. Never was a plant more deserving of its name.

I've made scientific history, Peter. Yes, this is one for the history books. OK, OK, it's not the discovery of gravity or electricity or anything as momentous as that. But I've achieved something that no one in the history of the world has ever managed to do, and that is to neutralize the toxins of the cruellest and most dangerous mushroom on earth. So let's hear it: three cheers for Arnold Trevellyan: hip, hip —

I need to grow more. I *have* to grow more. But now, of course, I'm worried that they're going to find the cave. It was yesterday, you see. We went back there. We hacked our way back up the mountain. And what did we find? Footprints. Or rather stonking great boot prints.

"They've been, Gilbertine. They've been."

"Who, sir?"

"Them."

She looked puzzled and then she laughed. "These are you're footprints, sir. And mine. Look, Your boot fits completely into the print."

It did. And yet still I don't believe it. Those were not my boot prints — that much I know for certain — and they were not Gilbertine's. Those boot prints belonged to intruders. We were being watched. Spied upon. Just as I'd thought.

You could see the footprints in the soggy moss. And in the mud. You could see where they'd cut through the jungle. I swear they'd slashed a path up the northern side of the mountain, which is even more tangled than the way we'd come.

Gilbertine refused to believe me. "That's the bandicoots, sir," she said. "That's a bandicoot trail. They cause much destruction."

But it wasn't, Peter. That trail was not made by bloody bandicoots. And I should know.

"I can tell you why they came that way," I said to Gilbertine. "It's because of their boat, Their boat must be almost directly below. It's close to the northern point."

"I don't understand, sir," said Gilbertine. And of course she didn't. I hadn't yet told her anything about the boat.

"Come," I said. "Let's follow them. Let's find out what they really want." And so down we went, down the northern flank, fighting our way through the shrubs and the giant ferns and the great tunnels of creepers and suckers. Gilbertine warned it was dangerous and that we needed to take care and that no one ever came to this side of the mountain. It was certainly tough going — steep as Machu Picchu — and there were these lichen-covered boulders that were as slimy as seaweed. And what with the heat and the humidity and the vicious acacia thorns that pricked us like needles — it really took it out of me. Legs aching. Knees trembling. Feet hurting. Head pumping. Sweat dripping. And then, after about twenty minutes of clambering down the rock-strewn slope, the canopy parted slightly and we found ourselves stepping into an enclosed grove that stood shoulder to shoulder with wild rhododendrons. Great knotted bushes, dark waxy leaves. And they were showered with flowers; these huge clusters of luminous pink blooms. Lit up like light bulbs. There were so many of them that you could see nothing except pink.

"Aeeeoike Maaleekai," said Gilbertine. "The royal bush, sir. It flowers four times a year."

She shook one of the clusters and a thick-as-soup odour oozed from the buds. "It attracts the honeybird," said Gilbertine. "You sometimes see hundreds in a single bush."

Whoever they were, they'd cut quite a trail through the jungle. Bandicoots — *my arse!* A bandicoot doesn't cut branches with a machete. A bandicoot doesn't snap roots underfoot. And it made me think that they perhaps wanted me to know they were here. Of course, they were trying to scare me. Psychological terror. They were trying to drive me away. What if Gilbertine — one of my own wives — was one of them? Who was to say that she hadn't switched sides? And then it suddenly dawned on me that perhaps my presence had become a nuisance to them. Perhaps they'd realized that I had the ability to ruin all their plans.

The sea. We could see the sea below us, glittering like silver foil. It was only a hundred feet further down, perhaps a little more, but that last clamber over those slimy, greasy rocks was pure treachery. I slipped — grated the skin on my leg. It came off in a long strip, like the skin of a cucumber. It began to swell almost immediately but I waded into the sea and cleaned off the slime and the salt water did it good. And then Gilbertine tied on some bark of the cau-cau tree.

I led her to the cove where their boat had been. "Nothing, sir," said Gilbertine. "There's nothing here." It was true. There was no boat. It had gone.

"But look; look, look," I said. "Look at the sand." There was a shallow line gouged into the beach like a slashed canvas. They'd pulled the boat out of the cove and into the water — and they must have done it since the turning of the tide.

"You'll have to be my eyes," I said to Gilbertine, pointing out to sea, where I could see nothing except the tinsel water and the glimmering sky. "You've got the sharpest sight of anyone on Tuva."

But Gilbertine swore she could see nothing — not even a minuscule speck on the far horizon.

"Are they leaving us?" I mused aloud. "Or hiding from us? Have they got something new up their sleeve?"

Gilbertine shrugged her shoulders. "I see nothing, sir. But I can swim out to sea — out to the horizon — if you want."

"*Swim!* The horizon must be several thousand bilks away."

"No trouble, Mr Husband, sir, if that's what you'd like."

"No," I said. I don't want to put you in any danger."

"Danger, sir, is my middle name."

That's what she said. And it *is*, Peter, it is! She's called Gilbertine Danger Kituwaia. Isn't that priceless!

But I must return to the banquet; that's where I left you. Or was I in bed? Whatever — it's not important. What *is* important is what happened in the days that followed the meal. You see, the whole business with Eastern Europe was reaching lift-off. The Order had been preparing the way — and now they were ready.

I can't give you the exact details because I don't know them. All I can say is that they had hundreds of agents and underground networks working for them. The scale of the thing was incredible. They'd wreaked havoc in a dozen different places — in Romania, in Prague, in Poland, in East Germany. They'd succeeded in bringing the Iron Curtain crashing down. Within the organization there was a very real feeling that they were an unstoppable force. But they needed to be prudent. They needed a back-up plan in case everything should go wrong. And this was where Lola and I came into the story. It was Tuva, you see. In one sense, the idea of restoring Lola to the throne of Tuva was strategically unimportant. It was not going to change the world. After all, we're talking about a tiny little realm that was lost somewhere unspeakably remote in the South Pacific. I do believe that half the members of the Order wouldn't have been able to point to it on a map. But it was its very isolation that made it so significant. The archipelago had long been mooted as a place of refuge if everything went belly up.

I've already told you that Lola's grandfather had offered sanctuary to the Order at the beginning of the century. In

288

many respects, it was the perfect place. You see, the military brains had realized that with very little weaponry they could defend the island from attack. It's almost impossible to land troops on Tuva because of the reefs that surround the island. And a handful of missiles would be enough to keep an armada of warships at bay. Besides, there were any number of monarchs willing to help in defending the place. The sultan of Oman had already donated vast sums of money and he was now offering troops as well. And both Denmark and Sweden had also given a great deal of logistical support. The only drawback was how to get people there in the event of disaster. Speed would be of the essence. And that's where Mitterrand stepped in: he offered to put his presidential plane at the disposal of the Order. He made it quite clear — I heard it from his own mouth — that if the need ever arose and everyone had to flee, then he would make his plane available.

But before Lola and I set off for Tuva, the Order wanted to send a signal to the outside world. They wanted to present Lola's return to Tuva as the democratic desire of the Tuvan people. They wanted to show that it was possible for monarchy to be re-embraced by countries which had functioned without a monarch for many decades. It was a PR exercise, nothing more, nothing less. And so they got me to contact the *Telegraph*. They asked me to send out a press release. And it worked like clockwork, because about a week or so later, a reporter turned up. He was called Tobias something-or-other. I forget his name. Nice-enough person, if a little bland. And we talked about mushrooms. A lot about mushrooms. And we talked about monarchs and trees and, before we knew it, it was about two in the morning. But still no Lola. She suddenly got cold feet. She refused to meet him.

She said she was worried about the idea of being in the newspaper and, well, the Order accepted her concerns. I have to confess that the journalist seemed a bit annoyed by all of this. "It would have been good to have a photo of her." That's what he said. "They might pull the piece if there's no photo." And I thought to myself, "You only want to run the piece so that you can stick a gigantic great picture of a beauty queen in your sodding newspaper."

I was surprised when he told me he worked on the foreign desk. He didn't know the capital of Botswana, nor could he name the longest river in Russia. In fact, he didn't seem to know very much at all. And that made me laugh.

CHAPTER
TWENTY-EIGHT

The phone rang. It was Philippa on the other end and I immediately knew that something was wrong.

"He's left," she said in a distraught voice. "He didn't come home last night and now he's left."

"Who? What?" I said.

"Peter. He's left. He's left."

I was stunned. And the normally composed Philippa was clearly in a terrible state.

"But have you heard from him?" I asked. "Why's he left?"

"Greener pastures. That's what he said to me. That's *all* he said to me. He's found greener pastures."

And immediately she said it, my mind was transported back to the time I'd had lunch in his office and a girl had brought in sandwiches. Even at the time, I'd picked up some — *complicity* — between them. And now, thinking back on it, I wondered if it was her that he'd gone off with. What was it she'd said to him? "I've brought you crisps, Mr Rushton. I know how you like them." And Peter had made some lewd comment about her.

But then, thinking about it further, Peter was always making crude comments. He was not the subtlest person on earth.

"Can you speak to him?" asked Philippa. "Can't you talk some sense into him? He won't listen to me but he might listen to you."

"But where is he?" I asked.

"Oh, he's at work. He's at the office. But he won't speak to me. He refuses to answer my calls." She paused for a moment before continuing in a very different tone of voice. "You know who *I* blame?" she said. "It's Arnold. It's *his* fault. It's his fault entirely. He's been sending these tapes — he's been telling Peter how he's run off with this bloody queen who's about half his age and who seems to want to jump on top of him every minute of the day along with half the other women on his island. And now — well — now Peter's gone and got ideas —"

"Oh, you can hardly blame Arnold for that," I said. "Surely not?"

But even as I said these words, it occurred to me that perhaps Philippa had a point. Perhaps Arnold could be blamed for this new turn of events. Perhaps it was yet one more example of the effect he was having on all our lives. Even now, thousands of miles away on Tuva, he had the ability to bring the marriage of his best and oldest friend crashing down.

"I *can* blame Arnold and I *do* blame Arnold," said Philippa. "I've always felt he's had a hold over Peter. Yes, Peter looks up to Arnold. He thinks that everything he does is wonderful. For him, Arnold can do no wrong — even when he walks out on the lovely Flora and abandons her for some floozy queen from the other side of the world. And, because he's done that, now Peter has to go and do the same."

"I'll see if I can speak to him," I said. "I'll see what I can do."

I was bemused by the fact that Philippa had turned to me for help in contacting her estranged husband. I'd only known her for a few months and only met her a few times, yet I'd suddenly become her greatest confidant.

It was several hours before I managed to get through to Peter and he sounded decidedly irritated by the idea of talking to me.

"It was Philippa who got you to ring," he said in a weary tone of voice. "You can admit it to me."

"Yes it was," I said, "but to be honest, Peter, I would have rung anyway. What's going on? It doesn't add up."

"Can't really explain, old boy," was his response. "But, well, everyone's at it, aren't they. Everyone's at it like rabbits. You only have to look over your shoulder. You and Flora. Arnold and Lola. And, well, I thought it was time for yours truly to have a shot at it."

"But Peter, you're married. And I thought you were happily married."

"Well, so was Arnold," said Peter, "and it hasn't stopped him. And now it's high time I had a slice of the action. Otherwise, the next thing I know, I'll be dropping dead of a heart attack and that'll be it."

"Yes, but —" I could hardly believe what I was hearing — "but do you really want to be like Arnold?"

I could hear Peter clearing his throat on the other end of the phone. I sensed I was beginning to annoy him. He didn't want to talk.

"Well, as I said, I don't see why I shouldn't have my slice of the fun," he said. "And, well, Deirdra has been only too willing to —"

Deirdra! So I'd guessed correctly! "But what about Philippa? And Peter — that girl — she's about half your age. Less. She can be scarcely out of her teens."

"Well, Lola's not exactly Arnold's age, is she?"

"*Peter!* Are you only doing this to compete with Arnold?"

And that was the moment when the phone went dead.

Peter had hung up on me.

CHAPTER
TWENTY-NINE

My dear Arnold,

How I'd like to address you in a more familiar manner, given that we've shared sixteen years of our lives together. But how can you be anything more than a formal "dear Arnold" after everything you've done?

I never wanted us to part like this and I never asked for it. I never instigated it. I am — and remain — ripped in two by everything that's come to pass.

You, dear Arnold, were the love of my life. You were the light that illuminated all the darker bits. You entertained me and amused me. Your passion for life — your zest — your love. I'd never met anyone like you and I doubt I ever shall again. You, dear Arnold, were my all. And I thought — I still believe — that I was yours.

We argued. Yes, we had big fights. But that's how we'd always been. As you said, there were often thunder clouds. You compared us to two weather fronts colliding in the sky. But the sunshine always arrived in the aftermath of the storm and the clouds scudded away. Oh, Arnold.

Life with you was a long happy moment punctured by the odd storm.

I've come to see that I have many flaws. And I'm doing all I can to repair them — of that I can promise you. But you, too, have a flaw, Arnold. And you have consistently — all your life — refused to confront it. And someone has to tell you, or you'll reach the end of the road and there'll be nothing but a wall. Arnold: you cannot and will not face the real world. And it's so frustrating for everyone who's close to you.

You have such creativity and potential. You are such fun to be with. You are a burst of colour and the reason I wanted to drag you away from Baddington's was so that you might do something worthy of yourself. But what have you done? You've gone off to pursue a fantasy and now it's ruining your life.

It's time to escape, Arnold. Not to Tuva or to any other little paradise you wish to name. No, it's time to escape the fantasy of Lola. To escape the mediocrity of Baddington's. To escape the shadow of Peter and Philippa. Wake up, Arnold, wake up.

All this to say that now, to my utter desolation and sadness and misery, we appear to have reached the end of the road. There was a storm — an almighty tempest — but on this occasion the sky didn't clear at the end of it.

I'm sorry to have walked out (I've learned to accept my share of the blame). Believe me, I've regretted it every single day since it happened. I'm sorry, dear Arnold, I'm sorry. But why — why — why — did you not come for me? Why did you not accept I was scared?

And so this is the end. Now I'm too weary to pick up the pieces. I intend to start from zero. And that means practicalities (how you hate practicalities).

I'm putting the house on the market — I've been told by the estate agent that several people are interested — and I sincerely hope that you will be in agreement when it comes to the paperwork and to dividing up the money and all those other hideous things that one has to go through when it comes to divorce.

Divorce, Arnold. Divorce. That's what now has to happen. What are you doing? What *are* you playing at? You get married, for God's sake. Twice. You marry without even getting divorced. That is the greatest insult of all. If only I could see you, I could at least scream at you. I could hurl every single bloody plate, bowl and mug that we possess at the wall. No, I would hurl them at *you*. We would have the storm of our lives. And then — surely — the sun would shine once again, as it always shone.

I worry for you. Yes, above all else — and despite all that's happened — I worry for you. Are you well? What nonsense are you telling Peter? Tell me one thing: are you doing what you truly want to do? Are you truly happy on a tiny island on the other side of the world? Are you truly happy with *that woman*?

I hope this letter finds you well. I hope you've found happiness. (How hard, though, to say such things.) I hope you're bringing joy to others as once you brought joy to me.

My only other news: I was pregnant. But I lost the baby.

Yours,
Flora

CHAPTER
THIRTY

And then one day there was a flurry of activity in the quarries. Everyone was on the move. People coming and going; meetings; conferences; endless discussions as to how, exactly, it was going to work.

I wasn't there, of course. Lola and I had left for Tuva months earlier. But I've been told all of this from people who were there, so it's as good a picture as you're going to get.

I'm told there was a real feeling of optimism. The Order believed it stood a very high chance of success with at least half of the monarchs, if not more. You must remember that everything, so far, had gone like clockwork. They'd successfully brought down the Iron Curtain. They'd wreaked havoc in East Germany, in Hungary, in Czechoslovakia and in Romania. Everything their agents had set out to achieve *had* been achieved. Stage one of the plan was complete: the old Soviet bloc was in total turmoil. It was in meltdown. Now, it was time to turn to stage two.

This was to be a softly-softly approach. And it was to differ with each individual country. King Michael of Romania had already left the quarries; it was felt that he stood the best chance of reclaiming his throne by making public appearances whenever possible. The people *wanted* him back, you see, so it was easy for him. King Simeon of Bulgaria had also gone public. He, too, remained popular. And he was not in danger. Of course, both of them had senior directors of the Order advising them, helping them, pulling strings behind the scenes. King Leka of Albania was receiving a great deal of help from the Order, and I know for a fact that there were several senior operatives fomenting unrest in Tirana and Shkoder. But it was felt that it would be several years before it would be possible for him to reclaim his throne. Mitterrand was also doing his bit — oh, yes, I've been reliably informed that he was operating at the most senior levels. He was determined to bring the entire Soviet Union crashing down. That's what he desperately wanted to achieve before he died. Then, and only then, could Ivan of Russia be sent back to Moscow.

Ivan of Russia: he was one of the ones still in the quarries on those last days in February. Prince Stanislaus of Poland, he was another. And so was Laszlo of Hungary and Mircea of Moldova. And all of them were in and out of meetings and receiving advice on how stage two was to unfold.

The Order's greatest concern was to have solid contingency plans in place in the event of everything going belly up. It had already been decided that the quarries were to be definitively abandoned. They were no longer deemed to be safe. We were hearing constant rumours of interlopers and trespassers. The cameras picked them up every time. More worrying was the fact that the Morvan was being overrun by more and more Dutch people buying holiday homes here, there and everywhere. It was increasingly felt that it would only be a matter of time before the whole shebang was discovered. But abandoning the quarries! You can imagine, Peter, what *that* entailed. Everything had to be dismantled.

Everything had to be boxed, packed up and shipped to — yes, to Tuva. We'd known about all of this for some months, as I've already told you. We'd been preparing for ages. Not just the missile stations, which were nearing completion, but a whole network of store-houses and buildings in which we could house the vast quantities of stuff coming from Creux.

The level of planning was quite extraordinary — it never ceased to amaze me. The Order had modelled the new Tuvan headquarters on the military base on Diego Garcia. Perhaps you know the one I'm talking about? It's in the middle of the Indian Ocean — a number of scattered atolls, rather like us out here, which were long ago converted into a British and American army and naval base. They, the Order, had a whole series of aerial reconnaissance photos taken and we used them pretty much as a blueprint for our own headquarters. It was a real master plan. I've sat around a table, Peter, looking at their drawings and, I tell you, it was extraordinary. The level of competence and expertise could rival that of any government.

But now I'm running ahead of myself. I'm forever running ahead of myself. I was telling you about the quarries; they were packing everything up when — bang — absolute disaster struck. It came like a bombshell from the heavens, except that it was far more sinister than that.

We must move the scene to the kitchens of the quarries: that's where we need to be. In the kitchens they were preparing lunch, just as they always did, day in, day out. Chopping, frying, grilling, toasting. The aroma of freshly chopped mint and Armagnac and woodchips. I'll leave it to your imagination. Just think in terms of wonderful, delicious appetite-building smells. Smells to get your juices going. And the constant chop-chop-chop of a dozen chefs and sous-chefs. It should have been the maestro, Jean-Claude, preparing the meal. He was always the one in charge. But Jean-Claude was poorly (I'm told he had a stomach bug, or something like that) and so François, his understudy, had stepped in. It was to be a normal working lunch — nothing fancy. Some pan-fried foie gras to start with. A little smoked cod with lentils and a chorizo marmalade (I've had that marmalade, Peter, and I can tell you, it's bloody delicious). And to follow there was sautéd pigeon served, as you'd expect, with a little compote of caesars.

But why am I telling you all this? That's what you're asking yourself. Well, Peter, you need to know all of this because it's the only way in which I can tell you why I now find myself living in my very own Pompeii. The walls, the ceiling, the entirety of my existence has come crashing down around me.

The mushrooms, Peter, the mushrooms. You need to imagine them on the kitchen work-surface. You need to imagine François slicing them with his razor-sharp Sabatier. Look at them carefully. Put on your glasses. Examine them, Peter, examine them. There's a great mound of caesars — as bright as any tangerine — and he's cutting them with infinite care. Not one slice is more than a millimetre in thickness. They're wafer thin, just as they should be. But turn your gaze to the left. What are those other mushrooms? What's that second, smaller pile. They're a pale tawny colour and they're slimy on the top of their caps. And, hey, why is François putting on gloves when he comes to chop this second pile? And why is he chopping them even smaller than the caesars? Slice, slice, chop, chop. By the time he's finished, they're completely unrecognizable.

302

You'd have spotted them immediately, Peter. You'd have known what they were. Deathcaps. A little over a pound of them. And that's enough to kill twenty men. Perhaps more. As you know, it takes just a small forkful of deathcaps to take out your internal organs. Goodbye and goodnight. It was nice to know you.

François. Who is François? It's a good question. He's been working here for two months and very good he is too. He has impeccable credentials — the Order saw to that. The vetting procedure, Peter, for anyone coming down into the quarries was quite incredible. I later learned that they knew everything about me. Yes, long before Flora and I had signed the contract for our odd little house in the woods, they knew my entire life story. And it should have been the same for François. He would have been vetted; his parents would have been vetted; his entire bloody family would have been scrutinized.

But *they* were clever as well. And the Order had underestimated them. They'd underestimated the counter-plotters, the ones who knew of the Order's existence. For more than a year they'd tried to infiltrate the quarries, but it was almost impossible. The place was under constant surveillance and you couldn't get near without being detected. And so François applies for the post of sous chef. And because he's known to Jean-Claude and he's well born and he's a cousin or something like that of the crown prince of Montenegro — well — he's allowed in. And from that moment on he's watching, observing, spying and reporting back. Oh, yes, he was the snake in the grass. And when he realizes what is happening; when he realizes that the Order is about to launch into stage two — and there's a very real chance that their master plan will work out — well, he seizes the moment. Slice-slice, chop-chop. The lunch gong rings. And a little assembled group of would-be monarchs — and several senior members of the Order — sit down to a lunch of pan-fried foie gras, smoked cod served with lentils and a chorizo marmalade and sautéd pigeon served with a delicate little compote composed of caesar mushrooms laced with a heavy dose of deathcaps.

They should have seen it coming. It was *exactly* what did for the Emperor Claudius. It was an exact replica of his last meal on earth. But none of them knew their history. For all their obsession with tradition and ritual and suchlike, no one saw the historical parallel. If only I'd been there, Peter, I could have saved the entire situation. If only I'd been there. But I was thousands of miles away on Tuva, so what could I do?

And it was fully two days before anyone realized there was something amiss. It wasn't until fully forty-eight hours after that terrible luncheon that King Laszlo suddenly and spectacularly spewed his guts out. And then — and only then — did they realize the terrible truth of what had happened. They'd been poisoned, all of them, and they were all going to die.

Or were they, Peter? Let's not forget your old pal Arnold Trevellyan on the southern Pacific island of Tuva. Let's not forget that he's been working hard on his antidote to the deathcap mushrooms. And let's not forget that he has personally eaten a large portion of deathcaps and is neither dead nor feeling remotely unwell. Quite the contrary. He's never felt better and is sitting in his deckchair on a rather breezy morning in March when he hears a call from Lola. She's calling from the top of the chapel and she's telling me that a large boat is approaching from the south. And this is

304

most unusual. We're not expecting anyone. And no one has any idea as to who it might be.

Twenty minutes later they were all on the beach. Deathly pale, sick as parrots, sweating profusely. Prince Mircea vomited a bowlful of green bile as soon as he stepped onto the beach. King Laszlo had to be steadied on his feet. And the three members of the Order — boy oh boy — they were advanced cases, Peter. They'd already been through the false remission. Those few days when you think you're OK. This lot were within seventy-two hours of a gruesome, lingering death.

Their journey to Tuva had been fraught with difficulty. They all knew that their only hope was to get here with the greatest possible speed. They knew all about my antidote because Lola had written to friends back in Creux. And they also knew that it was their only hope of salvation. But time was of the essence. They had no time to lose. They were battling against the hours. Tick, tick. Each second brought them closer to death.

They got to Paris, where Mitterrand's plane had been put at their disposal. But the counter-plotters had even managed to scupper that. They'd sabotaged the plane. Cut the fuel line or some such. And that caused yet more delay. They had to get a regular flight to Auckland. And then another to Tonga. And then a very choppy and uncomfortable boat ride to the Tuvan archipelago, where I, at that precise moment, was tanning my toes in the sun.

"Gilbertine," I cried, as soon as I realized the seriousness of their plight. "Gilbertine. We must go. Now. Quickly, quickly. We need the caesars. We need the milk thistles. We need to make the antidote. There's not a moment to lose."

"Mr Husband, sir," she replied, standing to attention. "I'm ready for you. Let's go."

She picked up her machete and off we went, up the familiar trail, hacking and slashing our way to the northern slope of the mountain. It was stinkingly hot, Peter, and horribly clammy. You know how it is when you shake someone's hand and their palm is disgustingly warm? Well, it was just like that. It was as if a clammy hand had been wrapped right around my body. And it was as if Nature had come down with a fever. As if the shrubs were sweating and the trees were convulsing and the creepers were shivering. There was a feeling of sickness in the air and everything smelled of death.

"Nearly there, sir," called Gilbertine, as she hacked at another creeper. It slumped to the ground and coiled itself round my leg. It felt alive, it really felt alive. And when I pulled it away. I could swear that I saw it slide off into the undergrowth.

And then we heard the birdsong and the monkeys and the crashing of water and we knew we were almost there. The cave was just twenty yards from where we stood.

I must say, Peter, I was a little nervous as to what we'd find. I was nervous that they'd have found the cave, that they'd have discovered all the secrets of my lab. And so it was with considerable relief that I noticed that none of the creepers and succulents that surrounded the cave had been touched.

"No footprints, sir," said Gilbertine. "No one's been here."

And then we poked our heads inside. And, my God, Peter — that was the moment when we got the shock of our lives. I blinked. I blinked again. And I pinched myself.

"*Aiaawio amaitistou*, sir!" exclaimed Gilbertine. "Holy sea cow!"

My caesars, my deathcaps, my amanitas and my milk thistles were nowhere to be seen. They were gone. Vanished into thin air. In their place — *in their place* — there was a thick rich carpet of bright yellow buttercups. Buttercups, for Christ's sake. Buttercups. My little Shangri-la, my microcosmic world of mushrooms and fungal decay, was carpeted in a flower that had never grown on Tuva. But how? And why? And who? And when? Nothing made any sort of sense. And there was only one certainty.

"They're all going to die." That's what I said to Gilbertine. "They're certain to die. There's no hope."

"Is there nothing, sir —?"

"No. There's nothing. I have none left. I used it all on myself. They will all die. They will die. Each and every one. It's the end, the end, the end. It's the end of everything."

"But who did this?" asked Gilbertine. "Who are these people? What do they want, sir?"

Well, it was clear to me what they wanted. Clear as the light of day. As Ivan had once said to me, "You're either with us or you're against us." And *they* were most definitely against us.

And that, Peter, is almost the end. The rest is almost too painful to recount. I've not got the heart to put any colour into the story — I shall merely give you the facts. Prince Mircea was the first to succumb. He'd been the most sickly when he arrived. He slumped into a coma within a few hours and he never recovered consciousness. King Laszlo was the next to go. He, too, slipped into a coma. Then it was the turn of the three members of the Order. One. Two. Three. Ashes to ashes. Dust to dust. And then it was Tsar Ivan. And Prince Stanislaus.

They all knew they were going to die. They all knew it was inevitable. And yet they went to their deaths with the greatest dignity. Calmly. Stoically. Without anger and apparently without pain. They just slipped away, one by one, like wilting flowers. We interred them — each and every one of them — in the little sandy plot that lies behind the Wesleyan chapel. And it was as if the curtain had fallen for the last time. All these people I'd got to know so well, all these friends, had just vanished like the breeze in the trees. And I'd never felt so very, very alone. Profoundly alone.

And now it's dark again and I can hear the crash of the lagoon, only it's softer than before and there's a gentle crash-sh-sh-sh of the waves licking at the coral. And so here I sit, at the uttermost ends of the earth, talking into a spool that's turning and turning and turning.

And I read and I re-read her letter; heaven knows, I've read it a hundred times and now I know it off by heart. And there's a question going round and round in my head — round and round like the spool of tape.

What do I do now, Peter? And how do I escape? I'm trapped in this strange little world and everything is collapsing and —

— so, what is it to be today. Monsieur Arnold? Le menu? Sorry if I am disturbing you. We 'ave a very good blanquette de veau served with sauté potatoes — it is chef's special — or we 'ave a very nice coq au vin — that comes served with rice — or if you want something more lighter there's — CLICK.

308

EPILOGUE

It was Saturday, 25 March, a day I will never forget. The date is indelibly printed on my mind. The setting is indelibly etched into my brain. And the turn of events — the sorry turn of events — continues to disturb my sleep, even though many months have gone by.

Flora and I were in Paris, a three-day break to help her recover from everything that had happened over the previous few weeks. It was around 12.30p.m., perhaps a little later, and we were looking forward to our lunch with a pleasure that was tinged with trepidation. The restaurant, you see, was Flora's choice. She wanted to go to Maison Lipuko, the place that Lola had mentioned in one of the tapes. It was, she'd said, the only place to get Tuvan food in the whole of Europe.

"So let's go," said Flora. "Let's see what it's all about."

Lola had said that it was on rue le Regrattier on the Ile St-Louis, a little street that runs from the north to the south of the island and is crossed by the rue St-Louis, which leads to the bridge of the same name. We were ravenously hungry, a hunger that was fuelled by the cold. It was one of those bitingly icy March days and the wind was whipping along the Parisian boulevards. The sky was bright, with a promise of sunshine in the east. But behind us, in the west, behind Notre Dame, a great stack of rain clouds was piling up. "I hope it doesn't tip down," said Flora.

She was looking at her most elegant — dark coat, boots, felt hat. "You can dress up in Paris," she'd said to me, "and I shall."

We turned into rue le Regrattier and looked out for Bonsai, a florist that specialized in tropical plants. Lola had said Maison Lipuko was directly opposite.

"I'm so hungry," said Flora, "I think I could eat a dozen raw fish."

"Then you shall," I said, "if you don't first get eaten by a giant whelk."

I remember passing an art gallery selling black and white photographs, a coffee shop and a boutique with a window display full of trinkets from Tibet and China. I remember it as if it were yesterday. There was a brasserie on the corner of rue des Deux Ponts and rue St-Louis. And there was a little store — very chic — selling fabrics and hand-printed wallpapers. And then —

"Here," said Flora. "It must be here." We were standing outside Bonsai. And our two sets of eyes immediately flashed across the road towards the Maison Lipuko.

It was not there. The building where it should have been was boarded up. It was clearly in the process of being renovated.

"Oh, no. It's shut down," said Flora in a disappointed tone. "How terribly upsetting. You see — we should have come here last time."

"Let's go and ask," I said. "Let's ask in the shop next door. Maybe it's moved."

We crossed the road and entered a little art shop selling Japanese papers and handmade boxes and pens and ink stands. I was about to ask the shopkeeper in my broken French about the disappearance of Maison Lipuko, but he initiated the conversation in perfect English.

"Can I be of any assistance?" he said. "Are you looking for anything in particular?"

"Well, yes." It was Flora speaking. "The restaurant next door — the Maison Lipuko — when did it close?"

The man looked puzzled.

"Restaurant?" He tutted in a way that only French people can ever really tut. "No, there's never been a restaurant there. At least, not for as long as I've been here. No — that was a *bijouterie* — a jewellery shop. But it closed last year. Not enough clientele."

"But — have you heard of Maison Lipuko?" asked Flora. "We were told it's on the Ile St-Louis. In fact, we were told it was here. It was definitely this street."

The man scratched his head and called to his assistant. "*Jacqueline — est-ce-que tu connais un restaurant qui s'appelle Maison Lipuko?*"

Jacqueline appeared from the office.

"*Non,*" she said. "*Il y a une maison de thé — rue Poulletier. Mais — non.*"

311

"Sorry," said the man. "I don't think we can help you further."

When we were back out in the street, Flora held her finger to her nose, as if she was deep in thought.

"That's strange," she said. "It was certainly this street. I even checked with Peter. And yet —"

She pulled up her collar as a few large spots of rain began to tumble from the sky.

"Well, it doesn't alter the fact that I'm hungry," she said. "We'd better find somewhere else to eat."

And it was as she said the word "eat" — exactly as she said the word "eat" — that I got the shock of my life.

"My God," I said under my breath. "*My God.*"

"What?" said Flora. "What's wrong?"

"Oh, my God, Flora. Look. Look. There. It's *him.*"

Her eyes followed mine down the street and she instantly recognized the figure coming towards us. And she let slip his name — not loudly, but loud enough.

"*Arnold* — "

I'll never forget the expression on his face when he heard her voice. He looked up and focused directly on Flora. Shock. Anguish. Fear. Surprise. And shock again. A dozen emotions were writ large on his face before they were replaced by a look of extreme agitation. He was by now less than ten feet from us. We hadn't moved. We'd remained rooted to the spot. And he couldn't turn and run. He was too close for that. And he couldn't hide from us because our eyes had made contact. And within less than two seconds he was going to be right in front of us and he was going to have no option but to engage us in conversation.

"Arnold."

Flora said his name for a second and third time, only this time in a less exclamatory fashion. "Arnold."

"Flora."

He spoke in a low voice, almost a whisper. It was as if he was slowly retrieving her name and image from the murky depths of his brain.

"Flora — Flora — I — didn't — expect — this — I — didn't — think . . ."

His words trailed away and were caught by the wind. She did nothing to fill the silence. We stood there, the three of us — awkward, hesitant, unsure of how to begin. And a few large raindrops splattered the pavement around us.

It was me who made the opening bid.

"We were looking for the Maison Lipuko," I said. "We thought —"

Arnold shook his head from side to side, but still he said nothing.

"But what are you doing here?" said Flora in a low voice. She had not yet overcome the shock of seeing him as a tangible presence; seeing Arnold as real flesh and blood; seeing the husband who had fled from her life.

"Why are you in Paris? Why are you not in Tuva? And where —?"

She stopped in mid-question. I knew what she'd intended to ask. She wanted to know about Lola. But she couldn't bring herself to speak her name.

Arnold looked at me — stared at me. "How strange to meet *you* here," he said, "and with Flora."

There was a pause. "We met," he added, for Flora's benefit. "Many, many months ago. In Burgundy. In our house." He was still half-lost, still half-trapped in a world of his own. "What a long time ago that was."

He was a different person from the one I'd met all those months before. The spark had fizzled. I found myself standing in front of a shell of a man who was clearly in a profound state of shock. He was confronting a past that had arrived without warning and was now standing right in front of him.

"I received your letter," he said. He had turned back towards Flora and was now speaking to her. "Thank you. I will never be able to thank you enough. You will never know how grateful — . You helped me more — . You said everything —"

He was about to speak in earnest — I could sense that he was on the point of talking, perhaps explaining. But the rain that had been threatening us for more than half an hour now began tipping down in earnest. It fell in wind-fuelled sheets — sheets of water that advanced in waves along the rue St-Louis.

"We must take shelter," he said. "Shall we?"

He pointed at the bar-brasserie on the corner of the street.

Flora nodded and so did I. I took her arm but she nudged it away slightly — unconsciously, perhaps, but I noticed it all the same. What storm, I wondered, was to follow?

314

Arnold opened the door to the brasserie and allowed Flora to pass in front of him.

"*Ah, bonjour, monsieur.*" The proprietor seemed to know him. "The corner table? Ah — *vous êtes trois.* Well, you choose."

Arnold led us to the table in the corner, the one that had been suggested, and the three of us sat down.

"I'll take your coats," said the proprietor, helping Flora out of hers. "What weather!" And then, turning once again to Arnold, he said, "You wouldn't get rain like that on Tuva."

He brought us menus and I noticed that he appeared to scrutinize Flora with unusual thoroughness. He was clearly wondering who she was. And Arnold studied his menu with the sort of attention to detail that you only ever display if you are on your own in a restaurant or if you are trying to avoid someone.

I, meanwhile, cast my gaze around the bar, half-noticing the coffee machine, the rows of bottles and the —

On the wall opposite, there was a photo of a tropical volcano with jungle-covered slopes and a steam-enveloped peak. I idly wondered if it was Tuva. And then, on the other wall — to our right — I noticed there was a stuffed fish mounted in a long glass case. And, at that very moment, I felt a slow wave of shivers pass right through my body. It was as if a cold liquid had filtered into my veins, as if a mathematical equation suddenly made sense.

"I'll turn it off," said the proprietor, pointing to the fan that was turning and whirring above our heads. It was rustling ever so slightly the napkins on the table. "I don't know why Jean-Claude turned it on in the first place."

He realized that we were not yet ready to order and said he'd come back in a few minutes. Flora offered a faint smile, as if she wanted to acknowledge his recognition of the fact that the three of us were clearly in an embarrassing situation.

"Arnold?" she said in a clear voice when the proprietor had gone back to the bar. "Arnold — what's going on. *Arnold?*"

Arnold looked up when she raised her voice; he, like me, was looking at the photo on the wall.

"I'm so sorry," he said under his breath. "Flora — truly — I'm sorry."

I noticed that he had tears in his eyes, but he did nothing to wipe them away. And his face was pale. And in that instance, just then, I felt that I was looking at a broken man. A man who had been crushed. A man who had gambled and lost. A man who had nothing left to his name.

"But what —?" Flora had also noticed the picture on the wall and the stuffed fish. And she, like me, had at that very moment spotted the poster for Gilbertine cocoa. It featured the smiling picture of a plump Balinese maiden who was carrying a jug of cocoa between her ample breasts. And Flora — and I — had a flash of recognition. "But what's —?"

"It went wrong," he said, speaking slowly, quietly, but with conviction. "It spun horribly, desperately out of control. I was no longer in command, Flora. It took

316

on a life of its own. It was a demon, Flora. A demon. With horns and pitchfork and everything. Believe me, Flora —" he was shaking his head — "believe me, Flora."

"But *what*, Arnold. What? What happened. *What* took on a life its own. What demon?"

"*Lola.*" It was the proprietor calling to the waitress. "*Table deux. Un pichet de rouge. Allez, allez. Et de l'eau —*"

"Lola! Lola! *That* is Lola?"

Arnold shook his head. "It's not what you think," he said. "It *is* Lola. And it's *not* Lola."

And that was the point at which Arnold Trevellyan began to recount to us the strange story of the last fifteen months of his life. He never raised his voice and nor did she. He was calm — though obviously distressed — and so was she. And for once — for the first time since I'd started listening to his tapes — everything he had to say rung absolutely, crystal-clear true.

It's hard to know where to begin, as I attempt to set down his story, because he spoke unceasingly for almost an hour. There was the occasional protestation from Flora, the occasional interruption from the waiter. But otherwise it was a long monologue, delivered in a quiet low voice that seemed completely uncharacteristic of the Arnold I had met all those months earlier in Burgundy. There was a world of difference between the Arnold now and the exuberant Arnold of the tapes.

"You are always right." Those were his opening words. "You are absolutely right. And I am absolutely wrong. And you, Flora — well, it was as if you were shaking me, shaking me, shaking me. And for that I will always be truly — deeply — profoundly — grateful. For as long as I live, for as many years as I have left on earth, I will always be grateful to you."

Flora looked at him intensely, but didn't speak. I could tell she had a lump in her throat. I could tell she was on the point of tears.

"We moved to Burgundy and, well, I don't know if it was the change of surroundings or the unfamiliar house or the strangeness of it all because — you see — I still can't really explain it. There are many things I can't explain, even though I've relived them time after time in my head. But I was lost, Flora, I was adrift. I was no longer in my own world. Clapham seemed light years away. And Baddington's; the work colleagues; the auctions at which I was the conductor of it all. Everything, Flora, *everything* that had anchored me had suddenly been whisked out from under me. A boat without a rudder. A boat without oars. And an approaching storm. A force ten monsoon. And I felt terribly, terribly vulnerable.

"I did it for you, Flora. Oh, yes, I moved to France for you. But I needed certainties in return. I desperately needed something to cling to. Something tangible. Something concrete. And you —" he looked Flora directly in the eye for the first time — "I felt that you didn't even want to understand. I felt that you had your own agenda.

"Flora — Flora — all my life has been a struggle to cling to something, to cling to anything. And then we

318

moved to the middle of nowhere. And all the certainties had gone — vanished forever — and I found myself lost.

"Now, of course, I can see what a terrible mess I've made of it all. What terrible mistakes I've made. Now, when it is too late, I can see clearly. Now, Flora, I see that what I once clung to as certainties — the routines, the humdrum, the great showmanship of it all — these, of course, were not certainties. Or they were the wrong certainties. They were nothings. But I clung to them — I clung to them for years — and when they were whisked away from me, well, I was lost. I had only you. You were my anchor in the world. Flora — Flora — believe me. I beg you. Even if you believe nothing else, believe this. I was lost, hopelessly lost. And I knew that you couldn't help because you didn't understand.

"And so I began to create a world where I could be certain of everything that happened. A world in which I was king of everything. It was a world in which everything and everyone was at my disposal. It fascinated me. In fact, it electrified me. I could kill people off; I could conjure them back to life. I could create a whole world that was entirely my own. My own little playground. And so, on that evening, with the red candles and the white candles —"

Flora looked at him intensely and then she whispered, "That was *you*?"

Arnold nodded slowly. "It was me — it was me — yes. It was me."

"But why, Arnold? I don't understand."

There was another length of silence.

"For a long time even I didn't know why. I didn't know what was driving me. But now, when it's too late, I know. You see, at first it was simple. I wanted to force us both to flee. To go back home. But then it became far darker. I wanted to see how far I could push you before you'd leave. I wanted to test you. I wanted to know that your love for me was real. I wanted proof. You see, I'd given up everything for you. My friends, my house, my world. And now I had to see what you would sacrifice for me."

"But why?" interrupteed Flora. "And besides, you hadn't given up everything for me. You hadn't given me the one thing I most wanted."

"I know," said Arnold. "I know that now, but I didn't at the time. So I wanted to test you. I wanted to see if you'd stay with me. I wanted to know if — when you were faced with a choice, a terrible, frightening choice — you'd still choose me. Or would you run away from me and from it?"

He stopped for a moment and stared at the table.

"How stupid I was. And how — *twisted*."

He said the word slowly — ponderously — as if he wished to feel the full weight of his anguish. It's the closest I've ever seen a person come to repentance.

"And the terrible thing was the discovery — *my* discovery — that it worked. The changing of the candles — it scared you. It really scared you. And it forced you to make choices. I'd pushed it *that* far. And there's another thing. In scaring you the whole fiction became dramatically real for me. Suddenly I felt there was someone out to get us. I believed — I genuinely

320

believed — that someone had come into our house and changed the candles. I came to believe my own fiction, even though I knew that it was me who had done it. Those candles — they were my first step into a whole new world. It was a parallel world. One that ran alongside reality and eventually became reality. It became the most real thing in my life —

"And then you left. And I knew I'd lost. I had gambled with your love but you had chosen to leave —"

"But, Arnold," said Flora, "I had no choice. I thought there was someone out to get us. How could I possibly understand you?"

She took a nervous sip of her wine. "And the quarries?" she asked, shifting the focus slightly. "And all the stories? The stories of the royals?"

"The quarries — ." Arnold toyed with his fork. He rearranged the food on his plate, as if he were hoping that this would help him arrange his thoughts as well. "The quarries exist. You saw them. And Soufflot really did have a hand in them. And the stone really was used for the Panthéon. And there really are archives to prove it —"

"But the Order? And the kings? And the princes? And everything?"

Arnold shook his head slowly from side to side.

I hadn't yet spoken. It was my turn to speak. "It sounded so real," I said. "So convincing. I've heard every one of your tapes. And it was as real as anything I've ever heard in my life."

"But exactly," said Arnold, suddenly getting animated. "It *was* real. In my head, it was absolutely real. It was a real world and they were real people and real situations arose."

"But what about the book?" I asked. "The book about King Louis the sixteenth. I read it. I held it in my own hands. I brushed the dust from its cover."

"And then the deception grew deeper and deeper," was Arnold's reply. "I was in a hole — I was in a deep hole — and I didn't know how to get out. I was Macbeth: 'I am in blood stepped in so far . . .'

"I'd moved up to Paris by then. I'd left Burgundy. And I'd come to live here. And it was on this very street — the rue des Deux Ponts — that I found one of those old presses. You know the ones? The old hand printing presses. With the letters. And the rollers. And the ink. And . . ."

He let out a long sigh.

"Well, I can hardly bring myself to tell you this, for I'm deeply ashamed. I printed it myself. And I had it bound together with a couple of other accounts. And then I stood back and looked at my handiwork and I had the shock of my life. Because the story of the French king, you see, had suddenly become dramatically real. In producing that book, yet another part of the story had taken on a reality of its own. And even *I* began to believe everything that was taking place in my head."

Arnold stopped speaking for a moment. I glanced at Flora and noticed that her face was absolutely without expression. She was listening — listening attentively — yet she betrayed not a hint of emotion.

In the pause that followed, the waiter came over and brought our main courses. He joked with Arnold, misjudging the mood of our table. "No tape recorder today?" he said. Arnold shook his head and asked for some water. And then he continued with his story.

"And now that I had convinced *myself*," he said, "I wanted to convince others as well. I wanted to see how far I could go. How big the deception could get. It became like an addiction. A sickness. Yes, I do believe it was an illness. I'm not trying to excuse myself. Flora, I will never try to excuse myself. But just like some people gamble and some people drink, I was addicted to deception. It was exciting. It was real. And it was easy. I chose to plant my book in the London Library because they have a card index and I knew that I could slip the book into the shelves and also add an entry to the index. I actually wrote an index card for the book that I'd created, complete with dates of publication and the authors' names and everything. It was all so easy."

"And you succeeded," I said. "*I* was taken in. That index card led me to the book. And I read the account. And I believed it."

"So it worked," said Arnold. The realization that his deception had succeeded seemed to make him more depressed than ever. "And I did the same with the Warlock book," he said, "the book on Tuva. I put it in the University of London library."

"But Tuva," interrupted Flora. "You *went* to Tuva? You *did* go to Tuva? Tell me you went to Tuva."

Arnold's eyes glanced back up to the picture on the wall and Flora's gaze and my gaze followed his. There was a moment's silence. And then an extraordinary chill as the full implications of his gaze sank in.

"You mean to say —"

"I never ever *ever* thought it would work," said Arnold. "Never in a million years did I think it would work. I thought it would all fall apart. That I'd be found out. And then the whole thing would all come to an end. And you'd come back. And — well . . . but then I sent the press release. And I recorded tape after tape. *And no one ever checked to see if Tuva existed.* That was the strangest thing of all. Just one glance at a map. Just one phone call. Anything — and my story would have crumpled to pieces. And that was my continual fear. And it was also the excitement. It kept me awake at night. How long, I wondered, could I get away with it? How long could my new reality be a reality for my friends as well? I knew that Peter wouldn't check, he's far too lazy. But *you* . . ."

He looked at me. "You were my greatest fear. I thought you'd check. I was sure you'd unmask me. And, well, then the time came when I actually wanted to be unmasked. I wanted to flee it all. I wanted to get out. And I found that needed help. Because I couldn't do it on my own. I needed help, Flora, I needed help. But there was no one to help."

"But the tapes," I said, "they came from Tonga. I've seen the envelopes, the stamps, the postmarks."

"That," said Arnold, "was all down to someone I know through work — a shipping insurance man —

who's based there. I'd send the tapes to him. And then he'd repackage them and send them on to Peter."

I could scarcely believe what he was telling me; it sounded like yet another of his stories.

"And Lola?" asked Flora. "Lola *does* exist. She's there. She's real. You've been having a —"

"No," said Arnold as he glanced at the waitress. "That *is* Lola. And she works here and she was kind and she's been going out with Jean-Claude, the chef, for about three years and they are engaged to be married."

"*What!*" Flora choked on her water. "You mean —"

"All she did — *all* she did — was help me with one or two of the tapes. She called it 'creative expression'. That was her phrase. All of them here, they all thought it was wonderful. I'd come here every day with my tape recorder and they'd bring me my lunch and I'd chat away into my cassettes. And after the second or third day they asked what I was doing. And I told them. And Lola, who's always wanted to be a writer, thought it was so creative that she wanted to take part. She called it a living novel. And she didn't see — she couldn't see — she still doesn't see — the danger of it all. She didn't see the consequences."

There was a pause as Arnold called to Lola and asked her to come over to the table. And then, apologetically, he introduced her. Flora glowered. She glowered in the way that a wife might glower at a mistress. And then Lola spoke. And when she spoke, it was the strangest thing. It was the same girl we'd heard on the tape — exactly the same — except that the picture of the Tuvan princess that I'd had in my head for many months had suddenly been replaced by that of the girl standing in front of me. And she was very, very French.

I was expecting Flora to explode, I'd been expecting her to explode all along. And yet still she said nothing. And when Lola had left the table and was busy serving on the other side of the restaurant, she said to Arnold, "But you were in love with her? Tell me you were in love with her?"

Arnold thought for a moment.

"No," he said. "I was in love with an image of her. With the *idea* of her. Like everything in my entire life, from my childhood to the present — I was in love with the fantasy. But the fantasy — oh, Flora. Can't you see? Can you really not see? The fantasy was you. All along the Lola of my mind was not the Lola you see here. The Lola of my mind was you. You have always been my princess — my queen. The queen of my entire world. And to think that I'd never even realized . . ." His voice trailed off.

"But there's one thing that doesn't add up," I said, filling the silence. "When I went to Romania, I met your contact. Andrei Georgescu. The friend of yours. The one you'd recommended. And he — I swear — he —"

And before Arnold had a chance to answer, it dawned on me; it suddenly dawned on me. Even *that* — even my trip to Romania — had been set up by Arnold.

"It was my wildest card," said Arnold. "You see, your involvement excited me. It added a whole new

326

dimension of risk to the story. The interview you did with me — and all of that — . But it also worried me. I felt sure that you'd expose me. And Andrei owed me a favour. And I asked him if he'd invent a story. I had no idea, of course, whether or not you'd contact him. But you did. And he took you to the bathhouse, I believe. Isn't that right? And it seems — well — it worked. And — what can I say but repeat, over and over, that I'm honestly — terribly — genuinely — sorry."

"And Albania?"

"*Albania?*" Arnold looked genuinely puzzled. "That was nothing to do with me. I had no part in it. What happened in Albania?"

I told him about the men with the map of Tuva.

Again he shook his head. "Think about what you *actually* saw," he said. "Did you *really* see a map of Tuva? Or did you *want* to see a map of Tuva. Were you imagining a map of Tuva? I've learned a lot about conspiracy theories, you see. And I've learned that people *want* to believe them. They create all manner of things in their own heads precisely so that they can believe in them. Consider my tape about the Romanovs. I didn't have to use much imagination to come up with the escape of Aleksei Romanov. And I knew it was believable. Ever since nineteen eighteen people have been wanting to believe that some of the Romanovs survived."

He stopped talking and moved his plate towards him. But then he pushed it back again. "I can't eat," he said. "I can't eat anything. Not while I'm shaking like this."

Also available in ISIS Large Print:

The News Where You Are

Catherine O'Flynn

As a presenter on Midlands TV's regional news, Frank Allcroft is a long way from journalism's cutting edge, and he knows it. Saddled with Cyril, a gag-writer he doesn't want but whose limp one-liners are supposed to liven up his reports, Frank is now officially "the unfunniest man on God's earth" and a local legend. It's not quite the career that he envisioned, but Frank thinks there are more important things in life: his wife Andrea, his mother Maureen and his daughter Mo. But as Frank reflects on his late father's legacy and the unexplained death of a much loved colleague, an unusual news report catches his eye. Compelled to investigate further, he finds the familiar concerns of middle age falling into perspective as he uncovers a bizarre and tragic tale of thwarted hopes . . .

ISBN 978-0-7531-8716-6 (hb)
ISBN 978-0-7531-8717-3 (pb)

Also available in ISIS Large Print:

The News Where You Are

Catherine O'Flynn

As a presenter on Midlands TV's regional news, Frank Allcroft is a long way from journalism's cutting edge, and he knows it. Saddled with Cyril, a gag-writer he doesn't want but whose limp one-liners are supposed to liven up his reports, Frank is now officially "the unfunniest man on God's earth" and a local legend. It's not quite the career that he envisioned, but Frank thinks there are more important things in life: his wife Andrea, his mother Maureen and his daughter Mo. But as Frank reflects on his late father's legacy and the unexplained death of a much loved colleague, an unusual news report catches his eye. Compelled to investigate further, he finds the familiar concerns of middle age falling into perspective as he uncovers a bizarre and tragic tale of thwarted hopes . . .

ISBN 978-0-7531-8716-6 (hb)
ISBN 978-0-7531-8717-3 (pb)

The Unnamed

Joshua Ferris

Clearly an important and individual work, a stage in the development of a significant talent
Daily Telegraph

Tim Farnsworth is a handsome, healthy man, ageing with the grace of a matinée idol. He loves his work. He loves his family. He loves his kitchen. And then one day he stands up and walks out on all of it. He cannot stop walking. And, as his body propels him relentlessly forward, deep into the unfamiliar outer reaches of the city, he begins to realise he is moving further and further from his old self, seemingly unable to turn back and retrieve what he has lost. In his extraordinary novel Joshua Ferris delineates with great tenderness and a rare and inimitable wit the devastating story of a life taken for granted and what happens when that life is torn away without explanation or warning.

ISBN 978-0-7531-8712-8 (hb)
ISBN 978-0-7531-8713-5 (pb)

The Road Taken

Michael Foss

From rural Canada to Spain and North Africa, and from jobs as a journeyman writer and reporter, Lew Holle's life follows an apparently random course. Without a plan beyond a determination to remain an outsider, he falls guiltlessly into the life of the drug smuggler, transporting ancient hashish dreams from old lands to modern, dissatisfied Western youth.

When a moment's incaution sends Lew out of the drug trade with a slam of prison doors, he finally makes an active choice about what to do next, electing to drop out even further from the main currents of life. In the forests of British Columbia, a cabin in the woods provides perfect insulation from the ugly and almost infectious world he rejects.

ISBN 978-0-7531-8530-8 (hb)
ISBN 978-0-7531-8531-5 (pb)

Edward Trencom's Nose

Giles Milton

The first foray into fiction for the author of Nathaniel's Nutmeg

Edward Trencom has bumbled through life, relying on his trusty nose to turn the family cheese shop into the most celebrated fromagerie in England. But his world is turned upside down when he stumbles across a crate of family papers. To his horror, Edward discovers that nine previous generations of the Trencom clan have come to sticky ends because of their noses.

When he investigates further, Edward finds himself caught up in a Byzantine riddle to which there is no obvious answer. Like his ancestors, he is hunted down by rival forces whose identity and purpose remain a total mystery. Trapped between the mad, the bad and a cheese to die for, the infamous Trencom nose must make a choice — and for the last nine generations it has made the catastrophically wrong decision.

ISBN 978-0-7531-7838-6 (hb)
ISBN 978-0-7531-7839-3 (pb)

White Gold

Giles Milton

The Extraordinary Story of Thomas Pellow and North Africa's One Million European Slaves. Giles Milton vividly reconstructs a disturbing, little known chapter of history.

This is the forgotten story of the million white Europeans enslaved by North African barbarians into a life of harsh servitude. Ignored by their own governments, very few lived to tell the tale. Giles Milton has written a gripping and brilliantly realised and researched account of this particular time in history, using the first-hand testimony of a Cornish cabin boy named Thomas Pellow.

ISBN 978-0-7531-5647-6 (hb)
ISBN 978-0-7531-5648-3 (pb)